.99

The Thousand Doors

The Thousand Doors

by Abraham Rothberg

HOLT, RINEHART AND WINSTON

NEW YORK   CHICAGO   SAN FRANCISCO

Designer: Ernst Reichl

87596-0115

Printed in the United States of America

To

Robert Cosgrove,

who knows the meaning of courage;
and

Edward Finkel,

who understands the nature of risk.

Grateful acknowledgment is made to John Calder (Publishers) Ltd. of London for permission to quote "A Prayer" by Edvard Kocbek from *Parnassus of Nations*.

The Thousand Doors

WARREN STONE awoke, the hair on his neck and arms bristling with the old sense of being stalked. Someone was in the room. He had been dreaming about the war, the same nightmare he had had a hundred times before. He had locked the head against his shoulder until it went limp, and his ears still echoed with the German's guttural strangling "Ich." He heard the carefully controlled breathing of someone hiding and frightened. As Stone slowly, carefully inched his hand toward the light cord on the bed table a hoarse voice whispered in heavily accented English. "Be not afraid. Make not the lamp. There is cause. I bring you the thing from Master Karst, but someone follows."

The sound of the gun and the stifled whisper broke together. A weight fell across his bed, a hand gripped his fingers and closed over them like a handshake, a tightening spasm, then lax. Before Stone could disengage his hand, he saw a shadow float from behind the armoire, then the silhouette against the French windows and the shivering curtains. He pulled his hand from the dead man's, and threw himself out of bed at the shadow in the best tackle he could manage with so little leverage.

The pain went burning through his head and Stone thought

he had missed and butted the bureau, but as he fell he saw the gun and realized that the shadow had side-stepped and clubbed him. The room spun, over him a black totem pole with hideous faces wavered, then danced through the French windows, and flowed over the wrought-iron balcony railing. Just as the sickness lurching in his stomach, and the plunging roller coaster behind his eyes crashed together in the back of his head, he saw sheet-white hands with hair like black grass across the fingers holding onto the balcony handrail. Then they too fell from sight into the shadows of the hotel park below, into the black dice of the shaped plane trees, and Stone passed out.

When he came to, he was sprawled on the floor, his head beating like his heart, and the police were there. Two stood over him, tall almost identical men in drab green sloppy uniforms, their expressionless mustached faces looking down at him. When they saw him looking up, one of them nudged his side with a heavy boot, and instinctively, Stone, who had just begun to feel his fear mingle with the sour taste in his mouth, shoved the leg back. It rose to stomp him and quickly, angrily, Stone grabbed the leg and slammed the man to the floor. By the time Stone was on his feet again, dizzy and wobbling, the other policeman had a gun in his belly and the one he had thrown was on one knee, a bayonet half-unsheathed from his belt.

There was a sharp flurry of speech and for the first time Stone saw a small man in the armchair watching. His legs were crossed, and his blue raincoated arms neatly folded on his chest, "We could have you killed for resisting arrest," he said in very British English.

"Arrest?" Stone asked dully, still unable to focus his eyes enough to see the man's face. "What for?"

12

The slight tilt of the man's head was almost imperceptible, but the light from the overhead chandelier on his glasses made them glint. Stone turned and saw the body, half on his bed, half-kneeling, looking as if the man had been killed in prayer. Dressed in brown homespun edged with black embroidery, he wore trousers that bloused at the thighs, then tightened around the calves into dirty white knitted heavy stockings which were held in place by leather thongs. His shoes were the moccasins with turned-up toes that only the day before Stone had learned were called *opankes*. Again the glasses flashed, and one of the policemen—the same one who had tried to stomp him—kicked the body over with his boot, his eyes fastened on Stone.

The brown homespun forage hat fell off the dead face of a boy no more than sixteen years old. Fair-skinned, almost beardless, with thick curling black hair framing it, the face lay there, black eyes staring up at the ornate cut-glass chandelier. Stone felt weak, sick, and he held his head up with both hands, afraid that if he didn't it might fall off, roll down his chest and land at his feet. How did I get into this? he thought. The turned-up toes of the scuffed leather moccasins, the forage cap askew on the mop of curly hair seemed bizarre and romantic, like a Browning poem, or a Hollywood costume-movie.

A clipped British accent asked, "Who is he?"

Stone turned and stared at the man, again noticing the strange glitter and shape of his glasses, and that he wore a blue raincoat not a uniform. Unable to speak, Stone shrugged.

A quiver of contempt pursed the almost blue lips, or had he imagined it? His eyes were still not quite focussing.

"The boy's name was Antun Vuk, Mister Stone."

Before Stone could ask how he knew the name, either name, the man with the eyeglasses rose and gave swift orders to

13

the two policemen. They tore the bloodstained blankets and sheets off the bed, rolled Antun Vuk's body in them, and then carried it like a sack of meal through the door. They did it with so little waste motion that Stone was sure they'd had a lot of practice.

The man with the eyeglasses sat down again and Stone went to the night table for a cigarette, but couldn't find his packet. The man gestured with his own pack, gilt-wrapped Benson & Hedges, and Stone helped himself. Then the man lit them both up with what Stone was sure was a gold Dunhill lighter.

"And now, Mister Stone," the man asked, "what are you doing in Yugoslavia?"

Stone walked to the windows and stood there, grateful for the familiar rasp of tobacco on his tongue and in his nostrils, looking out of the still open French windows into the park. Down there, shadows seemed to move, dividing and combining. What had happened to that totem-pole shadow? Stone strained his eyes to see something, someone, but there were only the formal walks of the hotel garden and the topiary cut of trees and shrubbery. Was there such a man? Stone turned, saw the bloodstained mattress cover and felt his hands trembling.

"Perhaps you had better put on your dressing gown, Mister Stone, and your slippers," the Eyeglasses said considerately, "it is a chilly night."

Automatically Stone obeyed, got his robe, put it on, and looked for his bedslippers, but, like his cigarettes, he couldn't find those either. Probably, they'd been kicked under the bed and he didn't feel like getting down on hands and knees to rummage for them, making himself look even more ridiculous.

"Your feet are bare, Mister Stone."

14

"Yes, yes, I know, but I'm fine now. Warm." He rubbed his arms, and drew the smoke into his lungs.

"You were going to tell me what you are doing here," the man persisted.

Stone tried to pull himself together. This was his world, his century, when killing was a specialty on a mass-production basis. Why be so upset by another dead sixteen-year-old boy? But such hard-boiled thinking was not his own, only the ill-fitting adopted attitudes he had learned during the war and at a hundred fights, sports events and moving pictures. What he wanted was for this man to go away, for the whole thing to go away, so he could crawl back into bed, pull the covers over his head and pretend in the morning that nothing had happened, that it was all a bad dream. But there weren't any covers left on the bed; the two policemen had taken them for the corpse, using them like an old hammock, and the little man was still there, his eyeglasses like tiny mirrors turned on him. And besides, Stone asked himself, what *was* he doing there anyway?

"I'm a literary agent," Stone said, by way of beginning to explain.

"What kind of agent?" the Eyeglasses asked sharply, bearing down heavily on the word *agent* and pronouncing it as a Frenchman might.

"No, not that kind of agent," Stone said in French. Stupid of me, he thought. I should have had more sense. In English, he went on, "I'm an *author's representative,* someone who sells writers' books to publishing houses and conducts their business arrangements."

"I see," Decani said, after a pause, not quite convinced, then continued, "at least that explains your passport."

"Now what the hell are you doing with my passport?" Stone

asked angrily, as the man held up the little green folder with the gold-eagle seal of state on it.

"We wanted to know who you were when we found the boy," the man said, unperturbed, "and the hotel management obliged us."

Stone realized that he had better control his temper, and his tongue. If he lost his head, he wasn't going to find out what was really happening, and he was going to be in deeper trouble than he already was. This was a foreign country, and he was a visitor.

From his pockets the man also took Stone's wallet, address book, and his various identification papers. He spread them out on the small table in front of his chair. "We also examined these while you were unconscious."

Slowly, he extracted a card from a small black leather card case. "My card," he said, proffering it between two outstretched fingers, a sardonic smirk glued to his face.

Stone took the card. It was expensive heavy paper and in the center was beautifully embossed in flowing script the name, Dr. Petar Decani. At the lower left-hand side was an address and telephone number. There was nothing more to identify him.

"You're from the police, Doctor Decani?"

Decani nodded.

"But you wear no uniform?"

"You might say I am an inspector, what you Americans, I think, call a detective."

"I see," Stone said, but he didn't see, at all. "Are you a medical doctor too?"

"No," Decani said, impatiently stubbing his cigarette out. "As you may or may not know," he grinned and looked suddenly much younger, in his early forties, a contemporary, Stone thought, "everyone east of Vienna who is a graduate of

16

a university is a doctor of some kind. I'm a doctor of law."

"Of law," Stone echoed, feeling stupid.

"Of law," Decani repeated, the same sardonic expression there and gone on his face.

Decani got up and walked past him. As he did, Stone saw that he was not actually so short, in fact, he was at least six feet tall, almost as tall as he himself was. The man's leanness and effortless loping walk was deceptive. "Like a wolf," Stone thought and was irritated with the cliché. He'd been reading too many of his own fifth-rate writers. Decani fanned the passport and papers out on the night table as if he were spreading a hand of cards, then picked up the phone. He waited, then began to speak rapidly. When he was done, he turned back and asked, "You came here straight from Germany?"

"Yes, I drove from Frankfurt."

"Frankfurt?"

"Yes, I was there at the *Buchmesse,* you know, the annual book fair, the publisher's conference. I go every year, or at least one of us goes, my partner or myself."

"What do you do there?"

"The usual things. Talk to writers and publishers and other agents. Try to sell foreign translations of our writers and perhaps arrange to represent some European authors in the United States."

"Business," Decani said, making the word an epithet.

"You might call it that," Stone said. "What's wrong with that? In fact, since you were asking, that's what I came here for."

"To this country?"

"Yes, to see if I could find some books, speak to some of your writers and represent them in America. There's a lot of interest in your country and your writers just now, and very little is known of either of them in my country."

"Did you have anyone particular in mind?" Decani asked, his voice so deliberately casual that Stone knew he was on sensitive ground.

"I don't know much about your writers or literature, but people in Frankfurt mentioned that there were many I ought to talk to," he replied carefully. "Here, let me see." Stone picked up his notebook from the table where Decani had laid it down, riffled the pages and then read, "Stefan Zica, Andrija Gora, Konstantin Karst, Gavrilo Iovanovic . . ." he broke off and looked up. "There are a good many other names, but they told me I could ask at the Writers' Association, the State Publishing House, and the Foreign Ministry, and that they would arrange for me to meet whoever I wanted."

Decani seemed not to have heard. "The people who gave you those names were Germans?"

"Some," Stone answered, "not all. An Austrian, several Frenchmen, a couple of Italians, some Englishmen. Why?"

"And they said Konstantin Karst?"

Because Stone remembered all too clearly Antun Vuk's whispered, "I bring you the thing from Master Karst" before he'd been shot, Stone forced himself to scan the notebook again, glad to see that his hands did not tremble as his finger ran down the column of names. "Karst? Karst. Yes, here it is. Konstantin Karst."

"They told you to see him, especially?"

"No, his was just one of the names mentioned."

"He hasn't written any books for years," Decani said, "since before the war, before he was Vice-President."

"Is he Vice-President?" Stone asked.

"I said *was* Vice-President," Decani spoke too softly. "He retired last year . . . for reasons of ill health. I do not think you will be able to see him."

"That's too bad. I was told he was a very gifted writer."

"Yes," Decani affirmed, "Konstantin Karst is a *very* gifted man."

The silence that followed was broken by a knock at the door. At Decani's word, the night porter and a middle-aged, tired-looking chambermaid came in carrying bed linen and blankets. The porter's face was slack with sleep and the chambermaid kept rubbing her red-rimmed eyes and trying to suppress her yawns. They did not look directly at him or Decani, yet seemed to see Decani's nod and glinting glasses, which set them to re-making the bed. By his silence, Decani indicated there was to be no further conversation until they left, and Stone was grateful for the chance to compose himself.

Certainly, Decani was suspicious. He would be himself under such circumstances, and besides these people were professionally suspicious. They had been cut off from his world too long, immersed in their own, a world of battling and hating nationalities, of national wars, civil wars, of spies, murder and violence. The Balkans. Once only the name for a chain of mountains, it had become an imprecation. And now they were cut off still further, not only by their heritage of violence and bloodshed, but by their new religion which made them still bloodthirstier. They were men who had found their fulcrum and were going to move the world, *had* moved it. If they couldn't persuade you, you were a prisoner, a pariah, or a corpse. The viewpoint wasn't unique to them, Stone thought bitterly. We've done our share of killing too, more than our share. The age of anxiety, they'd called it, but the age of murder was what it was. Well, to hell with it. He didn't care what they were, so long as they let him alone. It was no business of his. He had no part of it, and wanted none.

"In spite of Antun Vuk?" his own voice questioned him

silently. "In spite of Antun Vuk," he answered himself firmly. "What is he to me that I should weep for him?" For a moment, he was pleased with the Shakespearean echo, then disgusted with himself for playing with words in the face of a boy's death. Hamlet, the word player, had at least finally been able to kill a king.

But wasn't that why he had become a literary agent? A book man, as Valerie had put it so contemptuously: "I married a book man." Not a bookish man, he recalled, but a book man, something not much better than a bookie. Well, at least she no longer had to put up with his books and bookishness.

The porter and chambermaid worked swiftly. After they had stripped off the mattress cover, baring the last much smaller bloodstain beneath, they covered it over with fresh white sheets and in a few moments, for all you could see, Antun Vuk might never have died there. In the making, they moved the bed, exposing his bedslippers and cigarettes beneath. Stone pulled them out of the way, gratefully stuffed his cold feet into the slippers and the cigarette pack into the pocket of his robe. But the right slipper did not give to his foot, and only after his second impatient shove did Stone realize something was wedged into the toe. Unobtrusively, he tried to identify it by wiggling his big toe around it, but couldn't.

The chambermaid kept rubbing her eyes and the porter's cheek jumped like a frog's eyelid, but they were soon finished, bowing and curtsying briefly, and went toward the door. As they were closing it behind them, one of the chambermaid's eyes blinked shut, solemnly and only once, like a silent camera shutter. That and the thing wedged against his toe startled Stone, and Decani's barked order right after made him jump. The door opened again and the porter and chambermaid came back. Stone wondered if Decani could have seen that wink when his back was facing the door. Then, suddenly, Stone knew why the eyeglasses looked so strange and glinted so often and oddly: they had small side panels so that out of the corners of his eyes Decani could see behind him, and he had been watching the porter and chambermaid.

Decani's words to them were a slow icy stream. The porter shrugged and the chambermaid's face grew grim. She shook her head but said nothing. Decani spoke again, his sentence ending on a high note of questioning. Once more the woman shook her head and, looking down at his shoes, said a few halting words. Deliberately, Decani turned his back on them and said, "Mister Stone, did you see this woman wink at you?"

"Wink?" Stone asked, not knowing what to say. Had she admitted it or denied it. He looked over Decani's shoulder at her, but not a muscle in her face moved. She would not be caught that way again. "No, I don't think so," Stone said slowly, as if thinking it over. "I saw her rubbing her eyes as if she'd just been awakened. She may have been blinking, but not winking."

"Thank you, Mister Stone," Decani said politely. Then, whirling, in one motion, he brought his heel down sharply on her foot. The woman's scream was high-pitched and wild as she lurched and fell over, and Stone was sure that Decani had broken half a dozen small bones in her foot. Stone remembered being taught how to do it, on the small bones of the instep with your heel. He even remembered having to do it himself. For one instant he thought about moving forward to pick the chambermaid up, but he was neatly shouldered out of the way by Decani who said harshly, "You will not interfere, Mister Stone."

On one knee, her head bent, the woman had both her hands clasped over her instep. Decani, blue lips twitching, looked down at her and then took a beautiful pair of yellow pigskin gloves from his raincoat pocket and slapped them sharply across her face. Then again. And a third time. A small line of froth appeared on the woman's pale lips, like the line of surf on a beach, and her moaning was a sea sound, harsh and wracked. They stood like that, all of them frozen into a tableau, and something hysterical in Stone almost laughed aloud and had to be fought down. In a little while, Decani nodded, glasses glinting, and the porter leaned down, got his arm around the woman, and helped her limp from the room.

For a long time Decani silently paced the room, loping from the open French windows to the closed door, and Stone sat on the freshly made bed, trying to conquer his stomach's dry heaving. His throbbing head echoed his heart beat, and his big toe, whenever it touched what was in the bedslipper, recoiled. Outside, a soft wind moved in the trees. The smell of mist and wet shrubbery filled the room and then the cold, clear cry of a night bird convinced Stone that what was happening was real, that he was awake.

Decani finally sank into a chair and lighted another Benson & Hedges. "You didn't like that, did you Mister Stone?" he inquired too loudly, and without waiting for an answer, went on, "Well, neither did I."

Stone grimaced.

"Then why did I do it, you ask yourself? Why?" Decani took off his glasses, revealing ocean-green eyes whose chill somehow made his face more human and vulnerable. For an instant, he closed his eyes, pressing thumb and forefinger against the beating veins in the blue hollows where his eyes met the sides of his nose. Then, wearily, he dropped his hand away. "You don't know our people. They are savage. Proud, primitive, *you* might call them, and you would think, perhaps, that was a compliment, a flattery. But we bring law and order, and they have resisted law and order for centuries, against everyone—Turks, Greeks, Bulgarians, Germans—and against each other and themselves. The only law and order they understand is violent punishment: swift, inevitable, severe."

"Even when they're innocent?" Stone asked.

"Innocent?" Decani's eyes narrowed, his voice grew softer, silkier. "No one, Mister Stone, is innocent. Everyone wants to do what he wants to do. If that were permitted, no society would be stable. There would be no law, no order, no progress, no safety. Only chaos." Smoke poured from his nostrils and made his face look like a brutal unappeased idol's. "Have you ever heard of the Emperor Basil? An 11th-century Byzantine Greek Emperor, who defeated our equally savage neighbors, the Bulgarians, then sent ten thousand of their soldiers back to the Bulgarian king. A kindness, eh? Not at all. He had blinded all ten thousand and generously left one man with one eye to lead the others home to Ochrid." He paused, and looked past Stone out of the window. "It is told that when the Bulgarian king saw those soldiers, he had a heart attack and died. I almost wish I could believe that he was so grieved. More likely he killed most or all of the ten thousand who returned because they had lost his battle and because, as blind men, they were now useless. Worse than useless, they were liabilities." His voice fell away into silence.

"The way I heard the story," Stone said, "Basil left one man in every hundred to lead the other ninety-nine blinded back. That man he left with one eye. But it doesn't make much difference—either version makes the point."

"I see you know something of our history, Mister Stone,"

Decani said. "You listen to our stories, our folk songs, our poetry, and they're all like that. We grow up with it in our blood, like a sickness, like poison."

"People are like that everywhere," Stone said. "Not even the Emperor Basil could conceive an Auschwitz or a Dachau." He almost added, "a Vorkuta or a forced collectivization program that would kill millions of peasants," but restrained himself.

Decani looked at him without seeing him, nodding. Then he shook himself, put his glasses back on and rose. His voice was formal and official. "You will, Mister Stone, please come to see me tomorrow at the address on my card. We shall try to clear all this up. At two-thirty in the afternoon. Is it agreeable?"

"It won't be agreeable," Stone said, trying to smile, and also standing, "but I'll be there."

He followed Decani to the door. Deliberately, knowing Decani would be watching him over his shoulder through those sidepanel eyeglasses, Stone thumbed his nose at him. It was a childish, irresponsible gesture and he knew it, but he couldn't stop himself nor deny the small spurt of pleasure at Decani's stiffened shoulders.

"That was only a joke, Doctor Decani," Stone said, as Decani, lips bluer by contrast with his now blood-suffused cheeks, turned to face him. "It was only to tell you I recognized your intriguing glasses."

Decani's anger melted into a smile that was like a schoolboy's caught in a prank. "Clever, aren't they?"

"I don't know," Stone said, suddenly feeling that both of them were acting like "the boys" women always thought men were. "I knew another man once who had a pair of glasses like those and it didn't turn out well."

24

"No? What happened?"

"He kept looking over his shoulder, and he looked behind him once too often, and someone shot him in the stomach," Stone said wearily.

The silence was awkward. "Yes, Mister Stone, I see what you mean." Decani's head bent in what might have been either a nod or a bow. "You are a strange man, Mister Stone," he said. "A strange *literary agent*"—the accent was now equal on both words—"I think you called it. Good night. I hope you sleep well."

"Good night, Doctor Decani."

After the door closed, Stone turned the key in the lock, threw the bolt, and put his forehead against the door until his stomach stopped churning. After a time, he walked back to the bed and slumped down on it. He took off his right bedslipper, put his hand into the toe and withdrew a small piece of wadded material, the kind of nondescript dirty grey stuff easy to hide, easy to discard, easy to overlook, it could almost have been a large wad of accumulated dust. Stone shook it, gingerly, with two fingers, and a square of paper fell to the floor. He picked it up, unfolded it, and smoothed it out on the bed table. On it, in very old-fashioned handwriting, he read:

My dear Mister Stone:

Friends of mine in your country have written telling me of you and that you would be coming to my country. I am taking this strange way of inviting you to come to see me, but it is necessary. I think we shall have much in common that will be profitable to us both.

It would be best if you could arrange to visit me through official government channels, but if you think that will not come to pass, we must look for other ways. The bearer is completely trustworthy. Tell him a café or some other public place that you will go to where we can meet, so to speak, by accident.

Tell no one about this note. Lives are at stake if you do. Put nothing down on paper. *And destroy this.*

I apologize for this roundabout and clandestine invitation, but it will be a pleasure to meet you.

Konstantin Karst

Tell the bearer. *Antun Vuk.* No one would tell Antun Vuk anything any more. Being completely trustworthy had, as usual, paid badly. It's not my business, he told himself, not my responsibility. I didn't ask Karst to send the boy, nor even ask to see Karst. But he couldn't root out the recollection, and as he tried, the sharp image of Valerie's hard, half-turned beautiful face flowered in his mind, and she was telling him again about Matthew Byrd. "Why, Warren? You think you survived that war, but you're wrong. You're half-dead already, Warren."

Stone stood up and went to the windows, hoping with movement to shake loose the memory of Valerie. Not the slightest glimmer lit the eastern sky. Morning was still far away. In the garden below shadows still moved and Stone felt his own shadows stirring inside him. Why should he be thinking of Valerie? He hadn't thought of her for sometime, at least not during the days. But as he looked at that unnaturally neat garden—its formal sharp lines now blurred by shadow and mist—Stone remembered the many forgotten dreams of her in the nights, her mocking face and slashing silver nails which always left him lacerated and bleeding, like the painting of some medieval saint with his flayed skin in his hands and his bowels bared for all to see. "That's the way you think of yourself, Warren," Valerie would surely have pointed out, "as some kind of bloody saint. But it wouldn't be a saint in life.

No, not that. Of course not that, but a saint in a book or a picture."

"She's a bitch. What can a man like you see in such a bitch? Not that I expect you'd tell me even if you could. T'aint gentlemanly, is it?" Sam Gordon had always detested Valerie, but when, on occasion, Stone had worked late in the offices with Gordon in the curious but satisfying professional intimacy which had been one of the few remaining bulwarks of his life, all Stone could get on the subject was a frown and Sam's repeated ambiguous statement that Valerie was one of those women "who thought she had it coming." And Valerie had hated Gordon in return, always trying to dissolve their partnership by urging him to go into a more "important" and "masculine" business. Of Gordon she had said with that scathing contempt and the delighted use of the word that only a "good" school breeding like that of Wellesley could produce: "Sam Gordon! All he thinks women are good for is *to screw*!"

Even after the divorce Sam would say little more, nothing except that it was in the cards, then insist that this year Stone would have to go to the Frankfurt *Buchmesse* because Sam couldn't: he was in the midst of negotiating a couple of important and sticky contracts, and since he was the firm lawyer. ... Besides, though business was good and growing, they were getting too parochial. Too many American writers and not enough foreign ones. They could use a couple of good European writers to fill out their list. Had Stone ever been to Yugoslavia? The country was particularly interesting now, and they had a good crop of postwar writers. Though Stone had not mentioned it to Decani, it was then, for the first time, that he had heard Konstantin Karst's name. He knew that books about Eastern Europe didn't usually sell very well, but there might be a change now, and they'd be ahead of the wave. Stone could combine business and pleasure. Had he ever seen the Dalmatian Coast? Some of the loveliest landscape in the world. A great place for a vacation. And beautiful women.

Stone went to the bathroom, got a water glass, and then to his suitcase for a whisky bottle. He poured himself half the glass, took a big swallow, then sat down on the bed and carefully reread Konstantin Karst's note. "Friends of mine," he had written. Who? Which ones? Who knew of his trip anyway? Well, lots of people, Stone supposed, publishing was a small, gossipy business. At least they might have known about the Frankfurt *Buchmesse,* and he himself had gone around asking about Yugoslavia there, and about Yugoslav writers so anyone might have heard.

Sitting there, puzzling, Stone drank the rest of the whisky. Things would be clearer in the morning. Tomorrow, first thing, before he went to see Decani, he would go to the Embassy and get it all straightened out in the light of day. For a moment, he thought about keeping the note from Karst to show to the Embassy people, otherwise they might think he was imagining the whole thing. But he decided against it. Antun Vuk had died to deliver and hide that message, and Karst had instructed him to destroy it. Lives were at stake. They certainly had been.

Stone laid the note in a hotel ash tray and lit a match to it. He watched it burn down to cinders and carefully stirred the ashes before carrying the ashtray to the window to blow them into the night. Then, gratefully, he got into bed. As he lay there, waiting for the sleep that was so long in coming, Stone remembered with pleasure how he had lunged for the totem-pole shadow and slammed the policeman to the floor, his body moving of its own mindless muscular accord, as it used to before and during the war. Even as sleep came, Stone knew that he had not been quite awake, not thinking, or he would have performed neither act—perhaps could not—and he remembered with shame the way he had let Decani stop him from helping the chambermaid, because by then he *was* awake. He liked to think that the years had taught him to curb his violent temper and his swift resort to unthinking aggressive action. *He had learned to keep his head.* But even as sleep overtook him, Stone knew that keeping your head meant two separate and distinct things. More than most things, more than anything perhaps, you had to be sure to which meaning you were really committed.

THE EMBASSY flew the American flag and had the great Seal of State over the entryway. Immense heavily barred glass doors at least twenty feet high reminded Stone of a portcullis, and inside the light was dim and grey as it might be in a medieval castle. There was something Balkan about the atmosphere inside the building, as if it had taken on the coloration of the country. For a few moments the dimness and the sight of familiar American newspapers on the racks and magazines on the tables made him feel comfortable, but the receptionist instantly restored the Balkan tone. "The Ambassador is in Washington for consultations," she said in answer to Stone's request to see him. Her accent clearly indicated that she was Yugoslav by origin.

"Then I'd like to see the First Secretary," Stone persisted, "or whoever is the political officer."

The receptionist bent her head and looked over his card again. "You are a *literary* agent, Mister Stone?" she said, searching his face with her dark eyes.

Stone nodded. How did they always manage to get such women and put them where everyone could get a bad first impression?

"Then maybe you would like to see Mister Michael Townsend, the cultural attaché. I'll see if he is free." She turned to a small black portable switchboard on her desk. "Second door on your left, fourth floor," she told Stone, but as he made for the open grillwork elevator, she called after him. When he turned, he found as his escort a red-haired Marine sergeant in khakis, a holstered 45 at his waist. "Nice day, isn't it?" Stone said, as they stood facing each other on the rising elevator. The Marine looked at him with small suspicious yellow eyes almost buried in heavy folds of eyelid. "I guess it is," he said neutrally, his gravel voice blurred by an Alabama drawl. Another friendly, attractive type.

The cultural attaché was smooth and even colder. A tall, slender man in his thirties, his face came to a harsh point in an almost razor-edged nose. He was wearing a grey British tweed suit, heavy Scotch brogues, black knit tie and button-down white shirt. With that uniform went the brisk uniform manner. "So you're Warren Stone," he said, shaking hands with a clammy palm and dismissing the Marine with a nod at the same time. "I'm Michael Townsend, Second Secretary in charge of cultural affairs. We heard you were going to pay us a visit."

"You did?" Stone asked. "How?"

"Oh, you know, that kind of thing gets around." Townsend's thin mouth bared white even teeth but it was a smile that did not engage the flat grey eyes. "And now what can I do for you, Mister Stone?"

Before he could answer, Townsend went to a huge half-wall of black knobs and panel that looked like a short-wave radio transmitter and receiver and turned it on, holding his hand up for silence like an announcer about to begin a broadcast. When the music began, Strauss waltzes of all things, he nodded permission to speak. Swiftly, briefly, looking straight into those grey pebble eyes, Stone told Townsend what had happened the night before, leaving out only the boy's whispered message and the note from Karst. Townsend's face did not change expression. Not even his eyes blinked, he seemed so rapt, and only when Stone was through did he realize that Townsend had not asked him to sit down. They stood perhaps six feet apart, Townsend sitting on the edge of his desk, arms braced and legs nattily crossed to show grey and maroon argyle socks, but Townsend's eyes were now riveted on the intricate design of the oriental rug beneath their feet.

"And then you came here?" Townsend asked.

"Where else could I go?" Stone replied, beginning to feel his temper rise.

"Or course, of course," Townsend said soothingly, his lips going through the motions of what passed for a smile. Then, as if seeing him for the first time, the attaché asked him to sit down, pointing to a leather chair. Stone took out a cigarette offered Townsend one, and when he had declined, lighted up.

"Would you excuse me for a moment?" Townsend said. "I'll be right back."

Stone waited, smoking and staring at a picture of the President, a neatly framed formal photograph which hung over Townsend's desk. Why had he always hated those portraits, officially posed, taken and distributed for mounting like part of the furniture? Gordon and Stone were a fairly well-known agency in the publishing world, but nowhere else, and he himself was scarcely legendary. Townsend had heard he was coming to pay a visit. How? When Stone had applied for his passport, he hadn't given Yugoslavia as a destination at all, because he wasn't sure then that he'd go. He'd applied for a visa in Frankfurt at a Yugoslav consulate and had not told the American consul there anything.

Townsend returned with a man who might almost have been

deliberately designed to be his exact opposite, a squat, powerful, almost square man in his mid-forties whose white hair was cropped so close that his scalp showed through. The florid face and broken veins in the cheeks and nose bespoke the heavy drinker. An old slovenly Navy blue suit, creased, stained and spotted with food, dandruff and cigarette ashes hung loosely on him, and the man looked as if he had been sleeping in those same clothes for a month.

"This is our economic counselor," Townsend introduced them, "Maxim Grout."

Grout nodded, but did not offer to shake hands. When he spoke, it was in a heavy bass rumble and though his English was flawless, there was something remotely off-key in his intonation that made Stone certain that he was not American born.

"I'd like to hear your story once more, Mister Stone," Grout said, "that is, if you can bear to repeat it." Stone again told what had happened the night before, again leaving out Antun Vuk's words and Karst's note. When he was finished, Grout asked, "You are sure that the boy's name was Antun Vuk?" He spoke the name very slowly and distinctly.

Stone nodded.

"And you came directly here?"

"First thing this morning," Stone replied, trying to keep his temper from kindling again.

Grout turned and said to Stone, "Just what did you expect us to do?"

Stone bounded to his feet. "This *is* the American Embassy, isn't it? And you represent, or are supposed to represent American citizens and their interests in this country, or have I misunderstood what the job of an American Embassy abroad is?"

Again Stone saw their quickly exchanged glances.

"I want you to help me get this mess cleared up so I can get on with what I came here for."

"What did you come here for, Mister Stone?" Townsend asked, his grey eyes darkening into small ball-bearings in his face. Both he and Grout seemed almost crouched in anticipation of what he would say. Either these guys are nuts, Stone thought, or I am.

Slowly, controlling himself, Stone said, "I'm an author's agent, here looking for books and authors for translation in the States. I never heard of Antun Vuk and I didn't kill him. I thought someone from the American Embassy, *my* Embassy, might come to see Doctor Decani with me to get this whole mess straight since I am not eager to spend my time here in jail for a crime I didn't commit. Is that clear?"

"Have any criminal charges been placed?" Grout asked.

"I don't know," Stone said, "it only happened last night."

"Did you have any particular writers in mind you came to see?" Townsend asked. Again, the note was too casual.

Deliberately Stone took out his notebook, though by now he knew everyone of the two dozen or so names by heart, and read the list aloud to them. When he got to Konstantin Karst, speaking the name completely without emphasis, as he had the others, he heard their sharp intake of breath, but they did not interrupt and he continued reading the list through. "I also meant to come in to talk to you," he added, "and to see the Writers' Union, the State Publishing House, and so forth, to find out whom else I ought to see."

"I think I might be able to help you to see some of those people," Townsend said, suddenly and unaccountably.

"Perhaps," Stone retorted putting the notebook back into his pocket, "I ought to forget the whole thing, pack my bags, and get the first plane out of here."

34

Disdain and anxiety seemed to clash in Townsend's face, but Grout remained impassive. "If they don't want you to leave, Mister Stone," he said, "you couldn't even get out of your hotel lobby, much less on a plane, or any other vehicle. And if there are criminal charges against you, there isn't too much we can do." He pulled an old hand-carved cherrywood pipe from his pocket, then a small oilskin tobacco pouch, and began to fill the bowl. "But," he went on, the pipe between his teeth, "maybe that is exactly what they hoped last night would accomplish. Maybe they wanted to scare you off. Maybe they're hoping you'll do exactly that, pack up and leave."

"Well, by God, if that's what *they* wanted to do, *they* damn well succeeded," Stone snorted.

"You're afraid?" Townsend asked, his voice incredulous and his eyes even steelier.

"I'm scared stiff," Stone replied. Then, turning to Maxim Grout, he said, *"They, they,* who are *they?* And what have *they* got to do with me?"

Grout looked at him sternly. "You are right to be afraid, Mister Stone, but you must not lose your head."

Again that phrase, Stone thought. That's exactly what I'm trying to prevent, losing my head, and the simplest way to prevent it would be to get the very first plane out.

Grout had his pipe lit and a column of smoke pouring out of it. "Have you ever heard of Konstantin Karst?"

"Yes," Stone answered, feeling guilty about not having mentioned Karst's note, and almost impelled to tell them the contents. "He's one of the names on my list of writers."

"Is that all you know about him?"

"No," Stone hesitated, "Decani mentioned that Karst was once Vice-President of this country but that he'd retired because of ill health and that I probably wouldn't be able to see him."

"Is that what Decani said?" Townsend asked, leaning forward, his long sharp face like a hunting dog's. "Exactly what he said?"

"As close as I can remember."

"In the Balkans, Konstantin Karst is a legend," Maxim Grout said dreamily.

"Mister Stone," Townsend cut Grout off, "could I see your passport, please?"

"You said you knew I was arriving, but you want to see my passport?" Stone asked. This was more than initial caution; it was suspicion and unfriendliness, not merely the diplomatic cool formality that one might expect for having dropped a pot of trouble into their laps. It had been positive hostility.

"We were informed that someone named Warren Stone was coming to Belgrade," Grout said, "but how do we know you're Warren Stone?"

"I might somehow have gotten Stone's passport, then come here masquerading as him?" Stone asked incredulously.

"It's possible," Townsend said. "The passport, please, Mister Stone."

Slowly Stone removed the green passport from the black morocco leather wallet and handed it to him. "Do you think that if I weren't Stone I'd be so stupid as to come here?"

Townsend did not reply but began to examine the passport closely. Grout watched him attentively. Was it simply, Stone thought, not quite believing things were happening that way, that even the American Embassy gradually took on the character of the country it was in, and that this Embassy had been Balkanized?

"Do you live in New York?" Townsend asked. Stone noticed that he had been jotting notes on a little pad.

"The passport says so, doesn't it?" Stone replied.

Townsend finished scrutinizing the passport and gave it to Grout who looked at it for a moment before asking, as he handed it back, "What did you do during the war, Mister Stone?"

"I was in the paratroops," Stone said curtly.

"Not in OSS or Intelligence?" Townsend said.

"Or in the State Department?" Grout echoed.

"I was in the 82nd Airborne."

"Have you been in Washington recently?"

Stone nodded. "I was there about six weeks ago."

"For what?"

"What I did in Washington is really none of your business. If you must know, I was talking to a Senator about doing a book on American foreign policy. . . . Is all this really necessary?"

They exchanged glances once more and suddenly Stone realized that they, too, thought he was some kind of agent, as Decani had. Probably they imagined he was sent on a mission to Karst that they should have been asked to do themselves, and that he was in Belgrade by-passing them. Or perhaps they thought he might have been sent from Washington to review their competence and effectiveness. The whole idea was ridiculous but it was the only one that seemed to make any sense.

"And what's all this about Karst anyway?"

". . . Konstantin Karst is that peculiarly European combination," Grout replied, "the poet and politician, the man of action and the man of contemplation. A tradition from which our own intellectuals could very well learn and profit." He puffed his pipe meditatively for a while, as if considering the prospects of such a change in American culture, and then smiled ironically and self-mockingly. There was a feeling and intelligent man under the tough face and square bulk of Maxim Grout.

"Karst is a mountain man, brought up in the harsh mountain world of Montenegro. He has always had many of the mountain man's qualities: lyricism and violence, sentimentality and ruthlessness; poetry and death. But most of all that overriding mountain characteristic, hardheaded fanaticism. When he chooses a course, whichever one it is, it is likely to be an extreme, and he is sure to push it to its logical—or illogical"—again the mocking smile—"conclusion.

"When such men drink, they always get drunk. Karst drank, but what he drank was more fiery than even the local *rakija*. He drank Revolution, with a capital R, in this instance labelled Marxism-Leninism, and he became as drunk with that as most men become with whisky. Drunker. Because he was more sensitive and volatile, he became even drunker." Grout's teeth gritted on the pipe stem.

Townsend's voice was dry. "Konstantin Karst was born just before the first World War, which would make him somewhere in his early fifties now . . ."

". . . so that most of what he knew as he grew up was war and depression, depression and war," Grout said.

"There were others from Montenegro who didn't end up commissars or Communists or killers," Townsend said. "You can't blame Karst's career on the mountains . . . or on 'conditions.' "

"Blame?" Grout spoke as if the word had not occurred to him. "Karst's nature, his character, was his destiny, but the circumstances were crucial too. Everywhere Karst looked, and he looked with a poet's eye, he saw misery, poverty, oppression, corruption, brutality, violence. And though he began his adult life as a writer, before long he was trying to change matters with politics."

"You mean he joined the Communist Party," Townsend interjected sarcastically. "There were other places to go, Max, other parties, socialists, peasants, independent democrats . . ."

". . . there were, Michael, but only the Communists were extreme enough, violent enough to suit a man of Karst's temperament," Grout admitted. "Perhaps," he added grudgingly, "only the Communists were extreme and violent enough to suit the circumstances themselves."

"Nonsense!" Townsend exclaimed. "You simply don't admit the type of root-and-branch fanaticism that attracts some human beings to communism."

Grout held up his palms and with that shy mocking smile, said, "You see, we have our factional squabbles too."

Again Stone felt that they were playing a game, that they were trying to persuade him that their view of the local situation was correct, because he might be, just might be, higher up in the hierarchy than they were, the headquarters man come to see how the front-line boys were carrying out directives. The argument was scarcely new to him, but no other reason for going over it in front of him seemed sensible. Obviously, they had covered the ground many times before—and heatedly.

"You've never met Karst, or been in communication with him?" Townsend inquired abruptly.

"No. I never met him or wrote to him," Stone replied, aware of the hairline he was drawing between telling the truth and lying.

"Well, let's find out what it's all about," Grout said, rising and going to the phone. A few moments later he was saying, "Doctor Decani?" and then lapsing into Serbo-Croat. When

39

he hung up, he said, "Come on, we're going to pay Doctor Petar Decani a visit, *now*."

"He said this afternoon," Stone protested.

"He'll see us now," Grout said, with grim satisfaction.

"You think that's wise, Max?" Townsend asked softly.

"I don't know," Grout replied. "What else can we do?" Again there was just the flicker of a glance off him, and the instant pause in speech. "Would you rather *I* went?" Townsend asked, speaking as if Stone were not in the room.

"No, Michael, thank you. I think it had better be me."

Outside, daylight had settled into a gloomy, dim-grey morning. Streets and still leafless winter trees glistened with moisture and in the air a heavy wintry mist muffled sounds like snow. They passed foreign embassies and government offices, each identifiable by its polished brass plaque and its own small green-pointed wooden sentrybox, with armed soldiers as guards. They carried pistols, rifles, submachine guns, and one even had two German-type potato masher grenades clipped to his belt. Stiff, wooden-faced, looking straight ahead, they reminded Stone of the miniature soldiers he had had as a boy, and he felt he could reach out and pick them up and move them around as he had those toy soldiers in the attic of his mother's old Oyster Bay house. "They look like toy soldiers," Grout's voice intruded, as if he had been reading Stone's mind, "but they're some of the bravest, toughest fighters in the world."

Everywhere, too, there were automobiles parked on the broad, half-dirt, half-concrete sidewalks. Row after row side by side, except where tree trunks intervened, the cars were so numerous and so closely parked that they made it difficult to walk and Stone and Grout were forced off the

40

pavement. Most of the cars were heavy, sleek black Mercedes-Benz 220s. "Belgrade's Embassy Row and Government Alley," Grount grunted sardonically. "None of them walks, if he can help it, and they don't leave anyone else room to walk either. Those Mercedes-Benzes are the new ruling-class status symbol here."

"Some people will shove you off the pavement into the gutter," Stone remembered the line as if his grandfather had just spoken it, though Cartwright Stone had been dead almost twenty-five years. "I see them every day in court. They'll shoulder you off the street, push you through a door, or knock you down if they can—and enjoy it. They're just like that. They're those kind of people." As a fifteen-year-old, Stone had come to ask about the Nazis, and that answer to what kind of people they were had seemed to him an old man's foolish answer, even a form of middle-class snobbery. "*Those* people are just like *that*." It was a long time before Stone had learned not to scoff at that observation on mankind, and a long time too since he'd remembered his grandfather saying it.

Stone heard the sounds—the screech of tires, the racing engine, and Grout's booming, "Move, Stone! Run!" He saw the black heavy car bearing down on them, its chrome grill-work and headlights like some animal's gaping mouth and glaring eyes. A lone man in the driver's seat was hunched over the wheel, coat collar turned up and hat brim turned down, so that all Stone noted was a white line of nose in the shadows between the two, a nose that looked more like naked bone than flesh. At the same time, out of the corner of his eye, he saw Grout's square body move with unbelievable agility and speed, knocking them both to the ground and rolling them over on the pavement between two parked cars.

When Stone got to his feet the car was gone. Grout, on

one knee, was already peering at the wet cobblestones in the street. Stone joined him, feeling dry-mouthed and knee-shaky. Grout was saying clinically, "Up to their old tricks. Even using an old-style Tatra with Venetian blinds down and no plates. I'd think all those people got their training with Capone in Chicago, if I didn't know better. They could teach our gangsters a trick or three."

Grout stood up. "It's plain that they really don't want to have you see Konstantin Karst."

"Looks like they don't want me to see anything," Stone said, disliking the fear and self-pity he heard in his voice.

"They didn't want to hit you—or us—only scare you. Here, look at that," he pointed to the tire marks on the cobblestones. "That driver braked a long way before we jumped."

"Maybe he braked after we jumped and the cars on the sidewalk blocked his getting at us," Stone objected.

"If they wanted to kill, Mister Stone, a couple of smashed cars wouldn't stop them," Grout grinned crookedly, "and a couple of bullets would have done the trick too from that close. No, they wanted to frighten you off. Maybe me too. But they surely don't want you to get to Konstantin Karst."

While he was brushing his clothes, Grout began to talk, as if continuing a story. "By the time Karst entered the university, Yugoslavia had become a royal dictatorship, and Karst was in opposition. His two interests at the university were politics and literature. Only as a Communist did he believe they could be combined. He already had a small reputation as a poet in intellectual circles in Belgrade, which helped him, and which he deliberately used to organize an underground Communist youth group among the students, the first one in this country. It wasn't long before the police learned of it, and of him, and from then on he was a marked man.

"The Party was illegal and when the political police caught Karst, they had him dead to rights. Besides, he denied nothing. He made a fiery courtroom speech which was splendid but absolutely useless, and they sent him to prison for five years. There, what had begun as youthful and humanitarian rebellion against injustice, poverty and tyranny was turned into the hardened dogmatism of the professional revolutionary."

There was a long pause before Grout sighed, and as they began to walk, he continued, "In prison, Karst went on writing—poems, essays, a novel—which increased his literary reputation in this country, and even began to spread it abroad. In those days, however bad it was, you could write in prison, read, and even get out what you'd written to be published. These people," he nodded at a brace of green sentries they were passing, "no longer permit such prison luxuries." Grout's voice ran down, as if he were disheartened, and the shy mocking smile surfaced. "Two volumes of his poems and his novel were translated into French and German—that was the year before Hitler—and they even helped muster some Communist-manipulated public opinion abroad in favor of his release. But the royal government refused to release him."

"How can you be so sure it's Karst they want to frighten me away from?" Stone asked slowly, "and not some other writer?"

Grout's face was suddenly melancholy. "Come along," he said, taking Stone's arm, "Decani's waiting."

Stone shook off his hand and repeated the question.

"How can I be *sure?*" Grout asked. "I can't. There's only one clue, but it's a difficult one to ignore: *Antun Vuk.*"

The boy's name brought back the blood and the turned-up *opankes*. "Antun Vuk?" Stone repeated dully.

"Antun Vuk," Grout said very softly, "was Konstantin Karst's nephew, his sister's son."

"Oh, no!"

Grout nodded. "And I know he loved the boy. The boy's mother and father were killed during the war."

"The fool! Why did he send a boy to do a man's job!" Stone burst out angrily.

"Probably because he thought he had no other choice. He must want to see you very badly, and he must think it's very important. Essential." Grout began to take his pipe things out and to prepare a smoke. In spite of his deliberate manner, his calm voice and gestures, Stone saw that Grout was badly shaken too, that he needed not only the relief of the tobacco, but the precise routine of its preparation to restore his self-control.

He took up Karst's story again. "The rest is history. When Karst came out of prison, he was a Communist body and soul. In a few years, one of the usual Moscow purges of the local Party pushed him up the ladder, and he was elected to the Central Committee. Theoretically, he had always been a ruthless and dogmatic activist; now, with power, he was in fact worse. Everyone had to toe the Party line or else; and he crashed his boot down on every toe that didn't."

Stone saw Decani's whirl and the chambermaid's foaming mouth, her fingers clutching her foot. For seconds, he closed his eyes, hearing only the high-pitched scream in his ears, not what Grout was saying. Even when brutality was unnecessary, they used it. Coldly not hotly. Against the innocent and the guilty. It made everyone afraid, or almost everyone, and more tractable.

". . . then the war came, and Karst was a Partisan commander, brave and resourceful, but so bloody and merciless that he alienated even his own people. The Party had to yank

Karst out of the hill country where it had assigned him before he drove the local population into permanent opposition. After the war, Karst was everywhere, Ambassador, Minister of Culture, Politburo member, and finally Vice-President. The heir-apparent, the old man's favorite son. When the break with the Russians came in '48, Karst got the job of defending the country and attacking the Russians. Attack them, or counterattack them, he did it with the same ruthless, savage, passionate skill."

Grout puffed the pipe vigorously. "The more he attacked them, the more he saw he was attacking a mirror-image of the society he had helped to establish in his own country. And once the rose-colored glasses were off, Karst turned on that society, on his friends, former comrades, on what he himself had been, and began to cut them all to ribbons. He knew every lie, every evasion, every hypocrisy, every weak spot and double-think, and he began to probe them all."

"At first," Grout continued, "they let him use Party publications to criticize. Things weren't going well and they needed what they call criticism and self-criticism. They had to make themselves look different from the Russian Party, or lose their comrades to the Russians; and they wanted to loosen the reins a little to get the people on their side. The Russians had agents everywhere—in the Army, the police, the Party—all trying to stir up trouble.

"But Karst hit his comrades where it hurt—in the center of their power and their privilege—and they cut him down to size. They took away his jobs, his villas, his cars; they threatened him with prison if he didn't shut up, the same prison he'd been in before the war, under the King. They even took away his wartime decorations for bravery.

"There was almost no one left to defend him," Grout added harshly. "The so-called liberals and deviationists he'd stepped on never forgave him. The pro-Russians remembered his assault on the Soviet Party and the USSR. His friends in power, now the targets of his criticism, looked on him as a traitor. He was isolated, without friends, money or a job: absolutely alone.

"The laughable thing," Grout concluded, "was that Karst hadn't tried to set up a faction in the Party or any real opposition group. Completely unrealistic. He really thought they wanted to 'purify their socialism,' cauterize their abcesses."

"And Karst's books, his writing?" Stone asked, hearing as he did Valerie's laughter in his ears and what he knew would be her cutting comment, "That's what *you* would ask about! History being made. A country at stake. A man's life and career going under. And *you* ask about books."

"Nothing but polemics, political propaganda. Fiery, illogical, sometimes beautiful," Grout replied, his face downcast, "but no poetry, no novels. Or, if he did write anything, it didn't get into print."

"And all that time keeping other writers in line?"

"Yes," Grout nodded, "like a good commissar, he did that too."

It was so quiet Stone could hear their breathing, and the splayed sounds their soles made on the street. They walked several blocks before Stone brought himself to ask, "Why didn't you tell me about Antun Vuk before?"

"I shouldn't have done so now," Grout replied, "and if I hadn't been, well, upset, I wouldn't have. I thought it better for you not to know, especially with Decani."

"But I knew."

"You knew!" It was Grout's turn to be surprised. "You knew the boy was Karst's nephew?"

"No, not that," Stone hesitated, torn by the choice of whether or not to tell this man he had met only two hours before about the boy's whisper and Karst's message. "But I knew he had been sent by Karst." Stone told him the whole story then, about Antun Vuk's whispered words and Karst's note, but he felt guilty for betraying the confidence assumed in Karst's note. When Stone was finished, Grout's expression was rigid. "You should have told us that before, Mister Stone," he said, his voice frosty and formal.

"And you both should have told me who Antun Vuk was too, but you didn't, did you?" Stone retorted sharply.

Grout's face gradually relaxed into a smile. "No, we didn't, did we? I guess we're even." He put out his hand.

As he took the hand and shook it, Stone said slowly and very distinctly, "I haven't forgotten what you did back there, and I'm grateful."

"For what?" Grout replied. "I told you they were only trying to scare you."

They stood there grinning at each other, relieved, almost happy, their hands still gripped. "My name is Maxim, but no one ever calls me anything but Max," Grout said.

"Mine's Warren," said Stone.

Embarrassed, they laughed awkwardly, dropped their hands, and walked on, measuring their steps in stride. "I wonder how they knew where we were?" Stone said, deliberately casual.

"Not hard to figure out," Grout replied. "Decani knew we were on the way there. Only a couple of routes from the Embassy to his office, and this is the most direct and likely." But he was obviously thinking of something else. "That's why I don't think they wanted to kill. Not smart. Daylight. They'd have waited for night and not when we had an appointment to see one of their people."

"One of whose people?"

"Decani's. The political police. Secret police. Used to be

47

called the UDBA. They've got another set of initials now, but it's pretty much the same organization, though they stay out of the limelight these days and they don't throw their weight around any more the way they once did."

"That Tatra was pretty heavy," Stone said, trying to make a joke of it.

"It was that," Grout smiled. "But that kind of thing doesn't happen so often now. Things here have improved a great deal."

"Only one thing makes sense, ties the pieces together," Stone said finally, almost to himself. "Since his fall from the high places, or maybe even while he was up there, Karst was still writing. If his politics changed as radically as you said they had, then he's probably written a book his high and mighty former friends won't like. His former friends, no doubt, suspect that, but for one reason or another haven't been willing or able to do anything about it. I have no special qualifications that would make a man like Karst want to see me, except that I happen to be a literary agent. An American literary agent. Therefore, the only reason he could want to see me is a book."

"No other *special* qualifications, Warren?" Grout regarded him quizzically. "You're sure you weren't sent here *specifically* to see Karst? Because if you were, I think it would be better if you told me now."

"So help me, Max, I'm a *literary agent,* nothing more. As you could see back there with the Tatra, I'm not much good for this kind of thing."

"You'd be good enough," Grout said, looking levelly at him, "if you cared. The trouble is you don't give a damn."

"About politics? No, no more. The war cured me."

"*Cured* you?"

48

"Yes, cured me. I don't hunt. I don't fish. I don't kill . . .
any more."

"And you don't choose, Warren?"

"I choose to be left alone. If they're bad, and God knows
they are, we're not much better, are we? And I don't want to
fight or to do any killing to improve them either."

"Even if they are willing to kill to "improve" you, or are
not willing to let you alone, what then?"

"You mean Antun Vuk?"

Grout nodded. "Though that's the one part of the picture
that doesn't make sense."

"The boy?"

"Decani's men wouldn't have killed the boy."

"Why not?" Stone asked, remembering Decani's cold violence, and the skilled careless way the boy's body had been
disposed of by his men.

"They don't kill these days unless it's absolutely necessary,
and killing that boy wasn't necessary. It can only serve to make
Karst more determined, more stubborn, and they know that."
Stone felt Grout was holding something back.

"If they were going to kill, you mean they'd kill Karst?"

"No. Too much noise and publicity. But why the boy, I don't
understand."

Decani's offices were housed in a huge cream-colored building done in the style of the Nineties of the last century and
occupying almost half a square block close to the center of the
city. An imposing façade, Corinthian columns and an en-
tablature with an old-fashioned classical frieze showing blind
Justice and her scales seemed an anachronistic and ironic com-
mentary on the three green guard posts outside. Inside, the
windows were heavily curtained with dark grey velvet drapes

49

that kept one from seeing in or out but also permitted no daylight to enter. The huge hall was dimly lit instead with weak yellow lamps that cast startling shadows on the high ceilings and walls. Great wooden doors guarded the various entryways but all were closed off except one small door on the far left through which two lines of waiting people stretched past a small glass-enclosed cubicle.

Stone followed Grout onto the waiting line. In the glass cage two men sat, a Sten gun on the wall behind them and next to it a great square nailboard on which were hung little numbered brass checks. Each man going in presented an identity card and filled out a written slip stating who he was going to see and what his business was. In return he got a brass check permitting him to enter. Those coming out returned the numbered brass checks to get their identity papers back. The written slip remained on file. A simple, efficient method. "You can't say they're not careful," Grout whispered.

When their turn came, Grout spoke to the man seated at the desk inside the glass cubicle. Behind him, standing next to the Sten gun was a tall, terribly thin man with a face like a tomahawk. A heavy black mustache and a livid scar slashed diagonally across the bridge of his nose, from his right cheek to the left side of his forehead, made his face seem like it had been going in two directions at once and had only just been held together. His left hand nervously ran up and down the Sten gun barrel. For an instant his eyes met Stone's and Stone was sure of a flash of recognition. When he continued to stare, the other man deliberately and icily turned his eyes away but there was a sardonic hint of a smile in the turned-up corners of the mustache, and his hand stayed on the gun barrel.

"Damn foolishness," Grout grumbled. "Wrong entrance. We go round to the right."

Stone kept staring at the man, examining his face and wanting him to know it. Wave after wave of a hot anger burned through him, and Stone felt his muscles tense, as if he were an animal readying itself for a spring. He was absurdly gratified to see the man's eyes carefully watching him too, and the man's growing tension. His hand dropped away from the Sten gun, and he kept running a finger between his neck and the turtle-necked black sweater he wore under his shabby double-breasted jacket, as if he were wearing a collar too tight for him.

As they walked away from the line Stone asked Grout if he'd never been there before, a little surprised that he apparently didn't know his way around. Grout said it wasn't the kind of place he liked to visit. As they got to the door, Grout's voice rose slightly and he inquired gruffly, "What's the matter, Warren? You're white as a sheet, and your eyes are blazing."

Tossing his head in the direction of the glass cage, Stone ground out the words, "Don't turn now. But the man back there, next to the Sten gun."

Grout halted, and in a leisurely manner began to relight his pipe. As he struck the flame, he looked over the pipe bowl toward the cubicle. "I see him," he said softly.

"I think that's the totem-pole type who killed Antun Vuk."

Stone felt more than saw Grout's agitation, but the voice asked quietly and calmly, "Are you sure?"

"No. The room was pretty dark. But he's not exactly a run-of-the-mill size and shape."

"Remember him," Grout advised, puffing vigorously and snatching another quick look at the man. "I will too." Then, taking his arm, Grout said, "Come on, let's go see the good Doctor."

The right entrance for them turned out to be at the far

corner of the same building, but obviously set up for guests. Inside, tall leaded Romanesque windows were uncurtained, and through them daylight flooded into the two-story high cupolaed anteroom. Even the dim grey morning light made the room bright. On each side of two gracefully carved wooden doors three imposing caryatids stood, stone-faced and strong-bodied, as if they really held the building up on their heads and shoulders while their bare feet remained comfortably buried in the Turkish carpets that covered the floor. The cupolaed dome was painted with a fresco, strong light colors, which showed a glowing new city being erected in the background and in the foreground graceful naked men and women and children, tanned and muscular, carried beams, laid bricks, measured and constructed for the city behind them.

They were expected. From behind the only desk in the reception room, a French antique, a slender, dark-haired man in stylish, Italian-tailored clothes, rose and said in unaccented English, "Mister Grout, Mister Stone, good morning. Doctor Decani is waiting for you."

They followed him through the doors, up a marble staircase, to the first floor and were ushered into a large waiting room tastefully, if elaborately, furnished in Empire style. Heavy gilt-framed paintings of pastoral scenes that looked more French than Yugoslav decorated the walls, and small pieces of onyx and marble statuary sat on various small tables. In the corner of the room, there was an enormous and beautifully proportioned old porcelain stove. A male secretary tried to tell them in sign language to be seated, that Doctor Decani would be with them shortly. Grout in Serbo-Croat and Stone in German said yes, they understood, and sat down on one of the red plush divans. Relieved, the secretary said, *"Molim"* and *"Bitte"* and went back to his desk.

"The usual technique," Grout said under his breath, "is a good long wait, but today we'll be let in quickly."

They were. The words were scarcely out of Grout's mouth when the buzzer on the secretary's desk sounded. Painfully, in stammered English, he said to them, "Please to go in."

Politely, they both answered "Thank you" in English and stood up. The doors on the right led to Decani's office. When they opened them, another set of heavy doors padded with grey leather neatly fastened with a rectangle of thick brass studs faced them. The soundproofing and what it connoted made them hesitate a moment before opening that set of doors.

The contrast between the room they had just left and the one they had entered left Stone feeling he'd been elbowed in the solar plexus, and he realized that it was intended to do just that. As stripped-down as a military office or a cabin on a destroyer, the room was painted just a shade lighter than battleship grey and filled with the same color grey desk, carpet, and bank of metal filing cabinets—all modern, straight lines, unrelieved by decoration, and harshly lit by overhead fluorescent lights. Four spots of color stood out in the room like stains, and Stone's eyes sought them out in relief: three big, wine-colored leather chairs, with the same brass studding as had been on the grey leather doors, stood grouped around the desk, one behind and two in front; and a colored chromo portrait of Marshal Tito hung directly behind the desk just over Decani's head.

Dumbfounded by the room, Stone stood at the doorway, taking it in, and it was a moment before he was aware that Grout was already halfway across the room, and that Decani had come out from behind his desk to meet him. "Petar!" "Maxim!" The first-name greetings and flood of swiftly exchanged Serbo-Croat that came with a European-style embrace between the two men sent uneasy doubts flaring through Stone. These two greeted each other like long-lost brothers, or old friends. What was going on? Decani retreated a pace, still holding Grout by the shoulders though at arm's length, and said, "But we must speak English, Maxim, for Mister Stone's sake."

Grout also stepped back and Decani's arms fell naturally to his sides. "You've met Mister Stone," Grout said.

"Yes," Decani said, the blue lips smiling, the glasses glinting, "but under somewhat unfortunate circumstances, Maxim. We got a call last night from Mister Stone's hotel that there had been shooting heard and since I just happened to be working late I went along, with the others, to investigate."

"That was fortunate for Mister Stone," Grout commented.

"Yes, it was. You know some of my people. When there's a murder, or something of that sort, they get carried away. They're a little zealous, you might say . . ."

". . . still not used to the new methods, eh Petar?" Grout chuckled obligingly.

". . . exactly, Maxim, bad habits persist," Dencani said. "But we found someone had been killed in Mister Stone's room, an Antun Vuk . . ." Decani stopped in midsentence, his eyes glued to Grout's face.

"Vuk? Antun Vuk? The name isn't familiar. Did I know the man?" Grout inquired, blank-faced. "And you thought Mister Stone was involved, Petar?" Grout raised his voice and eyebrows together. It was a polished if somewhat theatrical performance.

"Well, Maxim, what could I think? The boy was in Mister Stone's room, dead, shot. You know, Maxim, tastes differ in these matters, some men do like young boys . . ."

54

". . . Doctor Decani," Stone cut in, his voice hard and definite, "I am *not* one of those men."

"No, Mister Stone, of course not. But you know that people connected with *literature*—" Decani enunciated the word almost mincingly "—sometimes are. Last night we couldn't be sure. Now we are."

"I'll bet you woke a lot of people in New York to find that out," Stone said sarcastically.

"We have our sources, Mister Stone. Your former wife was very cooperative," Decani grinned, "she told our man that *that* was not one of your problems."

"You called Valerie!" Stone said furiously, aware that he was as angry about the intrusion into his privacy as he was afraid of what she might have told Decani. "You had no right to do that." It had been almost a year and a half since the divorce and her remarriage and he had not been in touch with her once since. And to have the first time be like this. . . .

"But how else could we find out?" Decani asked innocently, his glasses reflecting straight bars of bluish light. "Now, to business," he went on briskly, "your trip here seems to be quite legitimate. My government is, therefore, very eager to help you. In fact, I've been asked to give you every assistance. The Ministry of Culture is delighted for you to meet our best writers, and we are going ahead to make some appointments for you. This afternoon, you have your first one. You will meet Eleanor Hvar, our foremost English and American translator. She will talk to you about the types of work available in our country and, we shall arrange for you to see any book or author you find interesting.

"Also, since you especially wanted to see Konstantin Karst, I, myself, will arrange an appointment for you with him."

Decani's blue lips fluttered in what was supposed to be a disarming smile, but remained a grimace.

"But I didn't want to see Karst, or anyone else, *especially*," Stone protested.

"Has Karst written a new book, Petar?" Grout asked.

"Perhaps, Maxim. I don't know. But after all, he *is* one of our best writers. Mister Stone should at least talk to him. Don't you agree?"

"He was once a very fine writer," Grout said.

"I'll have to ring you up about Karst at your hotel, Mister Stone, because I don't have his address and he doesn't have a telephone. Here," he picked a card off his desk, "is Miss Hvar's address. You can find her place very easily."

Suddenly all three of them seemed to realize that they were still standing. Decani said, "I'm sorry I can't ask you to sit down and enjoy our customary hospitality, some coffee and *rakija,* but it is a very busy day for me, and that Antun Vuk murder makes it even busier."

"Why do you think he was murdered, Petar?" Grout asked, as Decani herded them toward the door.

Decani shrugged. "Who knows? Perhaps he was trying to rob Mister Stone's hotel room with a friend, and the friend killed him. Some of the people at the hotel saw another man there, but not very clearly." He turned to Stone with a forced grin. "You know, some of our people—the young ones especially—think all Americans are rich."

"Well, aren't they?" Grout asked almost gaily.

"In some ways they are, Maxim," Decani said, unsmiling, "and in some ways they're not."

In the cupolaed waiting room downstairs, the young man in the Italian-style suit was nowhere to be seen. Stone walked to the outer door in front of Grout and pulled sharply at the door handle. The door, which he had expected to open easily, was locked and didn't give an inch so that Stone staggered back. Grout burst out laughing. "Warren, you're not used to this part of the world yet. Getting into these buildings is hard enough, but getting out is much harder. You don't exit from the scene until they're ready to let you." Grout walked to the antique French desk and began to run his hands along the bottom edge. Probably there's a little release mechanism here somewhere."

Feeling foolish, Stone looked up at the frescoed ceiling. Grout followed his glance. "That my friend, gave rise to one of the big jokes in town, at least among the common people. They said that it showed that to build socialism, the workers have to be kept naked."

"Pardon." It was the secretary in the Italian suit. He had come up so silently that neither of them had heard him. He reached past Grout, touched a part of the desk, a small buzz sounded and the door clicked open. Grout pulled it wide and stood aside for Stone to pass through; then, bowing slightly to the man at the buzzer, he followed.

"A matter of doors and postures," Stone said after they had walked several streets in silence. "I went in expecting all kinds of trouble from Decani, and he tells me he's eager to help me find books and authors, hands me an appointment with this translator woman, and even promises to arrange for me to see Konstantin Karst. I feel as if I were trying to knock a door down that someone opened just before my shoulder got there and I went flying on my face. Then, just when I'm beginning to feel that maybe the whole thing's a mistake, I'm baulked by a door that won't open when it should."

"Death hath a thousand doors to let out life. I shall find one," Grout quoted softly and sadly.

"You know that Massinger line!" Stone exclaimed. "It's haunted me for years, especially during the war."

"Don't forget it, Warren. Keep it in mind here all the time," Grout said emphatically. "All the time."

"But why? Everything seems straightened out now, doesn't it?"

"You don't really believe that mockery in there straightened anything out, do you Warren?" Grout showed an edge of impatience in his voice for the first time. "It's too true to be good, as the vulgar expression goes. That talk with Decani complicates matters. For one thing, I'm convinced—don't ask me why or how because I don't know—that Decani's boys didn't kill Antun Vuk, and that they're just as eager to find out who did as we are."

"We are?"

"We are. Good Christ, Warren, sometimes let your guts choose for you, like back there with that skinny hoodlum. Sometimes your guts have more brains than your head."

"You mean I'm stupid."

"No, you know that's not what I mean. It's just that you're trying so hard to be detached, that you're making yourself a zombie."

"That's what my ex-wife used to say all the time."

"Well, she might have been right. Julia, that's my former spouse, used to say I was a zealot, a Commissar *manqué*." He smiled wanly. "Maybe she was right. You know you care what happened to that boy, Antun Vuk."

"Well, maybe ex-wives are smarter than we give them credit for," Stone said, hurt because he knew how close to the bone Grout's comments were.

"They ought to be smart enough *not* to give strangers information about their ex-husbands," Grout said, obviously referring to Decani's people calling Valerie in New York.

58

"Amen! They damn well should," Stone replied feelingly.

"But somehow they never are." Grout shook his head wonderingly. "You'd be surprised what our unwary citizens will tell people who call about one of their friends. Just tell them he's being investigated for a job, or a credit rating at the local department store, and you get his most intimate history."

Grout changed the subject. "Remember something you said a little while back, about Karst's former high-powered friends? You said they suspected he had written a book about them and for one reason or another weren't willing or able to do anything about it?"

"Yes. So what?"

"I think you've just been picked to get Karst's book for them."

Stone thought that over. "You mean, Decani arranges for me to see Karst. Karst gives me the book. Then they take the book away from me. A, B, C."

"The plan has all the virtues of simplicity. And you do the dirty work for them. In the present circumstances they don't want to make Karst a hero, a focus for discontent or resistance. Most of all they don't want him to become a way of organizing a *second* political party. That's the crux. If they pick you up at the border with Karst's manuscript, they get you both. They get you for smuggling an illegal manuscript. They get him for violating their State Secrets law. That law is wide enough to drive a truck through. They could get Karst for that even if he gives you his date of birth."

"But why not just take it from Karst?"

"Probably, they think that if they did it that way it would look bad and might get them *more* organized opposition, not less. This way, you're a foreigner, an American imperialist no less, and he's collaborating with the enemies of the country."

"Well, what do I do now?"

"I don't know," Grout said. "I'll have to talk to Townsend first."

"Townsend? Why him? Is he your boss?"

"Not exactly, but I'll have to tell him what the situation is."

"You're not going to tell him about Karst's note to me, are you?"

"I must, Warren, it's my duty."

"I always thought duty was something you expected of others," Stone said bitterly, "or was that just a Wilde notion? I told you about those notes in confidence."

"It's for your own good, Warren. Decani knows that Karst tried to get in touch with you because he knows about Antun Vuk. Our people have to know too."

"I told you personally not officially, Maxim."

Grout lowered his eyes to the ground, then raised them and looked directly into Stone's face. "I'm an official representative of the United States government here," he said tiredly. "I've got a job to do. In that job there are no personal confidences and no personal friends."

"A commissar *manqué*." He saw Grout wince as he spoke the words. "Your job is to tell Townsend?"

"Yes."

"And if I mentioned to Decani or Townsend that you told me who Antun Vuk was?"

"I don't think you'd do that, and besides, it wouldn't do any good."

"No, probably not," Warren admitted. "Why Townsend?"

"At the Embassy he's in charge of this sort of thing. I can't tell you any more than that."

"You mean he's the intelligence officer, the CIA man?"

"I can't discuss that with you, Warren."

An unpleasant, uneasy quiet fell between them.

"I'm sorry, but that's the way it is. I must report what you said to me, even in confidence. You can't trust anyone anywhere, but certainly not here. Don't even trust me," Grout said bitterly in a harsh voice.

"I can see that now, and I'll remember it," Stone replied.

"Do you want me to go to see this translator with you?" Grout asked.

"So you can report what I say to Townsend?"

"That's not necessary, Warren."

"Do you know Eleanor Hvar?"

"No, I don't, but I have heard of her. And I've seen some of her translations. They're excellent."

"If I have to play a lone hand," Stone said, "I might as well start learning to play it. And since, as you so wisely pointed out, I ought not to trust anyone, not even you, I think I'd prefer to go by myself."

"Are you sure you trust yourself?" Grout asked, very softly.

"Not much. But more than I trust anyone else right now," Stone said promptly. "Zombie or no."

Grout put out his hand but Stone ignored it. Reluctantly, Grout lowered it, and began to take out his pipe things again. "I'll call you later in the day. Keep in touch, will you Warren?"

"I'll keep in touch," Stone agreed. "Besides, if you want me, Decani's sure to know where I am." Then he turned on his heel and walked away, leaving Grout refilling his pipe from the oilskin pouch, and followed by his soft-voiced advice, "Be careful, Warren, be very careful."

ELEANOR HVAR lived not far from Stone's hotel on one of those many narrow side streets that twisted and turned away from the center of the city as if in anguish. At first, because the streets were poorly marked and many houses had no numbers, Stone couldn't find her place. He had refused to ask anyone at the hotel how to get there, and had politely ignored the doorman's too quickly flagged waiting taxi as he left the hotel. Grout had warned him to be careful. Well, he was going to be careful, very careful. He had a street map of the city and he could find Eleanor Hvar's house by himself.

Stone wandered through streets filled with wretched hovels, such striking contrasts to the modern glass, aluminum and colored concrete buildings on the main thoroughfares—and some of the excellent private dwellings on other streets—that they might easily have come from another century. As he went, Stone watched to see if he was being followed, stopping to look into store windows where he could see what was behind him reflected, grimly remembering how handy Decani's trick glasses were. He felt melodramatic and foolish, as if he were acting a role in a Hitchcock movie. But his bumbling stops to look at street signs and numbers, and gawking in shop windows, paid off: someone *was* following him, a nondescript bland-faced man in a shabby loden coat, carrying an oddly weighted-down scuffed brown leather briefcase. Whichever way Stone turned, the loden coat followed, discreetly keeping a block or so behind him and occasionally switching from one side of the street to another.

When Stone found Eleanor Hvar's street, he deliberately passed it by and continued about three-quarters of the way to the next street. Then he stopped, trying to appear as confused as he could, and looked around. He made the first awkward steps as if he were going back the way he came and slowly, but quite naturally, the loden coat, now facing him, paused at a house entrance, rang and went inside. It was what Stone had counted on. He swivelled and sprinted down the rest of the street, turned sharply left, noting out of the corner of his eye that the loden coat had not come out yet. Stone raced up the other street until he found what he was looking for, houses with alleyways and yards through which he could backtrack to Eleanor Hvar's block. He went over a wooden fence, a hedge, past a chained dog, who looked so surprised that he didn't even bark, and was back on her street.

A high stone fence almost completely hid Eleanor Hvar's one-story house and Stone, still throwing glances behind him, breathlessly pushed the bell and pounded impatiently on the iron lattice-work gate. As he was about to try to force it, the gate was pulled open slightly from inside and a dark, large-eyed face looked out. Stone quickly shouldered through the opening, past the girl, and slammed the gate shut behind him. There was still no sign of the loden coat; for the moment at least he had eluded him. Taking the girl's arm, Stone towed her half-running after him up the path to the house and through the open door. Only in the darkened vestibule did he stop to catch his breath, softly close the door behind them, and apologize. "My regrets," he said in French. "I am Monsieur Warren Stone and I have an appointment with Madame Hvar. Would you please tell her that I have arrived?"

"But certainly, I shall tell her," the girl replied in husky accurate French, and for an instant Stone thought he caught an ironic note in her voice. "Will you come into the salon and catch your breath?"

"Yes, thank you very much," Stone said, aware now that he was breathing hard, and that his heart was pounding, but feeling his body alive and tingling with the effort and excitement.

He followed her stiff back and slapping red-leather clogs down a small corridor, through half-glazed French doors, into a sizable room whose high windows faced a small garden at the back of the house. There, gratefully, Stone slumped into an armchair and lit a cigarette, listening to the homely, comforting sound of the girl's retreating leather clogs and letting his breathing and blood pressure settle down to normal. The afternoon light poured monochrome greys into the room mottling a wall of books that went from floor to ceiling. Paintings and sculptures were everywhere. Some framed canvases hung on the walls, others were stacked against the armoires and bookcases. In the corner, on an easel, one canvas sat as if it had just been finished. They were skillful paintings of rural scenes in a dark, forbidding Rembrandt-like palette. Almost all of them had a somber dignity that showed individuals in highlight—a shepherd and his flock, a woman washing clothes at a creek, a boy in homespun carrying balanced loads on a carved wooden stave across his shoulders, the boy's curling hair and demeanor recalling Anton Vuk—but all of them were dwarfed by a background of mountains and melancholy pines.

The sculpture was mostly metal figures of soldiers in combat that might have been illustrations for Ambrose Bierce stories of the Civil War, or Stephen Crane's *The Red Badge of Courage*. One was magnificent. About two-feet high, it sat in solitary splendor on a large paper-littered desk, and was silhouetted against the grey light. It was a bronze of a naked man half-rising from his knees. His head, thrown back on a rigid neck, looked up to unconcerned heaven; his arms akimbo, the palms were bent back so far that they looked as if they had been crazily broken at the wrists. Where his chest and guts had been there was only an amoebic-shaped empty space, as if his center had been shot right out of him. Pleading and rebellious together, the figure was angry and powerful, and at the same time helpless and hopeless.

Stone rose and went to the desk. Lifting the sculpture, he was surprised to find it so heavy, but its rough texture and the cold feel of the metal pleased his fingers. As he raised it to the level of his eyes, it was wreathed in his cigarette smoke, which made it seem not only more dramatic, but as if, even with his insides blown away and the smoke of battle not yet cleared, that bronze man still could and would rise to his feet.

"Do you like it?" The sudden question in English so startled him that he almost dropped the bronze. Carefully, Stone set it back on the desk before turning to answer. He was even more disconcerted because facing him was the same girl who had let him in, only now she no longer wore the red clogs, but English walking shoes.

"You are Madame Hvar?"

"I'm Eleanor Hvar," she said, nodding. "Do you always make such entrances?"

"Someone was following me," Stone said abashed, knowing how ridiculous that sounded.

65

"A lady, I hope?" Eleanor Hvar grinned.

"Anyone following me, Madame Hvar, would *not* be a lady," Stone said, trying to take her bantering tone but not quite succeeding. "No, it was a man in a loden coat carrying a small brown briefcase."

"Everyone in Eastern Europe carries a briefcase, from ditch-diggers to tram drivers. It has the day's lunch in it, and it makes them feel important. And Americans in this part of the world always think they're being followed. The secret police, you know." She threw her head back and laughed, but her laugh did not ring true. Stone really looked at Eleanor Hvar for the first time. An aura of darkness came from her like a wave that threatened to overwhelm him. Her black hair was parted in the center and drawn tightly back under a white silk band into a hairpinned dark pool that lapped at the nape of her neck. She wore no makeup, which emphasized her heavily lashed black eyes. Her skin was dark. Neither the hint of pallor beneath nor the even white teeth of the too wide laughing mouth relieved the overall darkling sense of menace.

He offered her a cigarette which she took and tapped nervously against her fingernail. He lit the cigarette for her, then sat down and waited while Eleanor Hvar walked restlessly around the room, straightened some paintings, ran her fingers over some of the sculptures, looked out into the garden and finally returned to her desk and sat down behind it. She put on a pair of horn-rimmed glasses and in what seemed almost an official manner, asked, "And now what can I do for you, Mister Stone?"

"Are you afraid, Mrs. Hvar?" Stone stopped.

"Anyone who is not afraid in our world rapidly leaves it," she retorted. "And I'm *Miss* Hvar, not Mrs. That man," she pointed to the bronze on the desk, "was *not* afraid. He was

66

my husband, Mirko Sutnjak. He's dead. I have used my own name for a long time."

"I'm sorry," Stone said, but for what he wasn't quite sure.

They smoked in silence for a while until Eleanor Hvar said quite formally, "Doctor Decani said that you represented one of the best literary agencies in America."

"He flattered me. I'm a partner in a small literary agency. We are interested in adding some of your country's writers and books to our list," Stone replied, equally formal. "Doctor Decani said you were the country's foremost translator of English and American books, and of your own country's books into English. Because I know almost nothing of your modern literature, he thought you would be just the person to help me meet the right writers and buy the right books."

"Doctor Decani was also flattering me," she replied. "Are you interested in our books for political or literary reasons?"

This time Stone laughed. "I wondered how soon we'd get to that. I could give you a stock answer and say that I'm interested in books that make money. That would give the proper American materialist stereotype. But the fact is that I *like* books. And all kinds. I even like books whose politics and morals I don't agree with, simply because they are well-written or intensely felt. My wife—I mean my ex-wife—divorced me, she said, because I loved books better than anything else. . . ." Why was he so quick to remember Valerie and so indiscreet as to mention it? In New York he had rarely even mentioned her name, not even to Gordon, and now, here, what she said and thought seemed so close to the surface. ". . . and sometimes," he resumed lamely, "I think my partner will divorce me for my affection for good books that don't sell."

That seemed to ease the tension a little and she showed him her books, of which she obviously was very proud. Apparently it had taken a great deal of difficulty to collect them, and they represented a choice selection of the best in English and American literature, cheek by jowl with a collection of Russian and Soviet books. Not only did Eleanor Hvar have the 19th-century classics, Dickens and Thackeray, Hawthorne and Melville, Dostoyevsky and Tolstoy, but the up-to-date British "Angries" and American "Beats" as well as the "thaw" literature of the Soviet Union. She knew about Mailer and Styron, Ellison and James Jones, and about Braine, Wain, Silletoe and Kingsley Amis, some of whom she had already translated. Next to those was a large collection of Russian moderns, Ehrenburg and Sholokhov, Pasternak and Leonov, sharing shelves with such taboo authors as Orwell, Koestler, Silone and the undeservedly neglected Victor Serge. There were the French too, Left, Right and Center, Sartre, de Beauvoir, Camus, Mauriac and Céline, and there was a large section of shelves devoted to the works of her own country.

"That's a very non-partisan collection," Stone said, meaning it as a compliment.

"The Partisan days are over," Eleanor Hvar said bitterly, assuming a meaning of the word Stone had not intended. "I like your American writers," she continued, as if trying to make up for something, "and your books. They are strong and colorful and international, not like ours, which are only for this little world here, this small space of earth. But your books are like that sculpture"—she pointed to the bronze on the desk—"they have a hole in the middle"—she clutched her fists to her flat belly—"where there should be heart and hope."

"This is an age of negation," Stone commented, hearing the resounding hollowness of the words. "Our times and lives justify it."

"It is always hard to affirm," she said almost angrily, and

68

not talking altogether to him. "Life is never easy. To write you must transcend the time, seem to see beyond it, give affirmation to one's self and to others. Not falsely, by being *positive,* but by celebrating life, all of it, as it is."

Celebrating life? Stone thought. Even the phrase had the music of another time. That was in the age of the violin and piano; how did you celebrate life, all of it, as it is, in the age of the drum and the cymbal? What could be celebrated in an age of murder other than murder and evil? The Bogomils came into his head, back from the days when history, with big and little H, had been his passion. How they had fascinated him long ago, and now he was in the land of the Bogomils, those heretic martyrs of Bosnia, strange offspring of Gnostics and Manichaeans, who had been caught between the religious millstones of Islam and Roman Catholicism and ground into dust. They had found a way to celebrate life by denying it. If God was good, then evil could only come from that creation of the devil, man's flesh. In rejecting that devil in the flesh, in hallowing a cruel asceticism, those Bogomils had thought they were celebrating life. Death had a thousand doors to let out life, always, then as now, and so few doors to let in life.

"As it is?" Stone finally brought himself to ask aloud, only just managing to suppress the edge of irony in his voice.

"As it is," she replied sadly, "there is no other way."

Awkwardly, as if she had changed her mind about something, she stood up, took her glasses off, and said, "Would you like to have a walk, Mister Stone? I've been working since early morning and haven't been out in the fresh air. If you have not seen our Kalemegdan yet, I should enjoy showing it to you."

He had not seen Kalemegdan and said he would be glad for her company, for such an expert guide, but she ignored his half-jocular tone of gallantry and promised to return in a moment. Stone sat and smoked his cigarette down to a stub, wondering why he felt like a turtle on its back, undersides bare and vulnerable. This was the second person in a single day with whom he felt that small sunburst of intimacy and affection that he had not felt with others for years. Maxim Grout. And now Eleanor Hvar. Why now and here? Why so swiftly and abruptly? Why for people he was not even sure were friendly? Was it the shock of Antun Vuk's murder? The danger and the excitement of it? Or simply that in the course of events, the time had come for his shell to crack? No, he said to himself, No, these people don't concern me. But inside it was as if a strong wind was blowing through a narrow opening in a window and he couldn't get the sash slammed.

Eleanor Hvar came back into the room without his seeing or hearing her, so intent was he on repeating to himself the only German contemporary political slogan he enjoyed—*"Ohne mich, ohne mich"*—but now she was wearing perfume, a light lingering scent of lily of the valley, that reminded him of Paris and the *muguet,* and that told him she was there. Without speaking, he stood up and followed her out of the house, taking one last lingering look at the bronze on the desk, the light from the windows piercing its bowels like an ancient grey sword.

In the street, wary but casual, Stone looked to see if the loden coat had tracked him, but no one was visible. Still he was not relieved. As they walked, he only half-listened to Eleanor Hvar as she talked about how she hated Belgrade because, aside from Kalemegdan, there wasn't a building over one hundred and fifty years old in the city. And every day the city was growing more and more like Western ones, with big glass and concrete boxes that were supposed to be modern buildings, but were modern only in their ugliness and impersonality. The city she loved was Dubrovnik, old and walled, and in many ways still the same 17th century city of Ragusa. There she felt at home. She even kept a small flat in Dubrovnik, but of course, most of the publishing was in Belgrade, so she had to live there most of the year if she was to do her work.

Stone managed to nod at the proper intervals, to say that American publishing too was centered in New York, and if you were a translator it paid to live there or close by, but he was watching a small green Italian Fiat that seemed to be driving much too slowly behind them and in the same direction they were walking. As they turned off the street into Kalemegdan Park, the Fiat continued on its way and Stone was relieved. When he looked at Eleanor Hvar's dark profile, the short straight nose, the fine sculptured cheekbones, the almost too-determined jut of jaw, her features blended into a face that might have been carved on the bowspirit of one of those Ragusan galleys whose pictures he had seen in history books. Only then, by the face's beautiful remoteness, did Stone realize that Eleanor Hvar too was talking with only half her mind and thinking of other things.

Kalemegdan is the ridge overlooking the joining of the Danube and Sava rivers, the strategic high ground for which so many have fought and destroyed Belgrade: Avars, Celts, Goths and Romans; Turks, Hungarians, Austrians and Nazis; and a dozen others of which Stone had never heard. Telling of its history, which was really the history of the city and of Serbia and a good part of the fate of central Europe, Eleanor Hvar spoke in an emotionless voice that charged what she said with more feeling than it otherwise might have. Empires, Eastern and Western, had always met and clashed at Belgrade

71

because it lay athwart the classic invasion routes, the river valleys. Crusaders going south to the Holy Land to fight the infidel, Turks going north to fight the Christians, Ottoman Empire or Hapsburg, Nazis or Russians, the strategic confluence of Sava and Danube had to be taken—and there the city sat. "Belgrade," she said, "has been levelled some thirty-five times." And there was more than pity and anger in her voice; there was also a kind of perverse pride. For being levelled, or for rising again, Stone wondered, and remembered that bronze figure struggling to its feet.

"No wonder there are no buildings older than a hundred and fifty years for you to admire," Stone commented.

They were walking through the park where soldiers and lovers strolled in groups, and mothers with children, and old people, sat on the benches. It looked like Central Park in New York, or Fairmount Park in Philadelphia, only shabbier and smaller.

Quietly Eleanor Hvar told him what Belgrade was like on April 6, 1941, when the *Luftwaffe* smashed it to bits. She had been living in Belgrade with her parents then, her father an architect, her mother a lawyer, herself the only child of their middle age. "I was a school girl but one doesn't forget. Your Winston Churchill said Yugoslavia had found its soul, but to me then it only seemed that Belgrade was losing its body. The city was burning, dying and wounded people lay in the streets, with no one to help them. On my street a brown horse had been hit. It lay in the middle of the road, in a pool of black blood, its entrails out, trying to get up, shaking its straw-colored mane, beating its tail, its big eyes wide and a little crazed. But it kept trying to get on its feet, its hooves slipping on the bloody cobbles, and each time it fell back with a scream that sounded almost human.

"And nothing in the sky except those black gulls with their

72

hakenkreuzes and explosive eggs. They killed my parents, but even after I found them, saw them, I couldn't believe my father and mother were really dead. Only later, much later did it come home to me. It was the end of my life, I thought then, but it was only the end of my youth. And now, I can't even remember them, or their faces, or what they looked like dead. All I can remember of Belgrade and that time is that little brown horse slipping in its own blood and trying again and again to stand up. I was sixteen years old," she remarked wonderingly, as if it were impossible for her to contemplate ever having been so young.

Spontaneously, Stone reached out and touched her arm, but she jumped back as if she'd been burned. Her face darkened. "I don't know why I'm talking such rot," she said impatiently.

As she moved away from him, Stone knew he had touched something in her as she had in him that had made her speak of her youth unguardedly as he had spoken of Valerie and books. More for her than for himself, Stone tried to tell her what April 1941 had been like for him. He had just come home from college for Easter vacation to announce to his mother and grandfather that he was going to enlist in the Army. He had, in fact, already enlisted and was to report for duty after his graduation in June. His grandfather had advised him to wait, that there was no hurry and no war yet that the United States was involved in, but Stone had insisted that America should fight, and would, and he wanted to. To make it more palatable, he thought, Stone had told them he could get a commission as an officer if he went in right then, but they remained unimpressed.

"The commission is not the point," his grandfather had said, very slowly and gravely. "In war, the less time you're in, the better your chances to survive."

"Is survival the point?" Stone had asked.

"For the nation, winning is the point; for the individual, survival," his grandfather said wearily, a burned-out look in his eyes. "The two interests do not necessarily go together."

"He was right," Eleanor Hvar interjected.

"Yes," Stone said, "I suppose he was."

But he hadn't known that then. His grandfather had talked of his forebears who had fought, in the Civil War and the Mexican War, and of his own service in the Philippines during the Spanish-American War, as if somehow to make and emphasize the point of the family's bravery and service to country, and as if this time Stone was therefore relieved of some responsibility. Gingerly, the old man reminded him of how his own son, Stone's father, had come back from the first World War, after being gassed at the Meuse, to die of his seared lungs a decade later. "You're the last of my line," his grandfather had said.

"All the more reason for my going," Stone replied.

His mother, dry-eyed and downcast, her blue-veined arthritic hands twisted like white vines in her lap, finally spoke. "Do you *have* to go, Warren?"

"Yes, Mother, I do." He had kept his eyes on those knotty fingers and rigid knuckles, unable to look into her face.

"You may *feel* that you must go, Warren, but it is not your sense of duty, nor yet your politics," his grandfather had pronounced sentence on him, "but your desire for excitement, to prove yourself, and to be sure you don't miss the 'Big Show'."

"Maybe," he had admitted, half-guiltily, because he knew how close to right his grandfather was, "but it's more than the excitment or the 'Big Show.' The Nazis are evil. They have to be fought. You've said so yourself, a hundred times over."

The old man nodded, then stood up quietly, and Stone remembered that then he saw his grandfather's shoulders no longer had quite the military bearing they usually had. "I think I would like to be by myself for a while," his grandfather had excused himself, and had gone into his study, silently closing the door behind him. Once, before Stone went back to school, his grandfather made one last attempt to dissuade him. "You know, Warren," he said, "what this will do to your mother?" It was a plain statement of fact more than a question —and Stone had only winced, not answered.

Later, in a ditch next to the road that went up to Arnhem from Eindhoven, Stone had received his mother's letter with the news of his grandfather's death. His grandfather had not mentioned what it would do to him: he was not that kind of man. And in another April, that last green April of the war, so green after the bitter white winter, in a hospital in Troyes, the telegram from his grandfather's lawyer told him, with professional euphemism, that his mother "had passed on" and, as the sole surviving relative, the Stone estate was all his.

She barely grazed his coatsleeve with her fingernails, when he had finished, and it might even have been an accident. "You never had children with your wife?" she asked with that fine feminine irrelevance that Stone knew was anything but.

"No. Nor with anyone else, so far as I know," he replied, trying to grin. "I'm the last Stone of my house."

"And I the last of mine."

They had now climbed to the top of Kalemegdan ridge. Looming above them, on a high stone pillar and plinth stood a monumental grey stone statue, its back turned on them and the city, looking out into the distance to the north. "That," she said, pointing up at it, "is the famous Mestrovic statue,

The Victor, sometimes called *The Herald of Victory,* or *The Messenger of Victory,* depending on who does the translating, put up after the first World War . . ."

Their eyes met and even before she could finish the sentence, they began to laugh, laughing until tears came, unable to stop, while passersby, mostly young soldiers arm-in-arm with their girls, strolled past and looked at them curiously. When they were laughed out, though still trembling, they stood next to each other on the promontory, peering over the parapet, down the steep banks past the broken battlements, the scrub trees and shrubs, to the peacefully flowing grey-green Sava.

After an interval, Eleanor Hvar took up her role as guide once more, pointing out Zemun, Romania to the east, the New Belgrade growing up on the left bank of the Sava, the Danube, and beyond it, northwards, the fertile plain of the Voivodina, the black earth of the country's breadbasket that stretched far into Hungary to form what was known as the Pannonian Plain. She talked until Stone asked if there was a restaurant above, and when she said yes, he took her arm and they set out for it.

The restaurant was scarcely what Stone expected. A low-ceilinged room with bare walls, a few wooden chairs and tables without tablecloths, and a small bar. It was dingy and depressing. The only colorful thing in the room was the huge red and yellow and chrome jukebox which dominated it. They chose an empty table away from it, in the far corner, next to an open window. The waiter came and there was the momentary embarrassment and linguistic confusion of having her order for him. He told her he wanted coffee and *rakija,* and after she had ordered, they sat back to look around the room.

Only a few of the other tables were occupied, mostly by

young people, all clustered about the big illuminated jukebox. Glowing in the dusk, it seemed to Stone like some ritual camp-fire around which the savages made their ring. A few of them were in uniform, and the others all had a familiar look, their own special uniform, Stone had seen in New York and London and Frankfurt: duck-tail haircuts and pony tails, tight skirts and pants, both worn too short, smoking cigarettes dripping from their lips or hands; they even had bottles of Coca Cola on the table in front of them. One put a coin into the juke-box and its lights began to flash on the dirty walls, and the blaring music of the twist boomed. Until the record ended, they could not talk.

"It is hard to understand them," she said, biting her lip, and looking quizzically at them. "They are not at all like what we were."

They drank their coffee and *rakija* in silence. Out of the window Stone saw the silent green flow of the Sava, the few boats on the river, and the evening lowering. A strange sense of peace and quiet stole through him which he did not try to understand.

In front of the jukebox, a boy and girl began to twist, shaking as if with fever, their eyes and faces blank, not looking at one another and dancing apart, yet their movements co-ordinated as if their limbs were strung together with hidden cords. Again, Stone saw the barbarian rituals, some twitching muscular offering to appease the effigy of the new gods of industrialism: the jukebox. We're still here and alive, they seemed to be saying to the machine: Listen to us make noise! Look at us dance! But abruptly, too, Stone felt that their dancing was also a way of saying *ohne mich:* they didn't touch one another, theirs was a cold private frenzy, and that more than anything made it vulgar.

The yellow and red lights dimmed and stopped flashing, the twanging guitars and clanging brass ceased, and silence rushed headlong into the room. Heads huddled at one of the tables and faces turned to look at them, carefully scrutinizing his clothes, particularly his shoes and argyle socks. Another huddle and then one of the boys in faded tight blue jeans who, but for the Slavic cast of his features, might have been from Iowa, stood up and walked over to them. "American?" he said, pointing a finger at Stone's chest. Stone nodded, his muscles beginning to tense.

"T*v*ist?"

Stone shook his head.

The next question was not in English and Eleanor Hvar, without seeming to intrude, explained. "He wants to know if you are acquainted with Elvin Presley, Chubby Checker, and several other jazz musicians in America."

"Tell him I went out with Benny Goodman and 'The Big Apple,'" Stone grinned, relaxing again.

"What?" she asked, puzzled.

"Tell him I don't know any of the new jazz musicians."

She translated.

The boy's face fell. He half-turned back to his companions, who were watching, and in the air in front of Stone, with his two forefingers, he drew a square. Stone burst into laughter. He guessed he was a square, at that. The boy grinned, abashed, and stuck out his hand. Stone shook it and then the boy went back to his friends. Someone put another coin into the jukebox and Elvis Presley began to stomp.

The boy reminded Stone of Antun Vuk and the small feeling of peace that had stolen through him, born of the smell of Eleanor Hvar's perfumed presence, the Turkish coffee and the *rakija,* and the slow descent of darkness over the inscrutable pulse of the Sava, evaporated. It left as swiftly and mysteriously as it had come. Stone paid the check and they went out past the table of young people still smoking, nursing their cokes, and twisting. The boy who had talked to them smiled and waved good-by, and Stone waved back.

Outside, the evening hovered in the air. The moon, already out, was hidden behind a heavy cloud it had chalkily outlined. Walking down the narrow winding path and steep steps, Stone saw the round blob of the loden coat and the lean sway of the totem-pole shadow at the same instant, like some obscene silhouette of Don Quixote and Sancho Panza, coming up toward them. And as soon as he saw them he knew: it was here. Separate paths converged on where they stood between two of the Kalemegdan citadel's crenelated towers. From the right the two shadows came slowly at them; on the left, the path went across the drawbridge over the chasm that separated the fortress from the park and its lower reaches. Roughly, Stone took Eleanor Hvar's arm and pushed her toward the drawbridge path. "Run!" he whispered hoarsely. "Make believe you don't know me. Get away from here."

He felt her bicep flex and her legs brace. She didn't move. She too had seen them. "Are they coming for you?"

"Yes."

"You're sure?"

"Sure."

"Why?"

"I don't know. And this is no time for explanations. Run!" He gave her another shove, but she wouldn't budge.

It was too late anyway, because the totem pole had already cut across to block one path to the drawbridge; the loden coat stood bulking in the other. Stone pulled Eleanor Hvar behind him, against the citadel ramparts, and waited. From the restaurant above, Stone could hear the loud nasal braying of Elvis Presley, the plucking whine of his guitar and the faint muted clapping of hands in rhythm. Inexorably, yet leisurely, they moved up both paths, like two threatening clouds that must come together in a thunderclap. For an instant, the moon flashed out of the clouds and illuminated their faces, the pale unseeing otherworldly face of the loden coat, and the swarthy tomahawk countenance of the totem pole. There was no question now that the man he had seen with Grout that morning, the one in the glass cage of Decani's building, and the totem pole were the same man.

They were only a dozen feet from him now, keeping well away from one another, playing it very cautiously and professionally. The moon had plunged back into the clouds and Stone knew that in the shadows they could not see him too plainly. He reached his hand into his breast pocket, making his movements as broad and as menacing as possible, took his heavy passport wallet out and kicked his heel back against the rampart just missing Eleanor Hvar. At that distance, a black leather case might look a gun, and the kick might sound like he had clicked off the safety. He held the wallet in his fist as if it were a pistol.

They stopped, but hesitated only for a fraction of a minute. The totem pole's gun seemed to grow out of his hand, but the loden coat began to fumble with the brown brief case he was still carrying, trying to unsnap it. In that instant Stone moved. He slammed his wallet into the loden coat's face, lunged for the brief case as it dropped, scooped it up and with both hands threw its weight at the totem pole. As it knocked him off balance, Stone followed like a battering ram, hitting him sharply in the throat with his fist. The totem pole coughed, wheezing to catch his breath, and still trying to bring his gun arm around.

Stone clubbed the arm and heard the gun go clattering on the path. Before he could turn the loden coat had hit him from behind. His throat was caught and strangling in the crook of the loden coat's arm, his hair being pulled by strong fingers so hard that his scalp felt as if it were being torn away from his skull. He saw the totem pole looking for his gun, and then Eleanor Hvar leaping on him, throwing him back on his heels, pummeling him. Stone's body moved as it had once been trained. His elbow crashed back into the fat stomach, loosening the hold on his hair and neck as he enjoyed the "Oof!" that whistled past his ear. His heel stomped down on the man's foot, and as the gasp was followed by a cry, Stone pitched the fat man over his shoulder to the ground.

The totem pole had already reached the gun, but Eleanor Hvar was faster. She kicked it out of his reach once, then kicked it again. The gun flew over the side of the drawbridge into the chasm below, crashing through the underbrush like some small frightened animal. Angrily, the totem pole smashed Eleanor Hvar in the face and sent her reeling, then drove her back toward the edge of the drawbridge while she fought him with her fists. Stone went wild. He ran and with all his strength drove both fists into the totem pole's back right at the kidneys. The man wilted, sinking to his knees as if in prayer. Stone pulled him around by the hair, cuffing him with his open palm, back and forth, thinking of Antun Vuk, but remembering Decani slapping the chambermaid with his yellow pigskin gloves.

When Stone heard the yelling, he wasn't sure it was his own or Eleanor Hvar's, but he let the totem pole go and whirled to face what he thought would be another assault from the loden coat. The young people, and a couple of soldiers, were racing down from the restaurant and the loden coat was already scurrying away toward the first yellow flicker of the city lights below. On his feet once more, though weaving slightly, the totem pole had seen them coming too. For a moment they faced each other. "I will kill you next time," the totem pole, almost formally, promised in German. "I will kill you, Mister Stone." It was like an invitation with an R.S.V.P. Or was it an R.I.P.?

"Next time will be my turn," Stone replied, also in German, hearing with distaste the animal growl in his own voice. He moved to grab him, but the man was gone, so swiftly merged into the shadows of the clotting darkness that Stone could no longer see him.

Led by the boy in the faded blue jeans, the young people took them back up to the restaurant, and this time it looked lighter and friendlier to Stone, though all that had happened was that the dim jaundiced overhead bulbs had been turned on. The waiter brought more coffee and *rakija,* and the young people offered cigarettes. Stone gave them a pack of American ones in turn, and they seemed pleased. Their questions began and Eleanor Hvar again translated, interpreting as if she were not at all personally involved, but only there in some obscure professional capacity. "Who were they? Hooligans? What did they want? Your money? Your girl?" They peered at Eleanor Hvar but her face betrayed no embarrassment, no emotion at all. Stone looked at her, pale, except where the totem pole's finger marks were still red on her face. Their eyes caught and held, and they rose from the table together, as if at a signal, thanked the youngsters, and with the beating of the jukebox behind them, once more made their way out of the restaurant and then out of the fortress. As they passed the spot where they had fought, Stone put his arm around her shoulders, but she shrugged it off. He did not touch her again.

82

Just before the drawbridge, Stone found the loden coat's brief case lying in the path. He picked it up and tried to open it, but the catch still stuck. It had probably saved his life, perhaps their lives. He patted the heavy brown bag as if it were a dog. He was sure there were guns inside, but even as he carried it and felt weighted down he remembered how light it had seemed when he threw it at the totem pole.

They found a taxi at the Barjakli Mosque, at the foot of its Oriental minaret, which seemed like a cautioning finger in the night sky, its upturned crescent resembling a small scythe. The muezzin's balcony already was shrouded in darkness. Did anyone, Stone wondered, still summon the faithful to prayer five times a day with the wailing: "There is no God but God"? Not likely. If they did not kneel to the old Meccas in the East, they bowed to the new Meccas there and danced around the jukebox and the turret lathe.

They were silent driving to Eleanor Hvar's house. Stone helped her out of the cab and as he was about to climb back in, to go back to his hotel, she held him by his coat sleeve. "Don't go," she said, "Please don't go."

Stone paid the cab driver and watched him drive off down the street. Then he followed Eleanor Hvar through the gate and into the house. In the living room, only one small lamp lit, they sat and smoked. Stone stared at the bronze on the desk—its despair, outrage and helplessness so instinct in the distorted wrists—while his own barbarous howl as he drove his fists into that man's kidneys still rang in his ears. He had fought like a cornered animal, not merely trying to stay alive and unhurt, but wanting to kill them, grind their faces into the earth, especially when they had threatened Eleanor Hvar. If anything his own fighting had been a repetition and even an extension of Decani's brutality. The body was always a barbarian: it did not forget its own savage cunning and cruelty, nor the glands their own electrifying juices of anger and hatred. Perhaps the Bogomils had been right after all. But the mind was not exempt either: he had enjoyed his victory and their defeat.

Like a foot fallen asleep comes painfully awake when stamped on, his feeling for the dark, somber-faced woman who now sat absent-eyed across from him had come swiftly to the surface with the encounter. Was it because she had fought fiercely too, and in his behalf? He had put his arm around her in a way he knew was not casual and she had known too and shrugged it off.

She left the room and came back with a whisky bottle and glasses. After she had poured stiff drinks, she raised her glass to him and said, with a sincerity that could only be borne because it was so acidly etched with self-mockery and a sarcastic cinematic melodrama. "Thank you, Mister Stone, for saving my life."

"It was nothing, Miss Hvar," he said, taking the same moving-picture tone, "fair maidens in distress are my specialty."

"They are?"

"They are, but I do *not* seem to be theirs." His riposte had unwittingly been too sharp.

She turned her face half-way and drank her drink, and he followed suit. Back in her chair, she carefully arranged her legs and skirts, and lighted a new cigarette. The questions, he knew, would now begin. "Who were they, Mister Stone? What did they want?" Eleanor Hvar asked.

Grout had taught him a lesson again that in the past he had learned often and more often disregarded. *Be wary!* Who was Eleanor Hvar? What did he know of her except that he was instinctively drawn to her and wanted to trust her? All the more reason, then, for not doing so. That was undoubtedly part of her job, to be warm and attractive enough to invite confidence. But who did she work for and what were her allegiances? His own desire to talk to someone he could trust, candidly and openly, had already betrayed him once that day.

Carefully, Stone gave Eleanor Hvar an edited account of Antun Vuk's murder, of Decani's brutality, of seeing the totem pole in Decani's building, of the loden coat following him that afternoon from his hotel to her house, but he eliminated everything about Konstantin Karst—the note, Antun Vuk's whispered message—about Townsend and Grout, and their speculations about Karst. "Probably," Stone concluded, "those two men work for Doctor Decani."

"No," she said, "I don't think so."

"You don't? Why not?"

"I simply don't."

"Because they tried to kill you too?" Stone asked, trying to temper the cold question with a humorous intonation.

"And what do you mean by that, Mister Stone?"

"That you must work with or for Dr. Decani, Miss Hvar," Stone replied. "You're the first person with whom he makes an appointment for me. You're the foremost translator of English and American books in the country, he tells me, and looking at the work you've done"—he nodded at the bookshelves—"I believe him. But even setting aside the kind of cooperation it takes in your country to remain an *employed* translator, particularly of such 'dangerous' books as ours, it seems obvious that you are to be—how shall I put it?—my literary watchdog."

"Not a very flattering figure of speech. I have been called a bitch before, Mister Stone, but never in quite that way," she said, solemn and sardonic. "But if *they* work for Doctor Decani, and so do I, why should they try to kill me?"

Stone threw up his hands. "Who knows? I don't. A bluff, an act, maybe, to make me think so and trust you. Perhaps, they were even willing . . ." He stopped.

". . . to sacrifice me?" she finished the sentence for him.

"Look," he said, "I don't think they wanted to kill either of us. At least not to begin with, but I think matters got out of hand. They lost their heads. On the way to Decani's office this morning, a man tried to run us down in a car. If he really had wanted to, he could easily have killed us. The same was true up there at Kalemegdan. Those two could have waited quietly and simply shot me down. If they'd been hidden, or even careful, I wouldn't have noticed them. But they deliberately made a show."

"Then what *did* they want?"

"To scare me, I think. I'm not sure."

"Are you scared, Mister Stone?"

"Certainly. Shouldn't I be?"

"You didn't fight as if you were afraid." Her admiration was clear, if reluctantly tendered.

"You fought a good fight yourself," Stone returned the compliment. Then he went on. "Some kinds of fear make you fight better, the fear of disgracing yourself by cowardice, for instance. I was afraid every minute. Especially when it looked as if you would be knocked off that drawbridge."

"That's very gallant," she murmured.

"No, not gallant. I felt that it was my fault that you were there and that it would have been my responsibility."

"Even if I was in Doctor Decani's employ and therefore, as his minion, was with you on *his* initiative?" Her harsh laughter grated. "You're so old-fashioned, Mister Stone, so very Victorian."

"Is that what it is?"

"This is the Balkans," she rasped. "We don't reserve killing only for men. We kill men, women and children. And men, women and children kill. We've even been known to kill the unborn."

"The Balkans are not alone in any of that," Stone retorted sharply. He drank, and the rest of the whisky plunged hotly to the pit of his stomach. Fatigue overpowered him and his head seemed suddenly a foreign weight, too heavy for his neck and shoulders to carry. It nodded, then drooped, and Stone leaned forward, letting it fall, face down, into his hands. His muscles shuddered and his stomach rocked and pitched. The day stretched back interminably behind him and he was abruptly reminded that he had not eaten since an early breakfast before going to the Embassy.

Stone heard her get up and go to the desk. The receiver clicked, a dial tone whined, then the paced sounds of dialing staccatoed in the silent room. He recognized only the words *Doctor Decani* and *Petar* a few moments apart, the rest was a blur of foreign language, but he did not lift his head to look at her; he didn't even listen. When her perfume, warmed and chastened by the smell of her clothes and body, enveloped him he knew she had finished talking and was close. Hesitantly, her hands touched his hair, then strong fingers kneaded the back of his neck. "I called Decani," she seemed to be talking from a great distance and so softly that he had to strain to hear. "I told him what happened at Kalemegdan. Those were *not* his men. I described them and told him where you had seen the tall, thin one. He said he didn't know who they were, but he would find out."

The fingers paused, then skillfully began to massage his shoulders, loosening tightened knots of muscle. "You have your appointment with Karst tomorrow," she said after a while, so coolly indifferent that he knew it was important. The massaging stopped and Stone waited for what he knew was coming. First, her fingers began their healing probing once again, then her voice was like a caress: "Why don't you go to see him," there was only the slightest groping for his name, "Warren. Get Karst's manuscript and then give it to me?"

"Manuscript?" Stone looked up, knowing his eyes were wide with astonishment, his mouth a little agape, his face slack. He was so tired and disappointed, it wasn't even difficult to feign. "Has Karst got a manuscript?"

She handed him a small slip of paper on which was written an address. Only after a squinting and concerted effort did the letters cease to swim and take on the shape of "Konstantin Karst, 66 Kragujevac Street, 2 P.M." Eleanor Hvar gazed at him for a long time, her face so close to his, his eyes hurt to focus on it. Stray locks of luminous hair, loosened from their hairpins, made her look innocent and very *jeune fille*. "Konstantin Karst," she said slowly, "is no concern of yours, Warren." This time she spoke his name with authority.

"I've never even met the man, Eleanor," he replied, putting the paper in his pocket, and noticing how easily her name came to his tongue.

"Karst has written a book that we want . . . that we don't want published," she said.

"We?" he said. "You and Doctor Decani?"

"We means the government, the people."

"Karst, then, is not a person?"

Her hands fell away from his shoulders, and she stepped back from his chair. Stone stood up, making a conscious effort not to sway. His fatigue seemed heavier, like a burden that made him square his shoulders and throw back his head in order to carry it. "I'm sorry," he said.

"You mean, you won't give me the manuscript, Warren?" This time the name was almost personal.

"I don't have any manuscript, Eleanor. What I was sorry about was that you spoke."

"The telephone call?"

"No," he answered grimly, "the request." Swiftly he pulled her to him and kissed her mouth. She made no move to push him away but she was unresponsive. "It was my job," she said between clenched teeth, "my duty."

Duty again. He let her go. "Well," he said, "that wasn't duty. It was my pleasure."

She thought he had relented. "You will give it to me, then, won't you?"

"Give it to you? Give what to you?" he said, finally angry. "I've never met Konstantin Karst. I don't know if he has the manuscript you're telling me about. And if he has, I don't know why in the world he would give it to me."

"And if he does?" Her eyebrows rose questioningly.

Stone wanted to tell her that then it would be *his* job, *his* duty, to keep the manuscript and to see it published as a book. But such words had disturbed him for a long while, and twice in the same day Eleanor Hvar's and Maxim Grout's devotion to "their jobs" and to "doing their duty" made the expressions doubly disquieting. "*If* he does, *when* he does, I'll think about what to do," he answered quietly, "but not before."

He asked her to phone for a taxi and while she did, laid the loden coat's brief case on the desk in front of her and slammed his fist angrily down on the lock. It sprang open. Inside were three guns, a Luger, a Beretta, and a Webley-

Vickers, as international an arsenal as Eleanor Hvar's book collection. There were several boxes of ammunition for them, and two American pineapple-type hand grenades. Stone took the Luger out, loaded it, and stuck it into his belt.

"What's that for?" she asked as she put the phone down.

"Next time," he said, "Decani's men or whoever, I won't be caught off guard."

She looked unhappy. "This is not a game, you know."

"That point has already been well made."

"You'd better be careful, Warren, very careful," she said, in almost the same words and tone of combined menace and concern with which Grout had bid him farewell only a few hours earlier. Fatigue, hunger and irony combined to make him lightheaded, and Stone began to laugh. Eleanor Hvar was offended. "It's not funny," she said, and strode toward the front of the house. Stone picked up the brief case and followed her into the vestibule to wait for the taxi.

There was silence until, trying to revive a more natural atmosphere, Stone commented, "I wonder how those kids could hear anything with that jukebox noise going and that *tv*isting."

A sly grin lightened her face. "I screamed for help."

"Oh, I thought that was me screaming."

"No. You *roared*—like an angry bull. You didn't scream."

"That must have been a good yell," Stone said.

"It was. Roughly translated, it went like this: 'Comrades! Partisans! The Fascists are on us!' " She laughed outright and, helplessly, Stone began to laugh with her.

Just then the taxi tooted its horn softly. In spite of his objections she came out to give the driver instructions for him while he peered into the darkness and held the Luger at the ready hidden behind the loden coat's briefcase. Though a crescent moon made the atmosphere even more Balkan than it was, all was calm, the night quiet, and no one was visible on the street. As he stepped into the cab, Stone asked, "Will you have dinner with me tomorrow night?"

Her uncertainty was obvious, then slowly she nodded. The cab drew away and Stone looked out to watch her walk back into the house. As she closed the door, he wondered if she had consented because that would be after his appointment with Karst.

THE HOTEL was all lit up, people were drinking at the bar and in the coffee shop, and from the taverna below came the sounds of jazz music. Though it seemed like two in the morning, Stone realized that it was only ten o'clock. He stopped at the desk to get his key and order some dinner sent up to his room, and found a letter from Sam Gordon waiting for him. On his floor, he saw a man in the little alcove salon sitting in a modern red lounge chair, coat collar turned up, hat tilted over his face, apparently asleep. Stone took the Luger out again and clicked off the safety.

"Stone," a muffled voice called.

Stone turned, the Luger aimed and ready. It was Maxim Grout. Stone tucked the pistol back into his belt and Grout followed him silently down the corridor. When Stone pushed the door open, chaos greeted him. Everything had been over-turned. Closets were opened, the contents of drawers had been spilled over the floors, suitcases were jacknifed wide, and the mirrors turned facing the wall. The bed was torn up and, as the open French windows swayed back and forth in the night breeze, little puffs of down came out of the slit pillows. The medicine cabinet had been rifled too and someone had even tried his canned shaving cream on the bathroom mirror in a big white swirl that looked like a question mark. Grout went swiftly across the room and out on the balcony, then came back and closed the French windows behind him. In his hand was a heavy iron bar with a curved end sharpened to a spear point. It looked like a longshoreman's loading hook. "Some of *your* boys' work?" Stone queried, looking at the shambles around him. Grout looked hurt, and shook his head.

The last straw, Stone was thinking bitterly, the end of a perfect day. The nightmare world had presented its simple realities of crime and violence. Imperious and insistent: this is what *we* want; this is what *you* must do! He had wanted to be left alone, to mind his own business, to live his private life; but they wouldn't let him be.

"Looks like you're target for tonight, Warren," Grout said sympathetically. "And like they really mean business," he added, holding up the longshoreman's hook.

"Sit down, Maxim," Stone replied shortly. "What's on your mind? You didn't come here at this time of night just to chat."

"No," Grout said, and Stone could see his feelings were hurt, "but I might have." He seemed reluctant to continue. "Come on out on the balcony," he spoke up finally, "I'll show you where I found that hook." He turned out the lights, opened the French windows, and they both stood out on the small balcony. The sight of the garden below, reminded Stone of Antun Vuk and the totem pole, and depressed and enraged him still further. *They* wouldn't let him alone, but who was this they? Or who were those "theys?" Decani and Eleanor Hvar. The totem pole and the loden coat. Michael Townsend and Maxim Grout. And how about Konstantin Karst?

"Warren, I've been sent to see you officially and I didn't want to talk in there because the room may be, probably is, wired. There was a meeting at the Embassy this afternoon.

Townsend told the staff that if anyone got a manuscript from you, or from anyone else, written by Konstantin Karst, it was to be turned over to him immediately. What's more, no one is to send any manuscript out by diplomatic pouch for you without consulting him first."

"Can he make that stick?"

Grout nodded. "I was also instructed to tell you that you are to surrender any manuscript from Konstantiin Karst directly to Townsend or me."

"That's the second offer I've had this evening, and in some ways, many ways, the second best."

"Decani's translator?"

"Yes."

"It figures. I'll bet she was beautiful." Grout took his pipe out and began to pack it with tobacco. "Townsend knows you're going to see Karst tomorrow. He wants the manuscript right afterwards."

"Who elected Townsend President?" Stone asked angrily. "I didn't. I'm an American citizen here on legitimate business. I don't take orders from him, or from the CIA."

"Sssh!" Gout cautioned. "You won't be able to get the manuscript out of the country without the diplomatic pouch."

"And Townsend won't let me use the pouch to send the manuscript to my own office. Even if he promised, that wouldn't matter, I suppose. He'd simply send it where *he* wanted and that would be that."

"I didn't say that, Warren."

"No, Maxim, you didn't. But that's the way it would be."

"Your firm would be guaranteed its usual percentages, and you would be amply repaid for . . . the trouble you've gone to," Grout continued, looking embarrassed.

"For God's sake, Maxim, please shut up."

"This isn't my idea. I'm . . ."

". . . I know . . . just doing your job, your duty," Stone completed his sentence.

Grout lit up, his match making a small eye of flame in the night. "We could take your passport away," he said softly, "in the national interest."

"You just try that. I know a couple of people too, and I'll make a stink in the papers and in Congress that will make you wish you hadn't been born," Stone raged. "First you come here and try to order me around, then you try to bribe me, and now you threaten me. You think I'm a fool or a scoundrel or a coward. Well, I may be all three, but not this trip. If you'd had any brains, you'd simply have guaranteed me—in writing —the integrity of Konstantin Karst's text. That would have done the trick. The fact that that's the one thing you've avoided doing means that's exactly what you don't want. No, even if you promised it now, on a stack of Bibles, I wouldn't trust you."

Grout ran his fingers through his shorn white hair, his florid face saddened. A shower of sparks flew upward from his pipe. "Why don't you sleep on it, Warren, before you give me an answer."

"Was this your idea, Maxim?"

Grout shook his head slowly. "No," he said. "I suggested guaranteeing the text, and they said no. It's out of my hands."

A loud knocking at the door interrupted them. Hastily, they came in off the balcony and Stone flicked on the lights. "Do you *not* want to be seen here?" he asked Grout.

"You mean because I waited out there?" Grout pointed his pipestem. "No, there are a couple of entrances to the lobby and I didn't want to miss you."

"That's probably my dinner," Stone explained. It was. The

waiter rolled it in on a tray and when he saw the shambles almost jumped out of his white jacket. But he recovered himself quickly, and set about laying out the food swiftly and efficiently. Stone had no appetite, but after the first few bites, he found he was ravenously hungry. "Would you like to join me, Maxim?" he invited.

"No. I had my dinner earlier, thank you. But I could use a drink."

Stone found the whisky bottle. At least the intruders hadn't molested that. He poured Grout half a tumbler full and left the bottle at his elbow. As he ate Stone recounted the afternoon's events, the battle on Kalemegdan, Eleanor Hvar's offer and the call to Decani; then, though he couldn't say why, Stone talked about the bronze sculpture he had seen on her desk. As he described it, Grout snapped his fingers. "Mirko Sutnjak," he said, "that's *his* sculpture."

"She said that was her husband's name, I think, but he's been dead for a long time."

Grout's glance was odd, stunned and somehow moved. "Eleanor Sutnjak tonight," he marvelled, after a long silence, "and Konstantin Karst tomorrow."

"An honor and a privilege?"

"You don't know how much, Warren," Grout said, like a sleepwalker.

"Why, Maxim, I believe I've moved you. So that's your Achilles heel: women! And I thought it was politics . . . and duty," Stone teased him. His voice became deliberately inflated and oratorical. "She walks in beauty like the night," but even as he began the mockery, Stone realized how much the poetry sounded like what Eleanor Hvar was and he stopped.

"This gets more and more complicated," Grout said, his mouth moving from whisky glass to pipe and back again. "I think you're getting in over your head, Warren, way over your head."

"I have been all along."

Grout leaned his head back against the back of his chair, pipe smoke wreathing his white hair and fine alcohol-ravaged face so that he looked like some ancient, wise Dionysius recalling his days of Bacchanalian revelry. "Eleanor Sutnjak," he repeated, "Eleanor Sutnjak." The exaltation drained slowly out of his face and left it porous with sadness. "Mirko Sutnjak," he went on, "was once Konstantin Karst's best friend, though Karst was a mountain man from Montenegro and Sutnjak a Dalmatian from Dubrovnik. They went to the university together and Karst recruited Sutnjak into the Communist youth league, then into the Party. They were two of the brightest young hopefuls of their generation: Karst in literature, Sutnjak in painting and sculpture. They went to prison together, and when they came out they were Party leadership together.

"But Sutnjak was a different type. Perhaps, in the modern idiom, a more secure man. I don't know. But he didn't take orders easily. In the Party he was for resistance to the Nazis all along, and even spoke for Soviet intervention against the Reich when it looked like Britain would fall in 1940. Publicly, he swallowed the Ribbentrop-Molotov Pact, but there were persistent rumors that he had been severely censured because inside the Party he opposed it, bitterly and openly." Grout lapsed into silence, as if the recounting were simply too painful to be continued. His face grew harder, almost grief-stricken, and smoke poured from his pipe.

"And?" Stone coaxed, pouring them cups of coffee. Grout ignored the coffee, downed his whisky and poured himself another.

97

"And? When the Nazis attacked Yugoslavia, he didn't wait for the Party line to change on June 21, when the Soviet Union was invaded. He organized guerrillas, sabotage, fighting. In the winter of '41, the Party sent him to Dalmatia and Karst to Montenegro. Sutnjak's job was to set up supply lines and escape routes from the Dalmatian Coast through Bosnia into Serbia, then join Karst in Montenegro.

"The Party judgment was shrewd. Where they could, the Party leaders used men who knew the local conditions and people, and by their origins would be trusted. But, to give the Communists credit where it's due, though they sometimes exploited it, they generally fought against the nationalities hatreds that have scourged this part of the world for generations. They did try to get all the people together to fight the Germans and Italians, Serb, Croat, Slovene, Montenegrin alike."

"But under their banner?"

"Of course." Grout rubbed his fingers across bloodshot eyes. "In some ways, Warren, the names are symbolic. Montenegro means Black Mountain, the Italian version of the Slavic Tsrna Gora. Karst, as you probably know, is the name for the limestone outcroppings in those very same mountains. Karst and Montenegro was bound to be a rocky scrap."

"You know, my name is Stone, Maxim," he interjected, only half-humorously.

"I hadn't thought of that," Grout said, his face lighting up. "It is Stone, isn't it?" For a moment or two he looked intrigued, then commented, "From what Townsend said about your war record, that's appropriate too, I guess."

"Oh," Stone said acidly. "Townsend's been checking up, huh? First, Decani and my sex life. Now Townsend and my life as a warrior."

98

Grout looked uncomfortable. "You can be proud of that record."

"Sure, sure. Nations always seem to like their killers better than their more constructive citizens."

"Not always. And we're all killers," Grout said.

"That's exactly what Decani said, right here, the other night. My God, last night!"

"Which doesn't make it automatically untrue. Petar Decani is an intelligent man who's seen a lot of life."

"All of it red in tooth and claw."

"No. In fact, he's one example of that kind of man who hated violence at first and shrank from it, but steeled himself to endure it, and then inflicted it, because he thought circumstances would yield to no other solutions."

"And then he learned to like it."

"Maybe. Or maybe once he'd thrown away the restraints, there was no way back. Eden was barred by the flaming sword. He had chosen to live by the sword and he knew he'd have to go on living by it. He just learned that all men are killers, and that he was a man too."

"Like all men are mortal, eh Maxim? And each man kills what he loves best, is that what you mean?"

"The brave man with a sword. That couldn't apply more than to Konstantin Karst," Grout continued, obviously changing the subject. "He'd been away from Montenegro too long and gone too far. Between him and his own people stood the city, the university, prison, and most of all the Party. If he still spoke their language, he no longer spoke it with the home-grown accents. Or understood it.

"Montenegrins are tough and savage, and proud of it. They were the only people in this part of the world the Turks couldn't conquer. Their mountains are a natural stronghold, and they have a long history of guerrilla warfare. So Karst's job, in organizing them against the Italians, could have been an overwhelming success. Except for zeal, and Karst was always a zealot."

"And remains one?" Stone asked, genuinely curious.

Grout shrugged. "Who knows? Time changes people. He was much younger then and he's come a long hard road since."

His pipe had gone out and Grout relit it before continuing. "The Italians weren't the Germans, and the Chetniks and the Partisans, under Karst and Sutnjak, combined and damn near cleared their troops out of Montenegro. But the moment it looked like the battle was won, they quarrelled among themselves. They were already split every which way politically, but most resistance was nationalist not Communist. Instead of sticking to the Party line of a united national front against fascism, Karst blew the lid off by trying to make Chetniks into Communist Partisans, At first, he tried persuading them. When he couldn't and since time was short, he tried force, and also went ahead reorganizing parts of the area they controlled along Communist lines.

"Montenegrins don't force easily. Brutality and harshness only stiffens their backbones. A small civil war broke out. Here things get murky. Chetniks outnumbered Karst's men by far, and he set out to equalize their forces. He had some of his people make a number of bloody, horrible raids on the Italians who were holed up in the cities, and deliberately made the raids look like Chetnik operations to bring Italian retaliation down on their heads."

"That's keeping your nose to the limestone," Stone said, but Grout ignored his frivolity.

"Sutnjak was against the whole scheme. He argued for a common front with the Chetniks, insisting that Karst's methods would only alienate the whole province, and eventually drive the Chetniks into collaborating with the Italians. Which, of course, was exactly what did happen. In the mountains, when you're illegal and hiding out all the time, such a quarrel is hard to keep private. In time, all the men knew where the two of them stood, and had taken sides. You're cold, hungry, thirsty, dirty, and tempers are short. One day, after a particularly nasty business that led the Italians to shoot some fifty hostages, Karst and Sutnjak's quarrel became a fight. The men had to pull them apart. Some said Sutnjak had been drinking and it's true that he was a heavy drinker. They stopped talking to each other, and both of them, the story goes, appealed to the Party for a decision.

"Long before it came, Sutnjak was killed. No one knew how, but everyone was sure Karst had murdered him. The bullets were Italian, but that didn't matter much because most of their arms had been captured from the Italians. Karst said nothing, but the raids stopped. By then, morale was shot and the Chetniks and Italians working together had cut his forces to ribbons. He had alienated the local people, and the whole thing had become a fiasco. The Party withdrew him and the remainder of his men, and for two years, untiil 1943, they left Montenegro a Chetnik bastion where a Partisan couldn't show his nose."

Tears welled up in Grout's eyes and he bent over his pipe to hide them. He emptied the ashes into an ash tray and methodically went about refilling the bowl. Was Grout really so moved, Stone wondered, by men he didn't know in a tragedy in which he had played no part? Or was this the easy sentimentality that brought heavy drinkers so swiftly to tears? He knew Grout was trying to tell him something, but what? Was it simply a warning about getting involved with a man of Karst's fanatical and ruthless temperament? Was it a ruse to get him to turn over to Townsend whatever manuscript Karst gave him—

if there was a manuscript and Karst gave it to him? "What are you trying to tell me, Maxim?" Stone inquired gently.

Grout stared at him, his bloodshot eyes brimming with tears. "I don't know, Warren," he replied, his voice lost in his throat.

They sat unmoving and Stone thought about Eleanor Hvar and the magnificent bronze on her desk that Mirko Sutnjak had shaped out of his anguish and almost in prophecy of his fate. Thinking about them both he felt a personal sense of loss that a man who had molded such a bronze was dead, and a pang of jealousy that that man had also been Eleanor Hvar's husband. The other memories, older and more painful, stirred but he refused them recognition.

A knock at the door brought him back. Grout sat upright. It was the waiter to clear away his supper. With him he brought the same porter and chambermaid who had come the night before to remove the traces of Antun Vuk's death. Now they began to straighten the mess that had been made in his room. The chambermaid, dragging her right foot in a small cast from ankle to toe, looked the same as she had the night before, except paler.

Grout heaved himself to his feet. He looked white and tired, but his eyes flamed. Stone took him to the door. "You going to report this?" Grout asked.

"Doesn't seem much point," Stone answered. "Decani's right hand knows what his left is doing."

"They may not be Decani's men."

"If not his and not yours and Townsend's, then whose?"

"Karst has more enemies than you can shake a Luger at," Grout said, ignoring the dig about Townsend. "Whoever it is doesn't even want you to *see* Karst. That Tatra and those hoods on Kalemegdan were trying to scare you. Next time they might really try to stop you. That little hook there," he pointed to where he had left it on the chair, "looks like the real thing to me, the kind you use to kill not to scare. Decani doesn't want to stop you from seeing Karst, or he wouldn't have made the appointment for you. *He wants you to get the manuscript for him.* Those others don't care." As he turned to go, Grout asked if they would meet the next day.

"Is that official or personal, Maxim? Or can't you tell any more?"

"As you wish."

"That's no answer."

"I told you once, Warren, I'm an official representative of the American government here. I have no option. I also gave you Townsend's message. Sleep on it before you give us a final answer." His cautioning hand and warning glance at the porter and chambermaid cut off Stone's possibility of reply.

When Grout had gone, Stone called the desk. The desk clerk had already heard from the room-service waiter that his room had been broken into but wanted only to know if anything was missing. Stone had no idea but promised an account in the morning; and the desk clerk irritably replied that he would report it to the police then.

Stone sat heavily in a chair, exhaustion sweeping over him. The porter was putting his valises back into the luggage racks, the chambermaid had replaced his pillows with new ones and remade his bed. He watched them until they were finished, forcing his eyes to stay open. Then he gave them 500 dinars each and admired the way they bowed out gracefully. Feeling as if he was moving through water, Stone stripped off his clothing and got into his pajamas. Though he wanted a shower, he knew he couldn't manage it. He opened one valise and put the loden coat's brief-case arsenal into it, then carefully closed it from sight. He checked the Luger, took it to bed with him, and put it under his pillow. As he did, his hand brushed a slip of paper. "Oh no," something inside him cried, "not again. Not now." But he took the paper out, clumsily unfolding it. It was another note from Karst, brief but somehow exultant.

Dear Mister Stone:

We have an official appointment tomorrow at two. It is much better so. Don't worry: I have taken care of everything.

Yours,

Konstantin Karst

P.S. Burn this, please.

Wearily, Stone reread the note, thinking fuzzily that the chambermaid had put it there. Her dragging foot in the white cast, Antun Vuk's corpse, and Karst's European handwriting all materialized before his tired eyes. "Don't worry: I have taken care of everything." If that was the way Konstantin Karst took care of everything, he for one would do without. Laboriously, Stone got up, found his matches and burned the note. Then he flushed the ashes down the toilet and rinsed the ash tray.

Back in bed he remembered Gordon's letter but couldn't make himself get up again to read it. He turned off the lights, slipped one hand under the pillow, comforted by the feel of the Luger's steel barrel, and was almost at once asleep.

He was climbing a steep limestone cliff up from a slate sea. Ahead was Maxim Grout and both of them wore mountain-climbing equipment. They were tied together with thick rope looped and knotted around their waists which then serpentined up over the edge of the precipice above and disappeared where the sky sat blue on the brink. The pebbles came first, then the rolling rocks, leaping past them like great stone dolphins, alive and aimed and purposeful. When he slipped,

Grout grabbed him; their wrists, locked on each other's fore-arms, held. Grout's face, white as ice, melted and froze again into the totem pole's, the scar a ridge of shining snow. The ice axe in his hand split the totem pole's face neatly and blood-lessly into diagonal parts of a papier-mache mask that fell away from Grout's features and left them naked.

The German's head was so blond it was white. The chin strap bit into the cheeks as he pulled the head back until the neck, like a knuckle cracking, broke and the helmet lolled to light the white hair in the moonlight. The "Ich," guttural and expelled like smoke, also broke and strangled. "I," he thought, "I. To the very last moment."

"Descartes was an idiot," Slater said, as he waved the squad forward along both sides of the canal. A windmill with only three arms turned crookedly, silently, in the breeze. "*Cogito ergo sum*. Philosophers always get things asswise. *Sum ergo cogito*." Like Pluto from the underworld the Nazi came up from the canal, machine pistol in hand, his face covered with mud, but the same face of the white-haired boy in Normandy. "I killed him once," he thought, "back there in Normandy and now he's here in Holland." The machine-pistol fired like an old man belching and Slater fell, looking surprised at him, his "War . . ." cut off in mid-speaking, his mouth left open, already dead. His own carbine yapped like a dog. The Ger-man dropped. He fired again. The mud jumped. Again. The pot helmet and part of the skull fell away baring the bloodied brains. . . .

The phone rang tinnily as Stone fought his way up through the mud and nausea to reach it. The voice spoke his name but his tongue could shape no answering words. "Mister Stone, Mister Stone?" the voice asked. "It's Petar Decani. Are you all right?"

"I ... am ... all ... right," he heard himself say, each word a sentence and separate. The curtains fluttered back from the open French windows, the sun shone and filled the room with light, the numbered face's green hands on the bedside table said ten o'clock. He had slept ten hours and was still exhausted.

Decani apologized for waking him and offered to wait in the lobby until he got his breakfast. The hot shower and towelling revived him and drove away the memory of the dreams he had had during the night and the nausea that always came with them. He remembered the two usual ones, repeated he didn't know how many times since the war, but he wondered why he had dreamed about Grout and mountain climbing.

By the time Decani, and his breakfast arrived, Stone had taken advantage of the respite to hide the Luger and Sam Gordon's unopened letter beneath the mattress. Decani was brisk and over coffee came directly to the point, a point Eleanor Hvar, beautiful and perfumed, had made more effectively for him. "We want Karst's manuscript, Mister Stone, and I think you can see why. This country is united now, peaceful and doing quite well. Better every day. We have enough problems without reviving old hatreds. We don't want any troubles. Konstantin Karst is a troublemaker, a hot-headed Montenegrin, and this is a time for cool heads."

"Don't rock the boat?"

"Pardon?"

"An American expression which means to keep things on an even keel."

"Exactly. That's just what we want, to keep things at an even keel."

It was the same record: give us the manuscript because it's in the national interest—patriotism; we'll pay your expenses—

bribery; if you don't play ball, we have ways and means—threats.

Stone leaned back, enjoying his morning cigarette and Turkish coffee, and repeated what he had told Eleanor Hvar and Grout before, that he had not talked to Karst, didn't know if there was any manuscript, and was by no means sure Karst would offer it to him if there was.

"But if he does give it to you, what then?"

"It will depend on what conditions Mister Karst places on my accepting it," Stone replied.

Briefly Stone told Decani about the marauders of the night before, at Kalemegdan and at the hotel, describing the totem pole and the loden coat, and showing him the longshoreman's hook. Decani did not seem to be discomfited by the fact that the totem pole had worked in his own building, but when Stone described the attack on Eleanor Hvar, Decani's face paled and flushed, his blue lips writhed, and the glasses flashed ominously in the washed-out morning sunshine. "We shall find Mister Stevan Jazak," he promised and there was no mistaking the menace in his words.

"Was that his name?" Stone inquired.

"That was the name he used at the Ministry," Decani replied shortly, and rose to go.

When he had gone, though not without reminding Stone of the time and address of his appointment with Karst—which Stone dutifully wrote down again though he had it carefully stowed away in his wallet in Eleanor Hvar's handwriting—Stone methodically checked his possessions to see what was missing. Nothing was.

Sam Gordon's letter was mostly about business matters, but three things in it struck Stone. The first was an item about Valerie. "I saw your ex-wife in a restaurant the other night,"

Sam wrote, "and much though I hate to admit it, she looked marvelous. Pregnancy seems to have softened her lines. Here's hoping it will do as much for her temperament." So, Valerie was going to have a child. The day and the man had come. A week ago, he thought, such news would have devastated him, but now he was simply glad that he was not the father. The second item was also about women. "Have you tried any of the women there?" Sam wanted to know. "Remember you're on vacation and their women are fine, better than ours. The Slovenes are the most beautiful, but the Serbs are the way they always say they like their coffee: 'Hot as hell, black as night, and sweet as sin.' " Stone thought he'd remember to tell that to Eleanor Hvar. The third was a postscript and consequently stood out of the text most of all. It read: "Have you seen Konstantin Karst? I have it on good authority that he has a sure-fire bestseller in the drawer, so you'd better. If the bidding gets tough, just mention 'Flash' Gordon to him. I'm ashamed to say I was once known by that moniker."

Stone knew Sam Gordon better than he knew anyone alive, which he supposed didn't say much, but when had Gordon been in Yugoslavia? He was pretty sure Sam had not been there during the war—he'd been in Africa and Italy—but afterward, some time between 1946 and 1950, when they'd met and started the agency. Had Sam still been in the Army then, the Foreign Service, Intelligence? Had he actually known Konstantin Karst and Karst known him, or would only that comic-strip name be the connection? How elusive even the simplest facts were. And had Decani's men tampered with the envelope? He examined it but it seemed untouched.

It wasn't until he was about to leave that he noticed the longshoreman's hook was gone, and realized that Decani must have taken it.

K

ONSTANTIN KARST's house was on the outskirts of the city, though still in it, a one-story burnt-umber stucco building with a triangular red slate roof and a tombstone-thin slab of chimney. Set away from its neighbors and surrounded by a high stucco wall, the house had only one entrance, a wooden and iron grillwork door of odd proportions with a bell and clapper on it. When Stone rang he heard the faint echo somewhere inside, a short click, and the door swung open a few inches. He made a last-minute check to see that the Luger was properly hidden, and would be even when he took off his coat, then pushed open the door, went in, and clicked it shut behind him. He was in a garden which ran along the side of the house and opened out on a terrace and another garden in the rear. On the terrace, beneath clipped plane trees, were two concrete mushroom-shaped tables ringed by green wooden chairs. Beyond the rear wall, the land sloped sharply to give the house an eminence from which there was a magnificent view of the city spread out below, unobstructed by houses on the street directly behind. There, masses of huge lilac bushes grew in almost orderly profusion, as if tended and pruned, two twisted old walnut trees stood, and high uncut grass that bent in the slight breeze. An unseasonal sun threw lines and shadows into harsh relief and the earth gave off a bitter, tired smell that made Stone feel he was in the country.

The path led to the entrance, all the way round on the other side of the house, but before Stone reached it, a man came out and stood on the top step waiting for him. For the moment Stone was certain he had seen that face before, until he realized that he had, many times, in the newspapers, but a version flattened and made characterless by the combined efforts of camera lens and newsprint. Ascetic, almost unlined, its youthfulness clashed sharply with the short Lincolnesque black beard, the dark hair brushed straight back from a high thoughtful forehead and the shaggy sideburns, which needed cutting, glinting silvery in the sunlight. The eyes had that same opaque unfathomable quality one sees in moving-picture stars and politicians, as if one is looking into the shutter of a camera. It was not a face easily forgotten.

"Mister Stone?" Konstantin Karst said, coming down the steps from the house, hand outstretched. "I've looked forward to your arrival for a long time." His speech was precise, even flowing, with an undercurrent of vehemence and oddness of intonation that made Stone uneasy.

"I'm Warren Stone," he replied.

"And I am Konstantin Karst."

They shook hands and Stone noted that Karst had the practiced handshake of the professional politician: strong and hearty, but impersonal, giving nothing away.

Karst led him to one of the mushroom-shaped tables and gestured for him to be seated. They sat in the green chairs across from each other, shaded by the plane trees that made the light that fell between them a clear disembodied green. After silently offering a cigarette, as silently declined, Stone self-consciously lit one for himself, knowing he was being given Karst's unabashed and minute scrutiny. He sat back and looked at the lilacs, the gnarled walnut trees, struck by the beauty of the pale green light.

"Well," he said to Karst finally, "have I passed muster?"

"You must forgive my bad manners," Karst said soberly. "There is much to be learned from a man's face, and I wanted to be sure before we began our . . . talk. There is not much time."

"You're sure now?" Stone asked, skeptical.

There was only faint hesitation before Karst nodded. "As sure as this much can tell me. More time would tell me more, but time we have very little of." He paused. "The difficulty is to know where to begin. It will be simpler if you tell me what you have heard about me and what has happened to you since your arrival."

It was Stone's turn to look at Karst for a long time, knowing how skillfully Karst was turning the tables, testing his honesty, and also giving himself more time to make a judgment on how trustworthy he was. If he had not quite passed muster, this would be the final inspection and, though he couldn't tell why, it was an inspection he wanted to pass. Leaving out only that Townsend had sent Grout to ask for Karst's manuscript, Stone told him how he had come to Yugoslavia and what had happened since. Karst listened impassively except, as in the description of the murder of Antun Vuk and the story of Mirko Sutnjak's death, his flat, shutter-like black eyes seemed focussed on a flame, and widened and narrowed as if taking a photograph to be filed away for some future but not vague reference. In leaving out the fact that the Embassy wanted Karst's manuscript, Stone felt somehow that he was betraying Karst's trust and wondered if the omission was his apology for Maxim Grout, for his country, or for himself.

He felt even worse when, after a spell of silent consideration of what Stone had told him, Karst began to talk. "Mister Stone, we are going to have to trust each other. I know how difficult that is on short notice, between people of different backgrounds. In fact," his smile was controlled but genuine, "how difficult it is for any two people, even of similar backgrounds."

"First, there isn't *a* manuscript; there are *four* manuscripts. One is an autobiographical work on my time as a Party leader and Vice-President. The second is a political work, what we used to call a polemic, on the nature of socialism, class, the state and freedom. Third, there is a novel set during the collectivization drive here. And last there is a book of lyric poems dedicated to Mirko Sutnjak." After a moment, he added, ". . . the man I loved best in my life." He used the word love without an iota of self-consciousness or qualification, which Stone admired, even as he questioned if it was only Karst's shrewd tactic to reject the slightest implication in Sutnjak's death.

"The manuscripts are not here. Oh, don't be surprised, Mister Stone. They are completed. But keeping them in this house would be a mistake. I am entertaining you out here in the garden not for want of hospitality, but because I have no doubt that my house is wired, my phone tapped, my visitors carefully noted. In fact, it is what I would do to someone like me, if I were still with them. And Petar Decani is—how do you call it?—a methodical man. The manuscripts are well-hidden. If you agree, you shall have them all."

Agree to what? Stone wondered. Already he felt the fascination of the man, the combination of cold logic and passionate intensity, and the refusal to beat around the bush.

"First," Karst continued, raising his index finger, "let me try to clear up some of the mysteries. I knew you were coming to this country because someone delivered a message to your partner Gordon for me, and Gordon told him. 'Flash' Gordon we used to call him, after the comic-strip character, because of his tongue and his temper. Also because of his bravery and his way with women, our women." There was almost a note of ruefulness, of injury, in his voice. "He was like us, like a Montenegrin," Karst added, and Stone saw that that was almost the greatest compliment Karst could pay. "I owed Gordon a debt. He saved my life once. I also knew I could trust him. He was stationed here for almost three years, from 1947 through 1949, as part of the military attaché's staff, though probably he was working for your Intelligence service then. It was during that whole period when we were breaking away from the Russian bear-hug."

Stone was furious. Why the hell hadn't Sam told him? He'd have behaved with more circumspection, more sensibly. He hated being a patsy. "Will you draw some fire, Lieutenant Stone, we think they've got a machine-gun out there." His face must have shown his feelings.

"You mustn't be angry because he said nothing. That was one of my conditions. I wanted you to act normally for I thought it would be your best protection and mine," Karst said.

"And Antun Vuk's?" Stone asked angrily.

The face in front of him did not change. Karst didn't move a muscle, yet there was something so unnatural about his immobility that Stone felt it as a force, a tension, even a rebuke. Karst took up his story as if he had not broken it off.

"There were those among us who did not want to break away from the Russians. Some were sincere. They thought our destiny and history were on the side of the East. Some were in the Russians' pay. Some were both. One of them was a man who has dogged my footsteps like a *Doppelgänger*. I think he must be my fate. What his real name is I do not know, but he has

113

been Kucic, Vlakovich, Krupa, and now I think he is your Stevan Jazak.

"I met him first in prison, a Communist like myself, but a man I could not like in spite of it. He was not concerned with socialism so much as he was thrilled by revolution; he despised justice, but he worshipped power and violence. Simply, he was a murderer who had found a cause. Even then I suppose he was working for the Russians, though I did not suspect it in those days. Unlike Mirko and myself, and many others—we were such amateurs, Mister Stone, it almost seems unbelievable now —Kucic knew about false papers and passports, how to cross borders illegally, how to set up clandestine presses, and how to use weapons."

"A Comintern agent's training is its own kind of university," Stone said wryly. "It confers its own degree and *éclat.*"

Karst stood up and looked over the twisted walnut trees and breeze-bent grass toward the city below. "Sometimes, I think that Kucic, or whatever he calls himself now, and Mirko Sutnjak were my good and evil angels."

He shook himself impatiently and sat down again. "Kucic was Bosnian by birth, a Bogomil, I think, or from a Bogomil family, with all that crazed hatred of the flesh that made killing a religious act for him, violence and cruelty its sacraments. But it was not just that he was Bogomil: he was part of another Eastern tradition too, the nihilists and *Narodniki,* the tradition of the assassin with pistol, dynamite and bomb, of Vera Zasulich killing General Trepov, or a dozen other such martyrs. . . ."

". . . like Fanya Kaplan shooting Lenin?" Stone interrupted quietly.

Again he had piqued Karst. "Yes," Karst replied reluctantly, "I suppose like her, too."

Then he was no longer listening. "Kucic was in the mountains with us. He had helped Mirko in Bosnia. When Mirko and I quarrelled about strategy, or tactics, Kucic took my side. He was always on the side of killing. And I was angry because I thought Mirko was wrong, afraid to look severe because he was Dalmatian and the Montenegrins were my own people. I should have known better, but we were all going on nerves then, and we seemed to have no future. Mirko Sutnjak, Mister Stone, was simply more intelligent than I. Politically, humanly. He knew that what I was doing was humanly evil and politically a mistake. He knew what the killing would do and he hated killing.

"And Kucic hated him. He said Mirko was not like us, we mountain men, Bosnians and Montenegrins. He was soft, a Dalmatian from the coast, and everyone knew Dalmatians were half-Italian and effeminate. And a painter! What disturbed him most was Mirko's daring, his bravery; Mirko seemed to be afraid of nothing and he could never be accused of cowardice or lagging behind. Kucic said he lacked 'revolutionary vigilance'—that was the phrase at the time—and should be eliminated. But he said it in such a way I always thought he was joking.

"Then Mirko and I had that stupid fight. I should have known better, but Mirko was drinking and he made it an issue in front of the men. Though by then I knew he was right and I wrong, I was too proud to admit it before the others. We fought and the men separated us. We were both angry, very angry, though it would have blown over in a few days, as it always had blown over when we fought before, and I made my mind up to tell him then that he was right, that we would change our methods. We had fought many times in the past, over politics, books, girls, and always it was forgotten in a few days time.

"Only this time, Mirko was dead. Someone had given him

a whole magazine. Everyone thought it was I, everyone, so I said nothing. What was there to say? That I hadn't done it? That I had not killed my best friend? To do so would have been to dignify their accusations, even if unspoken, as having some merit, some weight. I would not lower myself like that.

"Only three of us could have killed Mirko, if it was one of us. Kucic was one of them. One thing, however, made no sense. It still doesn't. Why should he kill Mirko? If he was a Soviet agent—and I think he was, is—they wanted us to camouflage our political coloration in those days, to be nationalist patriots, not Communists. That should have put Kucic on Mirko's side, not mine, *if the instructions to kill him were theirs.*" He bore down heavily on the last words, and Stone could almost feel Karst turning the thing over and over again in his mind. He realized then that the story and these problems were things Karst had lived with for so long that they were thorns grown into flesh, flesh he tore in anguish, in guilt, to see where it had betrayed him, and Stone felt a sudden peevish pity for the man. He had not learned to live with the memory of Slater and that German boy either; he knew a little of what it was like.

"It was not until 1943, during the Fourth Offensive, that I met Kucic again. I was convinced he had killed Mirko, but I had no evidence and foolishly I accused him. He laughed in my face. He did not give me a yes or no, just laughed. My temper rose and I threw him to the ground. He tried to kill me and I cut his face open with an SS dagger that I had taken from a dead German. It was the kind of dramatic Wagnerian weapon the Germans love, one of those things with a silver haft whose end was shaped like the head and beak of the Nazi eagle, decorated with a silver *hakenkreuz.* It did at least one good deed: Kucic will bear that remembrance of me to his grave."

116

"He does, Mister Karst," Stone corroborated, and described the scar. "It is not a face that will make women admire him."

"Kucic never liked women, and Mirko loved them."

"You mean Eleanor Hvar?"

"No, Lili was something different. I don't think he loved her as one does a woman, but as a child, as a daughter, as one's hope. He let her come with his group when she was only a child, sixteen years old, because she had lost her parents and was alone and wanted to fight. In his bones, Mirko felt he was going to die. I know because he told me so once in a way a man does not forget. Lili was like the child he wanted to survive him and the war, to see the new world we were fighting for and going to build." His voice was pitted with acid. "So he slept with her and made her pregnant. And when he did, he married her, because he was like that, and because, as I said, in his own way he loved her.

"They were in Dubrovnik then. His assignment was to organize hiding places in the coastal islands where we could store arms and escape when we were pressed to the wall. Mirko did his job well. Later we used his arrangements to get arms from your people, and for a while, one of the islands was even our main headquarters. But when his job was done, he had to come to meet me, in the mountains, and Lili was already big with child and couldn't go. And he didn't want to take her. He left her in Dubrovnik with his parents."

The sound of a door closing interrupted. Karst's head turned and Stone followed his glance. A woman, fully as tall as Karst and almost as powerfully built, carried a tray down the steps from the house. She walked with a grace and pride that not even the coffee service and *rakija* bottle could unbalance; it reminded Stone of peasant women carrying baskets on their heads. Her fine dark head was thrown back, her spine straight,

117

her broad shoulders squared. Magnificent looking, her size in no way diminished the sense of her femininity; instead, it enhanced it. She looked like one of the imposing caryatids Stone remembered from Decani's reception hall, as if a building or a world could be sustained on her shoulders, a nation begotten on her loins. Her demure, Western-style grey suit seemed out of character, her bare legs and sandalled feet appropriate.

Though Karst remained seated, Stone stood up and she inclined her head slightly to him as she put the copper tray on the mushroom-shaped table between him and Karst. She stood next to her husband, her hands still, waiting, palms down on the table, the long fingers with their unpainted nails spread like a fan. Karst's hand stole over one of hers, covered it, and then, looking at her rather than at him, he said in French, "This is Madame Karst. Alexandra, this is Mister Warren Stone, the man I told you would come from America."

Stone had barely finished his *enchanté* when, without preliminaries, Alexandra Karst said in French, "I was hoping you would not come." Stone clumsily stood up from his chair, and she was embarrassed. "Please sit down," she said. "I did not mean that personally. Only it would be better if Konstantin, my husband, forgot about publishing those books abroad. They can only bring him disaster."

Karst's hand tightened on hers but did not stop her.

"They have done enough to him. And they will do more. They have taken everything away, his position, his honors, even this house. Soon we must find a flat now because this house is required by protocol"—she bit the word out—"for a foreign ambassador. And the nation's former Vice-President must go to live in a tiny flat with his wife and children."

"Alexandra!" Karst's voice warned.

"He should know," she said, addressing Karst. "Maybe he can speak sense to you." She turned her attention to Stone. "They can do nothing to him, he says, they would not dare. They *will* dare, and he knows they will. They will send him to rot in prison, or worse. He has sat in enough prisons and given enough of his life. *I* want him now," she said boldly. "I need him. And the children."

"*Point finale,*" Karst said evenly. He did not raise his voice, but it carried command.

She bit her lip, but was quiet. Then, to keep the command from sounding peremptory, Karst said, as if that was what they had been talking about, "I was just telling Mister Stone about Lili Sutnjak."

But he had made a mistake; he had given her anger another channel in which it could leap from her tongue unrestrained. Or *had* he made a mistake? "You told him what she did at the Writers' Association?" Before he could answer, Alexandra Karst continued, "She walked up and slapped Konstantin's face. It was an accusation of murder in front of seventy people, and while Konstantin was on the dais and guest of honor."

"Yes," Karst confirmed, "but she did it while I was still in power, Alexandra, not afterwards. She thought I killed Mirko. Can you blame her? It was her first opportunity," he explained to Stone. "I hadn't seen her for years, since before Mirko's death."

"Then she should have tried to kill you, not just slap your face," his wife replied fiercely, and Stone was convinced that in Eleanor Hvar's place Alexandra Karst would have done just that.

Eleanor Hvar's role took on new dimensions for Stone. Was this a job she had to do for Decani, or something she had her heart in, an act of revenge against Karst that might explain her fervor in trying to get him to promise her Karst's manuscript? Even as he thought it, Stone knew two things troubled him simultaneously: the first that she still felt so strongly about Mirko Sutnjak that she would connive against Karst after all those years; and the second that the feeling of intimacy he had felt between them might be spurious, only the displaced and convoluted hatred for Karst. He was troubled even more because both of his feelings seemed petty.

"And she did it after all the help Konstanty gave her," Alexandra Karst added.

"Help she didn't ask for, or even know came from me, Mister Stone," Karst said. "After the war, when I was in power, I hoped she would come to see me. Because of Mirko, I didn't think I should go to see her unless she came to me first, though now I'm sorry. But I wanted to help her."

"He did help her," Alexandra Karst said proudly. "Konstanty got her into university, and two separate scholarships for years abroad, to study in England, and later he arranged her first jobs in translating with the State Publishing House. And she never knew. She doesn't know now he paved the road for her."

"It was a bumpy road," Karst said evenly. "She had lost her parents, she lost Mirko, she lost their child. I owed it to Mirko to keep an eye on her. It was my duty." He leaned over to fill the three small glasses on the tray from the *rakija* bottle. He raised his own glass, and for an instant the sun caught it, and it shone like an ingot of green gold. "To freedom," he said unexpectedly.

"To freedom," Stone repeated, touching glasses, but Alexandra Karst had not picked up her glass, though her hand had retreated from beneath her husband's.

"Alexandra?" Karst said.

"I do not believe in words, Konstanty," she replied slowly, looking straight into his face. "Especially such large words."

"What do you believe in?" Karst asked, very softly, and Stone saw that he was witnessing part of a long, bitter quarrel.

"I believe in you . . ."

". . . but not in my words?"

She shook her dark head stubbornly. "I believe in you," she repeated, "in the children, in myself." Just then, almost as if it had been stage-managed, the cry of a child came from the house. She turned to Stone and said. "You must excuse me, Mister Stone, the children have probably gotten up from their naps." Gravely, without hurrying, she went back into the house, having left her glass on the copper tray untouched. Karst watched her until the door closed, then bolted his *rakija*. Stone followed suit.

"She does not believe in freedom," Karst said, as if talking to himself. "She believes only in what she can see and touch . . ."

". . . and feel?"

"And feel," Karst corroborated.

"Perhaps she is right."

"No," Karst said firmly. "No. Alexandra is wrong. She is quite wrong. *Only freedom is important.* Happiness, as distinct from pleasure, depends very little on material possessions once you are above a reasonable subsistence level. Beyond that, *freedom is everything.*"

That Karst was speaking from the depths of his conviction, Stone had no doubt. Here was a committed man, in both senses perhaps, and Stone was moved in spite of himself.

"It is my fault. She has heard me make too many speeches. She has seen me juggle too many abstractions. Now she believes in none of them, in nothing."

"She believes in you," Stone said. "My ex-wife believed in everything I said—well, almost everything—because she thought I was clever, but she did not believe in me."

For an instant Karst was taken out of himself and looked at him with more personal interest. "That's even worse."

"Much worse," Stone agreed. "That's the point I was trying to make."

"But Alexandra was a political, a Communist, a Partisan. So she saw too much, especially the cruelty and killing, and now she does not believe in politics at all. She simply moved away and, so to speak, left it all."

"I don't believe in politics either. And that's what I've tried to do too, but the world is on the side of killing and killers."

"You speak in pain," Karst said.

"Yes. I have done my own share of killing."

"In the United States?"

"No. During the war."

"That is a different thing."

"Not at all. Killing is killing."

"It is sometimes necessary to kill."

"Human beings?"

"Yes, human beings. Because they would make such a *merde* of the world otherwise. The Stevan Jazaks, for instance. To them, you must be merciless or the world is doomed. I have killed with my own hands and I am not ashamed of it."

"I have killed and not killed," Stone replied, "and I'm ashamed of both."

"You Americans are spoiled, Mister Stone. Death is not so horrible as life sometimes, and killing not so terrible as not killing. There are times when life is insupportable, not just disagreeable, but truly insupportable, when you cannot and must not stay your hand. Your people have violence without

122

the sense of tragedy, brutality without the sense of purpose."

"Perhaps so."

"And you don't understand about your finest political possession: *freedom, freedom!* What alarms me is not the ridiculous and irrelevant quarrel between the capitalism you don't have and the communism the Soviets don't have. The frightening thing in Eastern Europe is the similarity, sometimes even the identity, of Soviet and American influences here. The influence you bring to bear on our cultures is almost indistinguishable from that of the Russians.

"America and the West, of course, function better in the productive sphere. Which is not to be ignored. People have to be fed and clothed and housed. But more important, Western superiority is conceived and acknowledged—and propagandized—in terms on which both Soviets and Americans seem to be in full agreement."

"You mean we both want the same thing," Stone said, "only for the moment we do it better?"

Karst nodded emphatically. "You crow about our countries not fulfilling economic goals, because you do produce so much more and better, but you don't denounce *The Plan* itself as a monstrosity, the institutions of repression. Not planning in general, which is man's attempt to use his resources intelligently, but *The Plan,* which is political more than economic. There are few redeeming features in life under *The Plan."*

He leaned forward in his chair. "As I was gradually breaking away from my old beliefs, what impressed me most was the realization that people living under a totalitarian regime in many ways adopt the values of the regime unconsciously. Even opponents come to accept a lot of the *merde* which passes for fact and news and truth. They don't even realize that what is now called 'liberalization'—which heaven knows is a hundred times better than what came before—is still only a poor mockery of freedom. The result is a greyness in which people don't even have the fire of inner rebellion and passivity masquerades as contentment. All the ideology this side of Lenin can't change the simple fact that freedom means everything, and your people should be telling our people that."

Karst poured himself another *rakija* and looked apprehensively at the house.

"But many of us, your wife perhaps, and certainly I, myself, want the freedom to be left alone, to have a private life."

"The world is too small, Mister Stone, only a shrunken apple now. You will *not* be left alone. There's no such thing as a private life any more. That old and privileged world is dead. Today, public life touches private life everywhere. You can't escape it. And, therefore, you must make it the best public life you can, or your private life is doomed. The only way you can be left alone at all, the only way you can have even the shreds of a private life, is to fight for the best kind of public one."

"There is no cloister so sequestered as can keep politics out," Stone said.

"Jonathan Swift," Karst said, as if identifying a quotation in class. "And he was absolutely right."

They sat in the dappled green silence drinking the thick Turkish coffee from little white cups, the only sounds the buzzing of a single black horsefly attracted to the rim of Alexandra Karst's still full glass of *rakija,* and the muted sounds of children's voices from the house.

"You will take the manuscripts?" Karst asked finally, and for the first time Stone saw how desperately important to him it was, how much he was counting on it.

Why were *words* so important to revolutionaries as a preface to and explanation of their revolutionary *acts?* Why was a book so important in a world of violence? Was it really that only the war of words was possible?

"I will," Stone said, realizing that he would with a lurch, as if he had missed the last step on a flight of stairs. Karst the activist makes his last act spreading the word, and Stone the passivist once more moves into the world of action to pass along the word, Stone thought sardonically. How pertinent their talk of public and private lives had been! The public one had knocked and he had surrendered his long-cherished detachment like an impassioned virgin surrendered her virtue to the first importunate suitor, assuming a commitment he wasn't sure he could fulfill, and which might easily get him killed. Nor was he sure why he was doing it. For Karst? For Eleanor Hvar? For Sam Gordon? It wasn't so much *for* what or whom —Valerie could still enjoy calling him negative—as it was *against*. Against being pushed and prodded, chivvied and crowded, as he had been. Against Decani and Kucic; yes, and against Townsend too. And most of all against those who killed Antun Vuk. *Against.*

Karst contradicted himself, and he was a zealot. Certainly the picture he gave of his past was quite different from the ones Stone had gotten from Grout and Townsend, though the varied facets could be reconciled. Politicals, perhaps all of us, he thought, continue to rewrite their histories. Ordinary individuals do so privately; politicals are deprived of that luxury: they must do so publicly and embarrassingly. But he distrusted zeal and zealots, their narrow concentration and passionate intensity, for in the final analysis it always led to killing, to murder. There were those who killed for pleasure and those who killed because they thought it necessary, for a "cause," and those who combined both vices. All were monstrous, but a Karst was never a Kucic: they were different kinds of monsters. And both of them were quite different from Decani and Townsend, and those two in a different class from Grout.

At the back of his mind Stone recognized how much his decision resembled what he had said to his mother and grandfather before he went to war. This was, he knew, another war, another facet of life in which words were both means of communication and weapons; and that the war of words was both public and private. Was the war *for* freedom, or simply *against* tyranny? If it was only a choice of lesser evils, if it was *against* the latter, wasn't it necessarily, at least in part, *for* the former? Was choice ever couched in any but those terms?

Karst said nothing, only breathed deeply for a time. Then he glanced at his wrist watch and his voice became a conspiratorial whisper. "There isn't much time. You should not stay here too long with me. I will speak quickly. If you have questions, stop me. The manuscripts are in Dubrovnik. All of them. There are no copies. If these are lost, the books are altogether lost. I do not think I could reproduce them."

"No copies," Stone lamented, "but why?"

"It would have been too complicated and increased the chances for being found out. Also, if they found copies before you published, they could print and leave out what parts they didn't like, then accuse your edition of fraudulent interpolations."

"But you could deny . . ."

". . . they would permit no denials." The camera-dark eyes shuttered and looked away. "You must go to Dubrovnik as if you were on a vacation, or taking a tourist trip. Wait at least a week before you go, more if you can, to throw them off the track, but *not* more than three weeks. Stay at the Excelsior Hotel. Someone will come to you . . ."

"... how will I know him?" Stone interjected. "And he me?"

"He will say to you, 'Mirko Sutnjak is my brother.' He will be able to recognize you, never fear."

"And the manuscripts, how can I get them out of the country?" Stone asked. "Decani is watching me, Kucic or Jazak is, and ..." he stopped.

"... your own people will not help you. I surmised as much. They would like the manuscripts for their own purposes, to be printed in a form acceptable to them. I want you to promise me that the books will be published as I wrote them. I would not want you to take the manuscripts to your people unless they permitted the books to appear as they were written."

"Of course, that's the point."

"Yes," Karst said appreciatively, "that *is* the point. They will not leave you alone. When you walk out of here, and they find out that you haven't got the manuscripts, they are not going to let you out of their sight, or out of the country, if they can stop you, until they find them. Until they can make you tell them where the manuscripts are hidden, or until you lead them to them. That is why I am *not* going to tell you where the manuscripts are. It is as much for your protection as for mine.

"Give me your visiting card," Karst said, extending his palm. "In fact, give me two." Stone took two of his cards and laid them on the brown, lined palm. "I will tell them you came to ask me about manuscripts, mine and others. I had none and I gave none. I recommended none. But I did take your card so that in case I ever wrote again, or heard of something suitable, I could get in touch with you."

"That's the story. I'll stick to it," Stone promised.

"Good. Kucic will try to kill you," Karst continued.

"He promised he would the next time we met."

"He will try to keep his promise. You are armed?"

Stone drew his jacket aside so Karst could see the Luger. Karst nodded approvingly, matter of factly. "If you see him, kill him. Don't wait. He won't wait for you. Decani wants what he thinks is one manuscript so it can be destroyed, or at least kept from publication. There is the Revolution, the Party, the State, and my former Comrades to safeguard from my bile and slander. Kucic, I think, has orders to kill you once you have seen me, because I might have given you information and because that is the way they are, those are their methods. They know I have information which connects their present leaders with Stalin and his horrors. And if I told you, you might one day talk. In their mind, the only way to keep that from happening is to make you tongueless. That is also one of the reasons Decani wants the manuscript. Our government wants good relations with the Soviets now, it doesn't want to embarrass their leaders, who are now also eager to take them back into the fold, though my former comrades know that those in the Politburo in Moscow were all part of Stalin's *apparat*."

"And what about you?" Stone asked. "Once the books are published, and even before, when they find out, they will know that you gave them to me."

"Alexandra is right," Karst replied, with a quick, furtive glance at the house. "They will not leave me in peace. They will have to do something." His face grew somber. "Just what, I don't know."

"And your wife and children?"

"I don't think they will touch them. *I* will be enough."

Slowly, Stone leaned over and poured their glasses full of *rakija* again. They touched glasses and silently drank.

"Is it worth it?" Stone asked finally.

"I have no option because I must choose. That is what freedom is, the possibility and obligation to choose. And I have chosen."

For Karst there was no turning back; however tortuous and tortured the road he had taken, Karst would follow it to the end. Was that being a fanatic, or simply a brave and principled man? Stone knew that he was going to have to go along that same road for a good while, and that unlike Karst, who seemed to feel no fear, he was afraid. Where had he once read that John Huss had died for a technicality, that Galileo had been sensible and instead recanted before the Inquisition? Yet what had come down to men through history had been Huss' martyrdom, and not only that Galileo's science was right, but that apocryphal and moving story of his *"E pur si muove!"*

Alexandra Karst came out of the house with the children. She was now dressed in a peasant skirt and blouse and looked more natural. A boy of seven and a little girl of perhaps five each held one of her hands. On the top step, before descending in unison, they all hesitated and in that moment Stone saw them as Karst's triptych of hostages to fortune, a moving argument for not doing what he was doing. This time they both stood when Alexandra Karst arrived at the table, and she introduced the children to Stone. "This is Mirko," she said of the boy, and Stone just succeeded in repressing a start. If he needed further proof that Karst had not murdered Mirko Sutnjak, this was it. A man like Karst was neither sufficiently Machiavellian nor twisted to name his son after a man he had, himself, murdered. "And this is Lidija." Both children shook his hand gravely, too gravely Stone thought. Though the girl otherwise resembled her mother, and the boy his father, both had Karst's fathomless shutter-like black eyes. Karst bent down to them, crouching at their level, for the first time showing almost perfect white teeth in an unexpected smile, and speaking quickly in Serbo-Croat. The childrens' faces, which until that moment had had the impassive quality of Diego Rivera's paintings of Mexican Indian children, suddenly blossomed into laughter and language. Transfigured, they clung to their father as he tickled and teased them. When he stood up, they backed quickly to their mother, and their faces, like flowers without sun, seemed to close.

"Alexandra," Karst said, "I wish to show Mister Stone some things in the house. You will keep the children out here." He spoke in French so that, apparently, the children would not understand. Something seemed to pass between the two of them, the last sentence more than a request, yet not quite an order. Stone left his coat on the garden chair and followed Karst up the steps into the house.

It was cooler and dimmer inside and he almost tripped on an Oriental rug. When his eyesight adjusted, he was amazed to see modern Scandinavian furniture on those Turkish rugs, a daring juxtaposition of ancient and ultra-modern, of cool and brilliant colors, that had the same combination of qualities as Karst's personality. The paintings on the walls seemed familiar, but they went through the rooms to Karst's study too quickly for Stone to identify them. Karst's study was a second shock. Brightly lighted and windowless, it had the same stripped military-political monasticism of Decani's office, the straight lines unrelieved by color, only here everything was not of metal, but of dark wood. If not from a monk's cell, the dark old furniture might easily have come from an abbott's priory; so monastic was the feeling that Stone felt his eyes drawn up the plain white walls to where there should have been a crucifix, but found only another picture of Marshal Tito.

On the long refectory table that served Karst as a desk stood two bronzes, their bases lapped in papers. Together, they framed an old battered typewriter. Stone immediately knew the bronzes for Mirko Sutnjak's work. The first sculpture was of an old woman, undoubtedly a grandmother, and two young children, hurrying forward bent almost at a forty-five degree angle as if they were all leaning into a strong wind, fleeing hopelessly in the face of some catastrophe: flood or earthquake or war. The grandmother's head was covered with a peasant kerchief, but the childrens' hair, the long braids of a girl and the shorter locks of a boy, streamed behind them like defeated pennants. All were faceless, featureless, with a blind, bronze staring quality that most resembled the metal visor of a medieval knight.

The second sculpture was a young powerful man fallen on his knees, his legs splayed out behind so that his feet, with their ankle bones flat against the earth, were distorted and broken-looking. His chin was on his chest, his hair hung in front of his clenched eyes, his powerful shoulders were hunched, while his hands clawed at his vitals. Where they had been, from the middle of the chest to the apex of the groin, was only jagged empty space. Eleanor Hvar's and this one were brothers in bronze.

"Mirko's," Karst said tersely. "Part of a series he called *War.*"

"I recognized his work. I saw one of his bronzes at his . . . wife's." Stone forced himself past the last word.

"I'm glad Lili has some. These two were the only ones of Mirko's I could salvage."

"The children in that one somehow remind me of yours," Stone blurted, and then could have bitten his tongue.

Karst looked at him and nodded. "I know, I know. Life is a cruel wind. My old comrades, the fathers, are correct to me, but their sons are cruel to my children in school."

Hostages to fortune. No wonder their faces were wooden and withdrawn as Indians'. How could they fight an ostracism they didn't understand? The sins of the fathers, and the virtues, were visited on the children.

Karst was looking at his watch again and muttering, "Time, time." He closed the study door and put a cautioning finger to his lips, beckoning Stone to follow. Stone went with him to the wall where Karst gingerly lifted the portrait of Tito and showed a small area that looked like a place for a picture hook. Karst turned the picture hook a full 180 degrees and the wall suddenly and silently began to move, opening like a door on well-oiled hinges. Karst walked into the passageway behind, flicked a pale yellow light on, and Stone followed. Karst touched a second switch below the light switch and the wall moved silently closed behind them. The corridor they found themselves in dropped steeply down so that Stone had to keep himself from running, until they came to a very small room with paillasses neatly piled in diagonally opposite corners. Karst took two of them, dropped them in the center of the room, and squatted on one. Stone sat on the other. "This was built before the war," Karst explained. "During the war the man who owned the villa used it to help Jews and Partisans escape from the Germans. He was very brave and cool, and he saved hundreds of lives by himself."

"What happened to him?"

"We shot him."

"Why?"

"Only Mirko and I knew about his services. The third man in our cell was killed. Then Mirko. Those he helped never came back. The man was a bourgeois, a lawyer, and of course he was friendly to the Germans to divert suspicion. We shot him for collaboration."

"Couldn't *you* do anything?"

Karst shrugged. "It was after the war. Everyone was eager to pay off debts, to punish collaborators and enemies. When I came here to look for him, they told me that someone had reported him as a collaborator. Some of our people simply came and shot him. No trial, no formalities, just a bullet in the back of the neck."

"Justice."

Karst ignored that. "I took the villa myself then."

"You never told anyone about this tunnel and the room?"

"No." He rubbed his hands together, a harsh dry sound like autumn leaves. "Twice he saved my life, and once Mirko's."

Why, Stone thought, had he taken that particular villa? Was it like naming his son Mirko? Did Karst have to keep the evidence of injustice, or pain, or loss, always before him? To remind himself, or to torment himself, or both? And why had he never told anyone of the tunnel and the room? Had the future, even then, not beckoned so rosily?

Karst was telling him that the man who would meet him in Dubrovnik would lead him to the manuscripts, and after that to a hidden boat. Bari, in Italy, was only 70 or 80 miles across the Adriatic. It was easily crossed in a single night. "Do you know about boats?" Karst asked.

"I think I can manage."

"It is the old route that Mirko set up," Karst said. "It has worked for many people many times before."

Stone again felt that simultaneous envy and respect for Sutnjak that he had experienced with his wife and his sculpture.

Karst stood up and they went down the tunnel which still slanted steeply while Karst explained in a whisper that if Stone wanted to see him, this was the way. But he could come only in dire emergency. The passage came out in the hall of a house two streets away, and if Stone could get there without being followed, he could then come underground up to Karst's house without being seen, while if he came directly to the house it was almost always under surveillance. The tunnel could be entered the same way, by turning a picture hook behind a portrait of Tito. If he were seen in the house, it would not be too bad because the people who lived there were friends of his and minded their own business, but it was best not to be seen anyway.

When they came to the end wall, Karst motioned for silence again and pantomimed how one of the three switches worked a periscope fitted into the wall through which you could see if anyone was in the outside corridor. "My own improvement," Karst whispered proudly. "I built it myself." They both looked through and no one was there. Karst pressed the other two switches which moved the wall and turned out the tunnel lights. The shabby vestibule of an old house came into view as the wall fell noiselessly back. To the right was a small staircase that led to a second story; to the left, no more than fifteen feet away was the exit into the street. Stone looked both ways quickly, then Karst drew him back into the tunnel and closed the wall once more.

In the dark Karst said, "That chambermaid whose foot Decani broke in your room lives in that house. No known connection exists between us. Even they cannot watch everyone all the time." He switched on the light in the underground passageway and began to climb up toward the house. Stone strode after him, a perverted variant of the Lincoln adage running through his mind: You may watch all the people some of the time; you can even watch some of the people all the time; but you can't watch all the people all the time. Karst said he did not like to use women and children, and Stone knew he meant the chambermaid and Antun Vuk.

134

There were so many unanswered questions Stone wanted to ask, yet couldn't. And they were basic questions. Were any books, were all four of Karst's, worth the loss of Antun Vuk's life? By not dealing with the question, at least aloud, Karst had already dismissed it as unworthy of being asked: in short, he acted as if the books *were* worth more than a single life, or even several lives, and you had to take that on faith. He did not intimate that the lives lost, or those that might be, were a paltry payment; only of those in the distant past—the owner of the villa, Mirko Sutnjak—did he seem able to see the sacrifice. But suppose Karst were wrong, and the books not worth any human life? Even in posing the question to himself, Stone felt its self-mockery: it was so like what Valerie had said, perhaps less sententiously, all through their married life.

This time they didn't stop in the little room though Stone glanced sidelong at the two forlorn-looking paillasses lying there. Instead they returned to the house. Karst closed the wall behind them, then nicely arranged the balance of the Marshal's picture as Stone waited next to Sutnjak's sculpture of the grandmother and children, his fingers compulsively exploring their shape and texture.

Outside of the house, Alexandra Karst and the children were digging in a vegetable garden which lay some distance beyond the mushroom-shaped tables, and which Stone had not noticed before. Alexandra Karst waved and Stone waved back, then she returned to her digging; the children did not look up at all. Karst stopped at the tables and, keeping his voice low so that it would not carry, asked, "Then everything is clear?"

"No, not everything," Stone replied, "but the plan is clear. You don't want me to give the manuscripts to anyone, or to speak of them. You want them published exactly as they were written, their texts and intentions undisturbed. You don't want my Embassy or your former comrades to have any part of them. You want me to go to Dubrovnik in a week or two where a man will meet me, say, 'Mirko Sutjnak is my brother,' and then take me to where the manuscripts are. He will also show me a boat in which I can get across to Italy. Once in Italy I am on my own."

"Perfect," Karst approved. "Then what is *not* clear?"

For an instant Stone was tempted to sing, "Who is Karst, what is he, that all the swine offend him?" but such humor was out of place and the sign of his own mounting fear and apprehension. "Many things aren't clear, but there isn't enough time to clear them up now. Some business things must be decided, though. I shall take copyright to the books in your name, but what shall I do with your money?"

"I hadn't thought of that," Karst exclaimed, obviously irritated with himself. "They won't permit me to get it here, though it would be of use."

"How about a Swiss bank? I could put the money in an escrow account for you there. Perhaps," Stone hesitated, "it would be wiser to put the account in both your names. Then, either of you, or I, could get the money for you."

"You mean, if—yes, that is better. Then if Alexandra wants money, she can have it," Karst affirmed quickly.

"Should we be questioned, we will say we merely talked, but about what?"

"Books, of course. Literature. I recommended you read some of our old Serb epics, but I thought most of our new books too provincial for your audience. I did not mention names or titles. I told you I liked Malraux and Sartre, Faulkner and Hemingway, Kafka and Mann, because they refused to simplify man's motives or his estate. Mostly we talked about the Russians, Tolstoy, Dostoyevsky, Babel, Pasternak, Piln-yak, Akhmatova, and the others. They will recognize my hobby-horses," he said smiling, and Stone was struck by almost the first note of self-irony. "I also asked you about American books and you told me about the postwar American writers."

Stone nodded. "I'll need that. Decani and Townsend may not ask, but Grout will."

"Grout? Maxim Grout? Is he still here? You mean they haven't declared him *persona non grata* and thrown him out?" Karst's face lit up. "How marvelous! Our old friend Max."

Not knowing which of Karst's questions to answer first, Stone asked his own instead. "Do you know him? Why should he be *persona non grata?*"

"Because he knows more about us than almost any of your people. Or even the British. And he should. Didn't Max tell you?"

Stone shook his head.

"We were students together, Mirko, Max and I, in the last two years of the gymnazium, and then in the first two years of the university. When I came from my father's house in Montenegro, I stayed with Max's family in Belgrade until I found my own place to live. Old Nikola Grout, his father, was a doctor, a Socialist, and his mother was an American. Nikola had met her in England when he was in medical school—I think she was studying there, an upper-class Boston bluestocking—and he married her and brought her back to Belgrade. It was from Nikola that all three of us got our first lectures on socialism and our first books. Marx, Adler, Bernstein, Parvus, Herzen, Bakunin. Even, to give the old man credit, Lenin and Trotsky, though he hated both of them." They sat down and Karst refilled their *rakija* glasses. Stone was astonished at the youthfulness that had come across Karst's face and the almost lyrical quality of his voice.

"Nikola was a smart old man. In the mid-Thirties he saw

the war coming, and he took his family to America. His wife's family was there and had good connections, that made it easier. Max hated to go, because we were such close friends they called us 'The Three Musketeers.' I was a poet, Max was a novelist, Mirko was a painter and sculptor. But Nikola insisted, and Max loved his parents, so he went to the States. He finished his university there and then joined your foreign service. As I said, his mother had connections.

"We used to write at first, but our ways had separated, our lives were worlds apart, our views were opposed. At the university I had become a Communist, and later I recruited Mirko into the Party, but not Max. Old Nikola had inoculated Max well against our sickness: he hated the Communists with a passion. Then Nikola took Max to America. Looking back, that may even have been specifically to separate us, to keep Max from our ideas, for Max told us that our joining the Party almost broke the old man's heart. Max and I wrote for a long time, until I went to prison and he went into the foreign service. Then it would have been unwise for both of us, and we stopped. But he and Mirko wrote to the end."

"Communism," Stone said bitterly.

Karst was stung, "I'm grateful for once having breathed that honest and proud revolutionaries' air. Otherwise I think I'd have a less clear picture now of what I think man consists of, and a much lower idea of his capabilities." The lines were delivered as if his integrity had been impugned, and they fell just short of rhetoric, but he was obviously sincere.

Stone remembered his own first impression of Grout's literary English, yet curious intonation, and Townsend's tenderness with Grout. He remembered too the detailed accounts of Karst's life and Grout's unhappiness and unshed tears when he had told how Mirko Sutnjak died. It hadn't

138

been the sentimentality that came out of the bottle after all. Grout's remarkable and intimate knowledge of these men and the local scene made sense: the men were not only former countrymen, but his boyhood friends; and Grout knew the scene because he had lived in it long enough to hear the pitch and discern the tempo of the life.

And there was more. Karst told how Grout had been part of one of the first Allied missions parachuted into Yugoslavia during the war. He was an obvious choice. He knew the language, the landscape, and even some of the figures in it. Grout worked for a rapprochement between Chetniks and Partisans until, reluctantly, he had to admit that the Chetniks were hopelessly compromised by collaboration with the Italians and Germans. Even then, Grout had done everything in his power to keep America and Britain from abandoning anything but the Chetnik leadership, insisting that Allied arms shipments to the Partisans be used as leverage to force the Communists into a more representative coalition with the Chetnik resistance led by a new and untainted leadership. But he failed. Finally, in spring 1944, while leading a Partisan demolition group sent to blow up a railroad trestle, Grout was wounded by the Germans. Partisans brought him back to headquarters and he was evacuated to Italy.

Though Grout and Karst had seen each other from time to time during the war, and even fought in operations together, they usually avoided one another and rarely spoke. "Perhaps he, too, thought I was guilty of Mirko's death," Karst said reflectively, "though we never talked of that, or of Mirko, or of the old days."

He tugged at his little beard, his hands looking surprised to find it still there. "Later we stopped talking altogether. Because they knew we had been good friends, I was given orders to recruit Max as an agent for us. I argued that it was useless, that I knew Max, but they insisted. They were orders and Party discipline was Party discipline, so I tried. I failed, of course. Max immediately rejected my offer and reported it to the head of the American mission. It didn't help our relations much. We snubbed each other after that, but I sometimes had the feeling that Max was doing it more because he didn't want to compromise me than for his own protection."

The clear green light beneath the plane trees had muddied, and the murk seemed to invade Stone's spirit. Though he looked at his watch, Karst didn't seem to notice but went on saying that he had not seen Grout again until 1952, when Grout returned to Belgrade. Karst thought it shrewd to send Grout back because in the meantime he had been to Russia and Bulgaria and was now one of the most experienced people in the American foreign service. "By then," Karst continued, "I had begun to break away. Max and I saw each other on formal occasions, but only when necessary. Again, I think he did that more out of concern for compromising me than fear for himself. He knew that I was breaking away, from what I wrote, and he didn't want to give any of my people a chance to pin an espionage charge on me through him. Finally, after I was relieved of my government posts, and then only once, he spoke to me as he once had, as a friend. For the first time since the university he addressed me in the familiar form, and asked if he could help me."

"And?"

Karst shrugged. "There was no way to help—unless I wanted to leave the country and become an exile, an emigré, and I didn't."

Karst lapsed into silence, his eyes closed, and he leaned back unseeing in his chair. The murky green light made his face remote and somber, like something carved of stone; eyeless now, he looked like a sculpture of one of the ancient Caesars. Stone saw how much the afternoon had taken out of Karst, how much the pain of recollection and the difficulty of trying to explain had cost the man in expense of spirit. And Stone knew that he had stayed too long.

He got up, and picked his coat off the back of the chair. Karst's shuttered eyes opened and for a moment they mirrored his anguish. "I have involved you both in the Balkans and in history, Mister Stone, and both are cataclysms."

"No, Mister Karst, you have reinvolved me in life, though that too may be only a cataclysm," Stone replied.

Karst nodded, smiling. He understood. He stood up, his features again composing themselves into the face of the public figure. He called his wife and she came with the children to say good-by. They shook hands all around and Karst sent his best to Sam Gordon, "Flash." Alexandra Karst, as if relenting, said, "You may send Lili our regards when you see her." Stone agreed, moved by the effort it cost her, but more touched by the masked faces of Karst's children. Karst took him around the side of the house to the gate. Before opening it, he stopped and said, "I am greatly in your debt."

"And I in yours."

They shook hands again, urgently, as if they would not see one another again, then Stone was on the street, the gate clanging shut behind him.

THE MOMENT he looked around the empty street, he knew he should have called a taxi and been driven back to his hotel, but he was ashamed to ring Karst's bell once again. He looked up and down the empty street suspiciously though nothing except the silence seemed extraordinary. He put his hand inside his jacket and took the Luger out. Shielding it with his coat, he checked the ammunition and the safety, slung the coat over his forearm than tucked the Luger under it at the ready.

Stone walked downhill toward the city. The streets were narrow and winding, and ran between high walls or fences, many of them topped and covered with vines which hid the villas behind from prying eyes. Stone had the feeling he was being watched, that eyes followed every step he took, that all his movements were being gauged and measured, but he saw no one. It was a fine neighborhood—for an ambush. He walked quickly, on the balls of his feet, having all he could do to keep from breaking into a run, a preternaturally loud alarm-clock ticking in his head was only the pounding of his heart. A sudden flashing from the heavy ivy on top of one stucco wall across the street startled him. He tore his gun out from under his coat, but it was only a rush of swallows skimming skyward from their perch, veering and thrusting their way into the violet late-afternoon air.

Stone leaned against a high wooden fence and began to laugh with almost hysterical relief, and while he was still laughing, wood tearing sounded next to his cheek and a gouged-out piece of fence flicked past his face and into the air like a giant raw toothpick. Even as he threw himself flat on the ground, Stone realized that someone was shooting at him with a high-powered rifle. The second shot came a few moments later, splintering the fence a little on his other side. The rifleman had him bracketed. Stone picked out the street on the hillside above as the general area from which the shots had come, but he could not see his assailant; and in any event the distance was far beyond the range of his Luger. The third shot whined over his head, chipped the sidewalk just beyond his heels and riccocheted into the fence. Stone turned his body profile to the line of fire, offering less target, and began to inch along the pavement. He was no longer frightened. His mind worked coolly and clearly. At the end of the street, the road took a sharp bend; if he could make it, the turn would block the rifleman's field of fire.

Another bullet grooved the pavement in front of him spraying concrete fragments into his face and hair, and he stopped. The rifleman was not trying to kill him, but was toying with him, deliberately boxing him in, keeping him flattened on the ground. Since the man was apparently a crack shot, he must have something else in mind. The orderly chugging of an automobile engine made Stone turn his head. It was a small green Fiat like the one that had seemed to be following them when he and Eleanor Hvar had gone to Kalemegdan. His instinct told him it was the same car but he couldn't be sure. Should he try to kill the driver now before he got to him, or damage the car? But suppose it was not the same Fiat and the driver was an innocent man?

The Fiat came roaring down the street. Stone braced the Luger in his right hand with his left, using his elbows like the legs of a tripod, as the car neared him. But it didn't stop. Stone saw the bottle come flying out of the window toward him and knew what it was. Instinctively, he fired at it and simultaneously rolled away from where the bottle would land and smash if he had missed. He heard the splintering glass and roar of flame in the same instant, then saw his coat aflame. The smell of his own singed hair stank in his nostrils. He jerked his arm out from under the coat, but his jacket sleeve had already caught fire. Expecting the impact of a rifle bullet in his body at any moment, Stone leaped to his feet, tore the jacket off, stamped the fire out beneath his feet. An eight-or ten-foot pool of fire was searing the pavement black and melting the tar of the roadway. His shot had shattered the Molotov cocktail prematurely, so that only the outer edge of burning gasoline had touched his coat with flame.

Stone turned to look after the Fiat, his Luger ready, and he saw the end of the street blocked by a large black Tatra. The green Fiat's brakes screeched, tires whined, and then came the gnashing sound of tearing steel. The Fiat struck, seemed to bounce off the Tatra, then turned over on its side. So huge he seemed comic emerging from the small car, the loden coat climbed out of it, gun in hand, and began to run towards Stone. For a fat man he was very swift. From behind the Tatra came Petar Decani and two men in belted black raincoats, chasing him. The rifle up the hill barked and one of the belted black raincoats pitched forward and did not get up.

Another shot rang out, but nothing happened. Stone looked up to the hillside and saw two men struggling over a rifle pointed skyward. One of them he was sure was the totem pole, the other looked like Michael Townsend, but before he could tell for sure, the two grappling figures fell from sight.

The loden coat had seen them too, and he whirled, raising his arm to fire pointblank at Decani, when Stone shot him through the right shoulder. The gun fell out of the loden coat's hand, and as he bent to pick it up with his other hand, Decani charged. Running toward them, Stone saw the revolver in Decani's right fist and the metal rod in his left, which he raised and slammed down on the loden coat's neck. A bellow echoed down the street and the loden coat collapsed on his face like a felled bull, the longshoreman's hook sticking out just above his collarbone like a matador's *banderilla*. The man's great bulk shuddered once, a giant paroxysm, and then he lay still.

Decani stood over him, breathing hard, his eyes wild and dilated, his trick glasses catching and reflecting the rays of the setting sun. For a hideous moment Stone was sure that Decani would put his victorious foot on the loden coat's head. Instead, Decani stared at him, his eyes still unfocussed and perhaps unseeing, and said, "If they had used a grenade instead of a Molotov cocktail . . ." He didn't finish the sentence. Then, as if he was suddenly reminded of the rifleman on the hill, he put his palm over his eyes, Indian-style, and looked up.

"If that rifleman had wanted to kill me, he could have easily, as easily as with a grenade," Stone said, his insides shaking as if they were breaking away from their inner moorings. "I guess they had a warmer reception in mind." He put the Luger into his belt and began to search his pockets for a cigarette. Decani offered him one from a gilt packet of Ben-sen & Hedges and lit them both up with his gold Dunhill.

"Did you recognize the rifleman?" Decani asked.

"I only saw him for a moment. It looked like . . ." Stone almost said Kucic, but caught himself in time ". . . the same man on Kalemegdan, the one I saw working in your building."

"Stevan Jazak?"

"You said that was his name, I think."

The remaining black-belted raincoat said something to Decani in an undertone and Decani nodded. The man went back, made two trips dragging both bodies to the Tatra, but the door had been dented by the Fiat and wouldn't open. Each time he had to drag the bodies around to the far side of the car where he dumped them unceremoniously into the back seat, one on top of the other. Then he backed the big Tatra down the street and was gone.

They smoked their cigarettes down to the stubs while Decani scanned the hillside above them. "I wonder why he didn't shoot us down," he said. Stone muttered something about his getting frightened and walked back to pick up his jacket. When he did, the sleeve fell off in a small shower of blackened ash. "The ravel'd sleave of care . . . which can't be knit up," Stone thought, laughing sourly to himself. His wallet, with passport, papers and money, was untouched and he transferred it from the jacket breast pocket to his trousers. Nearby the Molotov cocktail was burning itself out, and the gutter had been melted into an oozing tar sea. They hadn't used a grenade because they wanted to burn up the manuscript with him. Thinking of the two bodies, the loden coat and the black-belted raincoat, he was reminded that three people had already died for Karst's manuscripts, one of them only a boy. He put the jacket on, his left shirt sleeve flapping where the tweed sleeve should be. "Sackcloth and ashes," he thought, "sackcloth and ashes."

146

"It doesn't seem worth it, does it, Mister Stone?" Decani asked abruptly.

"What doesn't?"

"Karst's manuscript. Did you get it, Mister Stone?" Decani asked casually.

"Do I look like I'm carrying a manuscript," Stone replied irritably, flapping his shirt sleeve. "Karst has no manuscript. Or if he does, he didn't give it to me."

Decani did not insist. After a parting glance at the over-turned Fiat and the still burning pool of gasoline, he led Stone to a big grey Mercedes-Benz parked a street away. Only when they had started, Decani poker-faced at the wheel, did Stone realize that in spite of the shots, flames and car crash, no one had ventured out into the street to see what was happening.

Decani gunned the engine and said, "Thanks for that shot."

"Lucky."

"Lucky for me. And your longshoreman's hook was lucky too."

"We were all lucky," Stone said, suppressing both a shudder and his own irony; the two dead men had not been so fortunate. To change the subject, Stone asked how they had gotten there, and Decani explained that after he had mentioned the green Fiat which followed them at Kalemegdan, they had traced it. It wasn't too difficult because there were few private cars in the city and still fewer green Fiats. They had trailed the loden coat all morning, then lost him on one of the turns going toward Karst's villa. Chrsto, the driver of the Tatra who had been killed, had figured out that the Fiat could only come that one way, the only downhill road, and that they could block him there. Chrsto was right. Right and dead, Stone thought. Quite right and quite dead.

At the hotel, Decani pulled the car up and looked Stone

over appraisingly. "You're sure Konstantin Karst gave you no manuscript?"

"Not a single one," Stone said, disliking the lie even if it only skirted the truth. "You can see for yourself. Now, if you can make some appointments for me with some of your writers who *do* have manuscripts and books, that would help."

Decani looked at him for a while longer, as if reassessing his qualities. "You'll have the rest of your appointment schedule tomorrow morning," he promised.

In his room Stone took off the one-sleeved jacket and his shirt and dropped them on the floor. When he had cleaned and reloaded the Luger, he put it next to him on an end table and sat staring out of the window at the orange sun settling. He saw the hair on his left arm and hand had been singed to a brittle stubble, but the skin was not even blistered. A close shave, he thought wryly, a very close shave.

He felt empty, drained. When he closed his eyes, the evening sun mixed pictures in his mind like a surrealistic nightmare, exploding, fragmenting, reshaping themselves from a blue flame of gasoline, the melting tar of the street and the burning sidewalk into the faces of Karst's children, the yellow-lit passageway that opened from a picture hook behind Tito's portrait, the matador Decani poised over the bull of the loden coat lying dead with a *banderilla* in his neck, the lolling head of Antun Vuk, the chambermaid's dragging plastered foot and the green-gold *rakija* glass in Karst's hand calling for *Freedom! Freedom!*

As he was about to slip off to sleep he heard a sound at the door and was instantly awake, alert and Luger in hand. In the semi-darkness he flattened himself against the wall next to the door until he heard a soft knock repeated twice and the sound of his name. "Who is it?" he asked hoarsely, keeping well to the side of the door. "Townsend," came the answer. Stone slid the bolt free, but held the Luger ready, safety off. Townsend pushed the door open, and Grout followed, flicking on the light switch as Stone flicked the Luger's safety catch back on. He bolted the door behind them and tucked the Luger back into his belt. Townsend's face and the big white square of adhesive tape over his cheekbone looked ominous. "What happened to you?" Stone asked.

"I met your friend, and we had a disagreement," Townsend said, wincing as he tried to grin. "But officially I walked into a door."

"Then it *was* you up on the hill?"

Townsend mock-bowed. "Let's sit," he said, "I'm feeling a little woozy."

Townsend and Grout sat down and Stone brought his whisky bottle and glasses, and poured them each triples. "I'm not feeling too sprightly myself," he said.

"Your health," Townsend toasted, and they drank. "Good bourbon," he commented.

"Drink up," Stone said. "I've still got three more quarts I bought on the plane."

"Your description, the totem pole, was good, Mister Stone. I recognized him immediately. Something totemic about the man, a natural savagery, an animal quality, half-snake, half-wolf. He could easily be the totem of a murderer's guild."

Stone realized that, like himself, Townsend was all wound up, and talking almost feverishly. Grout had not even said hello, and he sat there, his white sheared head bent over his bourbon, his eyes hooded.

Without transition, Townsend asked, "Did you get it?"

"Get what?"

"Don't let's play games. Karst's manuscript, of course."

Grout began to gesticulate broadly and silently, pointing to the walls and then to his ears. Townsend looked at him indifferently. With thumb and forefinger Grout held his right ear out from his head, and with his lips, but without sound, made the words: "The Big Ear!"

"There was no manuscript," Stone replied deliberately disregarding Grout's pantomime and shocked face. If Decani was tapping this, then let him hear that.

Grout stood up. "Let's not drink up all Mister Stone's whisky, Michael," he said smoothly. "Let's have another downstairs in the bar."

Townsend stood too. "This is no game, Mister Stone."

Reaching over, Stone picked his jacket from the floor and held it so Townsend could see the charred edges of the sleeveless shoulder. "I know," Stone retorted icily. If one more person told him that he ought to be careful, or that this was no game, he was going to punch his head.

"We'll wait for you in the bar," Townsend said, hostile. There was no mistaking the fact that he thought he was giving an order.

"You do that," Stone said.

The shower made him feel better. He shaved again, changed his clothes, and took his time doing it all. By God, let Townsend wait! His watch said he still had an hour and a half before he was to meet Eleanor Hvar, and the thought of that cheered him even more. He checked the Luger still another time, took two extra clips for it, and put them into his jacket breast pockets. Fortunately, he thought, I brought several suits and coats, but he knew he'd miss the burned one, an old Burberry he'd had for years.

At the hotel desk downstairs, Stone stopped to see if there

was any mail from Gordon. Instead, he found a note from Eleanor Hvar asking him to meet her at a *Balkan Restaurant* with an address that Stone quickly confirmed from the porter's map as being near the Danube. The envelope in which it had come looked irregularly sealed so that it might have been steamed open and reglued. Stone called her home number on the desk telephone but got no answer. He patted the Luger clips in his pockets for comfort, and decided he'd go to the *Balkan Restaurant* anyway, but would ask Grout first what kind of place it was.

Townsend and Grout were waiting in the bar, seated at a table close to the windows that looked out on the rear terrace and the formal gardens. The nearby tables were empty. They had already ordered a whisky for him and Townsend began to speak as soon as Stone was seated, slowly and very distinctly as if he had rehearsed every word. The interval had obviously given him time to bring himself under some control and to reconsider his method—that, and perhaps some advice from Grout. "Mister Stone," Townsend began, "I can't order you to give Karst's manuscript to me, but as an American, I think you'd want it to be in the right hands."

"Yours?" Stone asked.

"No, not mine, the American government's."

"So far as I know the government is not yet a commercial publisher."

"That manuscript is of prime political importance."

"Perhaps it is."

"And?"

"And nothing, Mister Townsend. I don't have a manuscript. Karst didn't give me one. If he had, I doubt I'd give it to you."

"But why?"

"For one thing it wouldn't be mine to give. If someone gives me a manuscript in trust to publish, I could no more give it to you than a lawyer can give his client's confidential papers to the police. I'd have to see that the manuscript was protected, published as the author instructed."

"Then Karst *did* give you instructions."

"Look, Townsend, I'm tired and I'm not very long on patience right now. Three attempts on my life have been made in the past two days and the last one came pretty close. *I have no manuscript of Karst's.*"

"I saved your life up there today," Townsend took another tack. "You know that."

"I'm grateful, very grateful."

"You don't show it."

"You saved my life because you thought I had Karst's book. Not for me, for my skin, but for the manuscript. So did Decani. Not for me, but for the manuscript. By your logic, I ought to show my appreciation by giving both of you the manuscript. How shall I do it, make copies and give you one each, or divide this manuscript I have never laid eyes on in two, the first half to you and the second half to him? Or the reverse."

"We want that manuscript," Townsend repeated stubbornly. "We want it and we propose to get it."

"I wish you luck."

"And you're going to cooperate . . ."

". . . Michael!" Grout said warningly.

"I'm taking the silk gloves off with this Mister Stone. Who does he think he is anyway? This is a matter of the gravest national interest," Townsend cried. "You literary wise guys messing in political things you don't have the first clue about. Well, its time we taught you a few things."

"If we're taking off the silk gloves, Townsend, let me tell you this. I'm tired of your stupid attempts to bribe, bully and blackmail me. And I'm tired of your presumption that you're the sole guardian and arbiter of the national interest," Stone said angrily. "You're going to teach me something, are you? Well, you go ahead and try, but you better stay out of my way, because I've had about as much of you as I'm going to take politely."

Townsend stood up, his fingers touching the white adhesive on his cheekbone. "Good night, Mister Stone," he said. "Are you coming, Max?"

Grout raised his eyes, his face non-committal. "Not just yet, Michael. I think I'll stay a while and talk to Mister Stone."

Townsend flushed. "Very well. As you wish. Good night, then." He turned on his heel and stalked out.

Grout sloshed the whisky in his glass, listening to the ice clink. "You've just made yourself a powerful enemy, Warren."

"I didn't ask for it."

"And lost yourself a powerful ally."

"Do you know a *Balkan Restaurant* down near the Danube?" Stone asked, to change the subject.

"Yes, why?"

"I have a dinner date there in a while and I wondered what kind of place it was."

"Posh hangout for tourists and Party bigwigs," Grout said. "Look, I'm not holding you up, am I?"

Stone looked at his watch. "No, I've got some time yet."

"Good. I'd like to talk for a bit and then, if you like, I can give you a lift down to the *Balkan.* My car's outside."

"Fine."

"Warren," Grout said after a pause, "I'm not going to apologize for Michael Townsend. He's got a job to do and he's doing it his way. I don't happen to work that way so I'll try it from another angle.

"Whatever a man like Karst writes is not only a literary mat-

153

ter, or even primarily a literary matter: it's a political matter. Our people are interested in what he says and so are his own people and the Soviets. The reason is that his book may influence tomorrow's policies and events . . ."

". . . don't all books, Maxim?"

"Perhaps, but usually in a longer run. I want to state the whole case as clearly as I can so you can see it. Karst is the rare Communist who has actually held top-leadership positions and, therefore, has top-leadership information—or what they call state secrets. He has broken with them and remains alive to talk about it. Only one other man had even a remotely similar position, Trotsky, and you know what happened to him and for how long 'Trotskyism' has been used as a bugaboo and still is. There is nothing like 'Karst-ism' yet. Karst did not try to *organize* opposition to the Party inside or out. He led no factions. Almost to the end, he believed he could reform the Party, *morally, from the inside.* This was his grandeur and his naiveté, his success even in failure. It may even explain why he is still alive, why he never got the pick-axe in the skull Trotsky did, or, I suppose, the bullet in the back of the head Bukharin did.

"Some months back, Karst turned in his Party card, openly, so it couldn't be hushed up. It symbolized the end of an era here, the end of the idealists in the Party. Perhaps it shouldn't have: Karst's idealism has taken many, many ugly and bloody turns in his time, and there are some, many, who would deny him idealism. Michael Townsend, for instance. But that is the way Karst thinks of himself, and the way lots of others see him.

"Now what's at stake, Warren? First, what happens to this country. Does it go East or West? That's a very important matter in the present balance of power, and what Karst writes about us and the Russians might be an important factor in tilting that balance. It will be listened to by many, especially the youth, but even by many of those who were idealists in his, the Partisan generation. Second, what he writes will influence the same kind of people all through the East-European Communist parties where he is known not only as a writer and poet, but as a political figure. It will influence people in the Russian Party, all those now struggling for what they call 'liberalization,' for change, for progress."

"I'd think any book of Karst's would simply be banned."

"It will, but what the book says, and the book itself will be circulated nonetheless. It's very complex. What's involved is not only our foreign relations with this country, Russia and all Eastern Europe, but also Yugoslavia's relations with us and with the USSR and all East Europe; and lastly Yugoslavia's own internal relations. What Karst does and says touches sensitive areas in all. And therefore we have orders to get that book."

"To be sure what it says favors us?"

Grout inclined his head.

"Whatever was in such a book would not be likely to harm us."

"We can't take that chance," Grout said.

"Can't?"

"Won't, perhaps. Frankly, Warren, though I'd deny it if quoted, I'd be perfectly willing to take any manuscript of Konstantin Karst's out in the diplomatic pouch and guarantee its textual integrity, because I think it would do us far more good than harm. Even if it criticized us, perhaps *especially* if it did, and we published it. But the decision was not mine. And to be honest, I don't think that even if we had been willing to guarantee the text, Karst would have dealt with us. He doesn't want them to be able to accuse him of being a 'capitalist lackey.' "

155

Grout raised his finger and a white-coated waiter appeared out of nowhere with two more whiskies. "They know me here," Grout explained, smiling. "Because of that," he continued, after the waiter had gone, "you're the logical choice. Three things connect you with Karst. First, the murder of Karst's nephew in your room. . . ."

". . . and that I stupidly told you about Karst's note," Stone interjected resentfully.

". . . second that you're a literary agent, someone who represents writers and gets them published. And third, that your partner is Sam Gordon. I did a little digging and found that he served here and knew Karst. In fact, he once saved Karst from some NKVD types who tried to kill him around the time of the split with the USSR."

"I still don't have any book, Maxim," Stone declared.

"Unlike Michael, I'm sure you don't. Karst is no fool. First, he wouldn't hide the manuscript in his house, even if he was working on it. Too easy to pick up. Second, he wouldn't be so stupid as to give it to you. But he might have, probably did, tell you where to find it. Decani will guess as much. Even Michael will realize that in a day or two. The others, the ones Decani tells me are Soviet agents, will know that too. They'll all be watching you like hawks, they won't let you out of their sight, and . . ."

". . . I know, Maxim, this is no game. I'd better be very careful," Stone said.

"As a matter of fact, Warren, I wasn't going to say that. You're in this game now and you're the kind that will stick it to the end. I don't think you were before you saw Karst, but something has changed in you. Before, you wanted simply to be left alone, but now you've made it your business. For better or worse. Of that I'm certain."

156

How Grout could be so sure Stone didn't comprehend. He wasn't altogether sure himself. Just why he had come so far in commitment in so short a time, or how, he couldn't say. All the things that had happened to him and to the others he had met, among whom Grout, himself, was no small factor, were part of it. That and something strange, wild and beautiful about the country and people that had touched a part of him long guarded against feeling and commitment.

Grout drove him to the *Balkan Restaurant* in a big, black American car with diplomatic license plates. During the ride Stone lay back, eyes closed, thinking that suppose he did give them one of Karst's manuscripts, the poems for example, could he get out with the others? He could pretend to give in to Eleanor Hvar—that wouldn't be difficult—or even to Maxim Grouts' persuasion—that would not be so very hard either—and then try to get out of the country with the other three manuscripts? But how? First, he'd have to elude them long enough to get the manuscripts in Dubrovnik. Then he'd have to hide the other three and copy the poems so he could give one set to both. Would they believe him? Would they let him out of their sight long enough to get all four and hide them? No, he answered himself, the real thing is getting out, and giving them one manuscript wouldn't help. Townsend wouldn't send the other three out by diplomatic pouch anyway, and Decani, being the kind of man he was, would search him thoroughly at the border no matter what, particularly if he revealed that Karst had given him anything at all. The others, whoever they were, would still try to kill him because to them the manuscript was secondary to what Karst might have told him. No, there was no point to that. He'd have to try it Karst's way.

A long, painful day. What he wanted was to be left alone with Eleanor Hvar, watch her face and listen to her talk, even if, as he was certain, she too, like Decani and Townsend, would be after Karst's manuscript. But he ought to invite Grout in to meet her and perhaps to have dinner with them, yet he did not want to share her. The smell of her hair and perfume, of the food and wine, he hoped would drive away the odor of burnt hair and flaming gasoline that was lodged in his throat. For their sakes, Stone knew he should introduce Eleanor Hvar and Maxim Grout now, for there might not be another opportunity. But would he be endangering them, and was he thinking that only in order to be left alone with her? He remembered Grout's marvelling face when he had said, "Eleanor Sutnjak tonight and Konstantin Karst tomorrow." Well, it made more sense now.

"Okay," Grout said, "you're here."

Stone opened his eyes and saw that they were parked next to a brownstone building, perhaps four stories high. A small blue and red neon sign flickered in the dingy darkness announcing the single word, *Balkan,* and the neon outlines of a curved sword half-drawn from its scabbard flashed on and off.

"Why," Stone finally asked, "don't you join us for a drink?"

"Us?"

"Yes, Eleanor Hvar and me."

"Lili Sutnjak," Grout whispered hoarsely.

"You'll come?"

"I've wanted to meet her for a long time," Grout smiled shyly, his face working.

The restaurant was down a flight of steps, a series of three beautifully wainscoted connected rooms that looked as if once, long ago, they might have been a wine cave. Lamplight played on the high polish of the wainscoting and the huge, square wooden beams in the ceiling. The whitewashed walls were softened by great hangings of dark red velvet and textured by swords and scabbards, daggers and pistols and a variety of shields, all quite old, graceful, very beautiful and warlike. In the far corner of the room, on a small raised platform, their Western dress clothes altogether out of place, five musicians in tuxedos played a haunting melody that sounded like a mixture of Arab keening and a Russian love song.

Eleanor Hvar was already seated at a table. The halo of darkness around her was almost tangible. She wore a black dress of stiff material whose modest decolletage and short sleeves showed her dark skin. Her black hair, now high on her head and held in place by a shimmering pearl barette, left her neck exposed and made her seem terribly young and vulnerable. Her darkness, intensified by a masked but discernible furor, exaggerated her every slightest movement. When she saw him, she raised her hand, a terse reluctant gesture, her long fingers cupped as if they held a wine glass, and there was—or did he imagine it?—the faintest leap of irritation that thinned her lips at the sight of someone arriving with him.

"Maxim," Stone said, when they reached her table, "this is Eleanor Hvar. Eleanor, this is Maxim Grout, First Secretary of the American Embassy."

Eleanor Hvar's face flushed, paled, and she began to stammer. In a faint voice, as if she were going to cry, she finally murmured, "Oh, Max, Max."

"Lili," Grout said, bending over her right hand and kissing it, while she patted his cheek awkwardly with her left, still murmuring, "Max, Max." Grout sat down, holding her hand, her palm on his face. "I didn't know you were here," she said haltingly.

"I came back again only last year," Grout told her, his face altered by a tenderness that stripped age, fat and drink from his features, and left the strong bones and clear eyes prominent that at twenty-five must have made him a very handsome man indeed.

"I got your messages," she said tremulously, "but I never seemed to be in the same part of the country you were. When I did manage to come to you, you'd been wounded and evacuated to Italy."

"But I wrote you from there, and from the States," Grout said. "And I had no answer."

"I never got the letters," she said simply.

"Didn't Konstanty tell you?"

"I never spoke to him," she replied.

"You never saw him?" Grout was astonished.

"Yes, once." She blushed again. "I slapped his face at a Writers' Association dinner where he was guest speaker."

"Oh my God! Because of Mirko?"

She nodded. "I was a fool, but I'm not sorry." Yet Stone sensed that she was sorry. For a moment, he wanted to tell her how Karst had helped her, been the overseer of her career, but he held his tongue.

"I thought you were dead," Grout said softly. "I made some inquiries, not too many because I thought it might not be . . . good for you, but there was no Lili Sutnjak."

"Didn't Konstanty tell *you*?"

"No." Grout's face was sad. "We didn't talk much even during the war, and almost never personally after."

"Because of Mirko?"

"Because of that . . . and politics." Now Grout was blushing and looked ashamed.

"Oh," she said. "I started to use my family name again, right after the war . . ."

". . . I saw the name Eleanor Hvar on books from time to time, but I never connected it with Lili Sutnjak, until yesterday, Warren . . ." Grout stopped, and suddenly, simultaneously, they were aware of his presence. Stone saw Eleanor Hvar's eyes shining, her teeth gleaming between half-parted lips, and Grout's rejuvenated face. Stone was glad he'd asked Grout to join them even if, because of it, he felt superfluous. Karst, he thought, Karst should be here, not me. Or . . . Mirko Sutnjak.

"Warren," Eleanor Hvar—or was it Lili Sutnjak?—said, "you couldn't have pleased me more." She squeezed his arm, but brought her other hand into Grout's.

"Not even if I gave you Karst's manuscript?" Stone joked lamely. His sense of being superfluous had made him even more awkward.

"Not even that," she replied without an instant's hesitation. And then, with something different in her emphasis, "Perhaps, not that particularly."

"Besides, he hasn't got it, Lili," Grout said gruffly.

They laughed as if that was really funny. Grout and Eleanor Hvar made a ceremony of ordering the dinner, assuring him that it would be the very best he'd tasted since arriving in the country, and it was. They began with delicious Danube sturgeon black cavair and had ice-cold, light-green wine with it that was a perfect accompaniment. They mixed the national dish of varied hot spiced meats, *cevapcici,* with a Turkish *musaka* and washed both down with a local dry red wine that was not even bottled. Only over the tart cherry

161

strudel and hot black coffee, and then over the still hotter *slivovicz* afterward, did they begin to talk of the war, and once more Stone felt his exclusion. Even his war had not been so bitter; at least, in the main, it had not included women, children and old people.

Eleanor Hvar told how she met Mirko in Belgrade after the Germans came. Her parents were dead and she was living with a Communist youth league girl friend who had her own flat, and who took her to meet Mirko in a café. Mirko needed couriers, and though she was not a Communist, Eleanor Hvar had joined the other girl in carrying messages, then arms, around Belgrade in their brief cases and among their school books until several months later her friend was caught by the Gestapo. They threw her down a flight of stairs then kicked out her front teeth, and she told them about Mirko and the group. The Gestapo surrounded both houses—the girl's and Mirko's—but forewarned, Eleanor Hvar and Mirko Sutjnak had not returned to their flats. They met in the usual way, at a café—a new one was decided each time they parted —and Mirko had taken her with him to another hiding place. So she had become a part of his group, then his mistress, then the mother of his child, and finally his wife.

When Mirko was ordered to leave Belgrade for Dalmatia, he had taken her to Dubrovnik with him, to his parents. After his assignment there was finished, he went to meet Karst in the Montenegrin mountains and she stayed behind. She was sixth months pregnant and couldn't go along; besides, she could see that he didn't want her to come to him even after the child was born. He wanted her to stay in Dubrovnik so that she and the child would be safe. Because of that, she remained there with his parents and some weeks later some- one had reported them all as the family of the filthy Bolshevik traitor, Mirko Sutnjak. Italian Army units picked them up one night, but turned them over to the Gestapo. They wanted Mirko, they said, and if his parents would tell them where he was, or even better, if she would write that she was sick and needed him to come back to Dubrovnik, they would capture him and let the rest of them go free. They even promised no harm would come to Mirko: he would only go to prison or to a labor camp. None of them told, however, because none of them knew, so the Gestapo shot Mirko's father and broke four of his mother's ribs and her arm in the interrogation. His mother got pleurisy, then pneumonia—one of the ribs had pierced the lining of the lungs—and in a matter of weeks, she was dead.

For Eleanor Hvar the Gestapo reserved their special "persuasion," because they realized that the old people really might not know, but what man would leave his pregnant wife without telling her where to reach him in an emergency? They beat her with leather-tipped bicycle spokes until she collapsed and hermorrhaged on the floor. By the time she arrived at the *Wehrmacht* hospital in Sarajevo, she was in labor: the child, a boy, was born premature . . . and dead.

She told the story straightforwardly, without embellishment or histrionics, but tears flowed down her cheeks. Grout drank more and more *slivovicz* from the bottle they had ordered, and Stone joined him, hoping the alcohol would stifle the heaving of his stomach and his mind. Grout poured Eleanor Hvar a glassful too, and she sipped it slowly.

When she recovered, the Germans drove her down to Gestapo headquarters a second time, but on the way the car was ambushed by Partisans. They knew about her, and they were waiting. They killed the driver and her guards and, freed, she went with them. "It was a miracle," she said hoarsely. "When they stopped the car, it was one of our people in a *Wehrmacht* uniform, but before I knew it they were all around the car, yelling, *'Death to Fascism! Liberty to the People!'* and the Gestapo in the car were dead even before they could get their weapons out. I was sure it was Mirko."

"That was Petar Decani's group?" Grout asked, it was a statement not a question.

"Yes."

"And he told you about Mirko?"

She nodded. "I didn't believe him. I was so weak I couldn't tell if it was all a nightmare or real. Then I got a fever and for weeks they thought I'd die. We had no doctor—we were illegal—and almost no medicine, but Petar nursed me and brought me through."

Listening to her, Stone found it hard to picture the Decani who had killed the loden coat with that *banderilla* that same afternoon, and who the other night had stomped that chambermaid's foot and swatted her face with his gloves, as the same man who had solicitously watched over Eleanor Hvar. Yet, they were. Again, the mystery of what worlds one man contained. The story also partly explained why Decani had chosen Eleanor Hvar to be his "literary guide."

Grout told her how, when Decani was transferred to Partisan headquarters, he had brought the first news of her. "Konstanty sent him to me, you know," Grout remarked. "We weren't talking much then, but he knew I was anxious for any information about you. It was Petar, though, who told me that they had sent you to Slovenia." As if apologizing for something, Grout went on to explain that Karst had also saved his life. They went out on a mission to blow up a railroad trestle, Karst as point, Grout as rear guard.

But though they succeeded, they ran into a German patrol on their way back. Grout, bringing up the rear, had been cut off and wounded by grenade fragments, his companion killed. Though they were outnumbered, and the sensible thing to do was cut and run, Karst had come back for him, and while the Partisans laid down covering fire, had crawled to Grout and dragged him out. Somehow, they had fought their way through and Karst had carried Grout to their own lines on his back.

So *that* was how it happened, Stone thought. Karst had not mentioned his part in it, that it was he who had saved Grout's life, but now Stone understood even better why they had delegated Karst to try to recruit Grout as an agent for them. Little wonder, too, that Karst, out of pride as well as friendship, had been reluctant. Grout also grew in stature from the incident: it took a lot more guts to resist a boyhood friend *and* a man who had saved your life; but he had. He had to give more credence to Grout's use of that word *duty*.

Grout wanted to know why she hadn't written to him, or somehow tried to reach him, and she explained, a little abashed, that she hadn't wanted to trouble him and that she was afraid it might get him, get both of them, into difficulties. "Yes," Grout commented sardonically, "it wouldn't do for us to be friendly, or keep in touch too much, would it? Especially since we don't have any official business together."

Well, you do now, Stone thought, but he did not say it.

In recounting the years since the war, Eleanor Hvar gave them a pall of greyness, almost of despair. She told how she had worked and studied, been sent to England for two years on fellowships, and now was and had for a long time been a translator, an "expert"—she used the term ironically—on American and British literature. Again, Stone was tempted to tell her the role Karst had played in her life, and again he refrained.

"*Only* worked and studied?" Grout looked askance.

"Mostly worked and studied," she replied shyly, not looking at him.

"That's not enough. Was that enough? Is it enough?" Grout persisted heatedly. "Why didn't you marry? have children? Mirko would surely have wanted you to."

"I don't know," she answered, with a quick, almost furtive glance at Stone, as if to see if he was listening and how he was taking what was said. "It was not that simple."

"It never is," Stone said, attempting to reassure her, "but Maxim is right. And you are still a young woman." Even as he spoke, he wondered what those years had really been like for her, and vividly, the figures of Mirko Sutnjak's sculpture came back, with their guts torn out and blue-grey air filling the empty spaces where their vitals had pulsed.

It was late and they were all glassy-eyed with fatigue. Stone suggested they leave and Grout offered to drive them both home. Sitting close together in the car's front seat, they were all silent until they reached her house. Stone took the Luger out and Grout came with them, his hand held casually in his pocket. So, Grout was apparently armed too. They escorted her inside and systematically searched the house while Eleanor Hvar laughingly protested that they would frighten her lovers away.

In parting she kissed them both on the cheek and said good night, yet Stone sensed she had expected something more of him, though what he couldn't tell.

On the way to the hotel, Grout finally grumbled aloud, "That complicates matters still further."

"What does?"

"Lili Sutjnak."

"Why?"

"Why, Warren? Because she was Mirko's wife and, therefore, must hate Karst. Because she and Petar Decani are old friends—she is deeply in his debt—and she must be working for or with him. Because you are obviously very fond of her."

"I thought *you* liked her too," Stone replied, hearing the double-edge of the comment.

"I do, of course, but what's that got to do with it?"

Grout was perfectly right, he realized. In those terms, liking Eleanor Hvar had nothing to do with it. Here the difference between him and them—Townsend, Karst, Decani, Grout, perhaps even Eleanor Hvar—was that in his terms, it did make a difference. He lacked their detachment; that made them professionals and him an amateur. And for this situation what he needed was that cold, analytic calculation which could see people as pieces on a chessboard, their behavior as gambits toward a goal, yet never forget that they were still people. Perhaps Grout and Karst were more skillful and smarter than Townsend and Decani, in that they never mistook the chessboard for life, even if they played it like one, nor ever forgot that the pieces, even the pawns, were complicated, unpredictable, individual human beings.

"Some pieces still don't fit the pattern," Grout said doggedly, as much thinking aloud as talking to him. "You say this totem-pole character tried to kill Lili too at Kalemegdan?"

"Yes," Stone replied, trying to keep the picture from recurring.

"Then they know she's working for Decani and Decani knows too. Why isn't he protecting her? Or is he and we don't know how? Also who turned them in to the Gestapo—the Sutnjaks, I mean? An accident? I don't believe in those kinds of accidents, especially when the timing was so good. Was that person an anti-Communist, anti-Mirko, anti-Lili, or what?"

"Don't you ever stop?" Stone asked.

"Stop? No, I guess not. If I did, I'd either be dead, or my usefulness would be over—or both." He laughed. "It's my job and by now my second nature. If someone does something spontaneous and unforced, it knocks things out of kilter. I try to figure out the balance, the purpose, the portents, the calculations, the 'What's in it for me?' "

"And?"

"And in most cases, it works. With politicals and in political matters, it almost never fails. It even works most often in personal matters, too. But in some cases, as with you, for instance, or with Mirko Sutnjak, it didn't. It didn't work with my wife, Julia, either. I told you she said I was a commissar *manqué*. None of you wanted anything in the orthodox patterns, and that's always harder to figure. With Karst it was always straightforward. He was that kind of man, and I could tell what he wanted . . ."

". . . even when he wanted you to spy for them?"

". . . especially then," Grout said, betraying no surprise. "So, he told you?"

"Yes, that and much more," Stone said casually.

"What?"

"About you, and him, and Mirko Sutnjak."

"Oh," Grout grunted, then lapsed into silence. It was clear he did not want to hear about what Karst had said, even if Stone had been willing to repeat it, which he wasn't.

At the hotel, Grout stopped the car but kept the motor running. "Thanks for dinner," he said, "I owe you a debt for introducing me to Mirko's wife. You see, I promised him I'd look after her and the child if anything happened to him, and I felt guilty, not even knowing if she was alive."

"And Karst didn't tell you?"

Grout shook his head. "Maybe he thought I knew. I don't know."

"Why didn't you ask Decani, then?" Stone finally said.

"But I did," Grout replied. "He told me she was dead." Then, with a subdued roar, the car and Grout were gone.

DECANI was as good as his word. Stone's schedule of appointments was delivered at breakfast in the hotel the next morning Its arrangements covered an entire fortnight, more than two dozen writers, five cities—none of them Dubrovnik—state and regional publishing houses, local and national writers' associations, and critics, reviewers and university professors. Attached was a brief note from Decani saying that Eleanor Hvar would accompany him as interpreter, since many of the writers he would meet spoke no English, or any other foreign language, and as a guide, since that way getting around the country would be simplified and swifter. He, Decani, wished him a pleasant and fruitful journey.

When Stone got back from breakfast, Eleanor Hvar was on the telephone to say that she, too, had received a copy of his schedule from Petar Decani and would be at his disposal for the next fortnight. She would pick him up in half an hour to take him for his first appointment, which was at the university. She arrived exactly on time in a small blue Fiat, all business, dressed in a prim blue-grey tweed suit of obviously British cut, and with English walking shoes which accentuated her slender, tapering ankles.

And she remained all business all through that fortnight.

Though she called him Warren when they were alone, it carried no trace of personal feeling, and when she interpreted for him, or when they were with others, it was always Mister Stone. She took him to villas and to slums, to old mansions that now housed Writers' Unions, and to jerry-built modern student hostels, with plaster peeling from the walls, that stank of unwashed linen, mold and cheap disinfectant. She drove him in her blue Fiat or a rented Mercedes; or arranged for them to take planes, trains, busses to other cities. She was efficient, competent and remote.

From the first, without ever speaking a word, Eleanor Hvar made it clear how she wanted things done, and their days quickly settled into a routine that she had defined and he accepted. They had breakfast, separately, in their rooms, then met in the hotel lobby to go to their first appointment. Usually, they had lunch with writers or editors or critics, when she interpreted, and then more appointments in the afternoons. Dinner was at the hotel or some restaurant of her choosing, during which they talked over the results of the day, or argued formally about choice of foods and wines, and almost always planned the next day's schedule. After dinner they went to the hotel's public rooms with some of the books and manuscripts they'd acquired during the day. When she knew the book, she would give him a brief summary of its contents, setting and characters, then translate at sight and aloud into English a chapter or two to give him the "feel" of the book while he sat smoking and listening. She was a remarkable linguist, knew the local languages, and also English so well that her translations were almost fluent, and it seemed as if she was simply reading aloud to him from an English book. But if she had opinions of the books' worth, she kept them to herself. At about ten, she would get up, say goodnight, sometimes formally shaking hands, and go up to her room by herself. She had made it plain that she didn't want him to accompany her to her room, though because he was afraid that the totem pole and others were still following them, he protested at first until she showed him the small business-like Walther automatic she carried in her purse. Stone usually lingered, having a brandy nightcap, and where there were translations into French or German, reading until his eyes grew heavy, and he too went up to bed.

During the days he sometimes caught a glimpse of her severe almost grim face when she wasn't looking, and wondered what it was she was trying so hard to prove or demonstrate. She scrupulously avoided touching him, and when by accident, going through a door or being helped into her chair at dinner, they did touch, she shrank from him as if he had the plague. At first he was exasperated, but when he saw her unswerving resolution he was somehow moved by it, and his feeling for her grew rather than diminished. If there was the renewed urgency of physical desire for her which occasionally made him brusque or sullen, he never permitted it to become an issue between them. Twice, when his flesh and loneliness were kindled by her being in an adjoining room, and through the poorly-built walls he heard her own restless turning in bed, he drank himself to sleep. Otherwise he managed the formal courtesy and distant camaraderie she seemed determined to impose.

Slowly, piece by piece, a picture of the state of the country's letters emerged from their talks and travels. The older writers were mired in the past, either the heroic past of the Partisan struggle against the Nazis in World War II, or the remoter past of the resistance to the Ottoman, Hapsburg and Byzantine oppressions. The younger writers seemed not yet to have found their voices, or their roots. Virtually no one wrote books about the present; the few they found were so politically orthodox as to be inhuman and absurd, and even in these there was the ever-present gingerliness that spelled fear. Only among the poets did Stone discover a few genuine and feeling voices, small, fluting personal music of the laments and triumphs in private worlds cut off from the larger orchestra of the public world outside. And the poetry would be difficult to translate and impossible to sell. Altogether, it was a parochial literature, rooted in region and regional language, and not even transcending local boundaries enough to become a truly national literature, much less to be of international interest and meaning. Though Stone had collected a suitcase full of books and manuscripts, he knew that less than a half a dozen would be of real interest in the West, and perhaps half of those in the United States.

When the trip was over and they were flying back to Belgrade, Stone became aware of how really tired he was. They had worked hard, it was true, but the strain of the relationship with Eleanor Hvar, the tension of watching to see if they were followed, and the anxiety of waiting for another attempt on their lives had told even more. He sensed they were being followed all the time, but he could never actually pick out by whom. This time, those who did the surveillance were thoroughly professional: they were unobtrusive, and the faces must have been changed so often that he could make no connections between them. In reality, it was the totem pole he looked and waited for; Stone knew that when the real showdown came, it would be with him. Logically that made little sense, for Decani had the men and the apparatus, and probably even Townsend had more forces at his disposal than did Kucic, or Jazak, or whatever he called himself, though he no doubt had what he needed too. Nevertheless, there was something demented about Kucic's concentration on the task, a fanaticism which he shared with Townsend and Decani, though not in the same degree. And the degree counted: here increase in quantity did indeed become change in quality. Kucic was somehow larger than life, like Iago or Claggart—how Valerie would roar at such bookish comparisons!—with all the inevitability of an avalanche and the surprise of a flash flood, a fount of perverted Bogomil passion and puritanism that flowed almost motiveless from the wellsprings of his character as natural or unnatural evil. Or was he embroidering the fact that Decani and Townsend only wanted the manuscript, and Kucic wanted to kill him?

Next to him Eleanor Hvar had fallen asleep. Her face, gaunt from the past fortnight, with dark hollows under the eyes, was weary, her regular breathing occasionally punctuated by a sigh. The "Fasten Your Seat Belt—No Smoking" sign flashed red and Stone gently touched her arm to wake her. Her body turned toward him, and she groaned, then was instantly awake and rigid. She said something in another language, then sharply, "What is it?" her hand already into her pocketbook reaching for the Walther automatic, though her eyes were still wide and unfocussed. "We're landing," he replied softly. "You have to fasten your safety belt." Without looking at him again, she did and they sat silent until the plane was on the ground.

While he waited for their baggage, Eleanor Hvar disappeared and Stone, ruefully, wondered if she had gone to check in with Decani. She was a long time in returning, and Stone carried the bags to a couch in one of the lounges and settled back for a smoke. When she did appear, she was white and staggering. Quickly, he sat her next to him, lit another cigarette and gave it to her. She drew on it deeply, two or three quick nervous breaths, then stubbed out the cigarette. Finally, she stretched her arms straight out in front of her, like a sleepwalker, her fingers spread to their fullest, staring at them as if all great Neptune's ocean would never wash them clean; then her arms went limp, her helpless hands dropped unyielding into her lap. "They have put Konstanty Karst into a lunatic asylum," she said, her voice quavering. "The paper says he had a nervous collapse." Even as he heard her, Stone registered the personal *Konstanty*. Her newspaper had dropped to the floor and now, noticing it, she leaned forward to pick it up and would, but for Stone's sustaining hand, have pitched forward on her face. Stone kept his arm around her shoulders, tightening his grip to still her trembling. She found the item, a small but distinct two inches of type on page three, and translated the brief announcement for him that Konstantin Karst, former Vice-President of the Republic, as a consequence of his anxiety concerning his separation from his comrades, the Party, and the nation, in the tasks of building socialism, and as a result of overwork on a book he was writing, had three nights earlier suffered a nervous collapse. He had for a long time before been showing signs of severe mental disturbance. Because his illness was very serious, he required prolonged treatment and had, therefore, been confined to the psycho-neurological institute of the Visegrad Clinic in the city's suburbs. The gravity of his condition prevented his receiving visitors of any kind.

"Karst is no more insane than I am," Stone raged.

"Perhaps you're both insane," she said, trying to smile. "In this part of the world, mental hospitals are for dissident intellectuals."

"Dissidence is not dementia," Stone growled, "nor intellect necessarily insanity."

"Perhaps in our society, dissidence *is* insanity. Frankly, intellect seems to be insanity in most societies, and so does dissidence. Here, if you put Karst in a lunatic asylum, you are treating him kindly, taking care of him. And most people are only too eager to think of intellectuals as a little"—she searched for the word—"crazy. This way, instead of putting him in prison, where he might become a political martyr, even a political threat, and have all sorts of fuss raised about him at home and abroad, he is a poor, sick man who must be treated, sheltered and shielded from the public. He ceases being a political problem, and becomes a medical one."

In the cab she suddenly seized his coat lapels as if pleading for something, then turned her face into his chest and began to sob. He held her until she was cried out and her sobbing over, and by then they were at her house. Silently she insisted he come with her and he dismissed the cab and carried the luggage inside. She slumped into the chair behind her desk while Stone, with a passing glance at Mirko Sutnjak's sculpture of outrage, searched the house. In her bedroom he heard the phone ring, and then her muted "Warren" called him. When he returned to the living room, she was standing with her back to him looking out into the garden. "Petar wants to talk to you," she said, not turning around.

The phone receiver on the desk squawked and Stone put it to his ear and said, "Stone speaking."

"Ah, good evening, Mister Stone," Decani said silkily. "Lili tells me that you already saw that item in the newspapers about poor Karst."

"I did but I didn't understand it," Stone said. "Karst is no more insane than you are. Why have you got him locked up there?"

"You'd like to see him released?"

"Of course. Who wants to see a sane man locked up in a madhouse?"

"Aren't we all sane men shut up in this madhouse world?" Decani inquired philosophically.

Stone was scarcely in the mood for that kind of tone. "Is there something you wanted, Doctor Decani? I'm exhausted. It's been a long trip and I'd like to get back to the hotel to bed."

"Back to the hotel?" Decani said. There was something so snide, yet jealous, in the phrasing that Stone was brought up short. "Let me be frank with you," Decani continued, "if you want Karst released, you can help. Turn over that manuscript to us, and we'll let him out. If not, he's due for a long stay."

"But I have no manuscript," Stone protested.

"Perhaps not. Then Karst must have told you where it was, and you can tell us, *hein?*"

"If Karst told you that," Stone replied, "why didn't he tell *you* where the manuscript was?"

"You know what a bull-headed Montenegrin he is. He refused absolutely to discuss it," Decani said, his tone considerably less silken now.

"I don't know where any manuscript is," Stone said dully. "But I have a trunkful, of new ones I brought back from the trip you so kindly arranged. You're welcome to any of those if you'll release him."

"I'm afraid none of those will do, Mister Stone. However, sleep on my offer—and sleep well." His laughter had a snarl in it, and then the line went dead.

"Why don't you give it to him?" Eleanor Hvar spoke from the window.

"Because I don't have it," Stone said, "and it wouldn't be mine to give even if I did."

Again they had outwitted him and even outfoxed Karst. By putting Karst into an insane asylum, they not only minimized the possibilities of his becoming a domestic political threat, but they clouded the possible influence of his book.

They were prepared to declare him a lunatic if the books did get out of the country and were published. And, Stone saw, they had a powerful lever to persuade him to give them the manuscript, or at least tell them where it was, to bail Karst out of the booby hatch. But he couldn't tell them where it was, because he didn't know, and he wouldn't tell them about the rendezvous Karst had arranged because that inevitably involved another man, or more than one, who would all go to prison or to lunatic asylums. Karst had been diabolically clever in the arrangements.

What did Karst want anyway? From what Decani had told him over the phone, Stone was almost certain Karst was still sticking to the plan. But he couldn't be certain. Perhaps he didn't want to endanger the other man, or men, either, and wanted to get out of the asylum with the manuscripts, and wanted him, Stone, to give them up for him without endangering the others. It was far-fetched, all right, but possible. And how about Alexandra Karst and those children? Should he go to see her? Pehaps Karst had left new instructions with her. He couldn't telephone her, because the lines were surely tapped, and they'd be watching her house doubly carefully now for any visitor. Then he remembered the hidden passage.

Eleanor Hvar was before him, drawing his face down to hers. She kissed him, her lips dry and harsh, her teeth clashing against his, and the room's horizons shifted and fell, remolded in a geometry of planes at whose center was a trapezoidal black mass. As their mouths separated, from its depths of certainty, the words came, scalding his mouth, "Decani is your lover, isn't he?"

She nodded mutely.

"And others too—since Mirko?" The first name was a true sacrilege for him, perhaps for her too.

"Many others," she responded savagely. "It's been long and lonely, and I like to sleep."

The pitiless, relentless needs: loneliness and liking to sleep. She meant having to sleep. To talk and sleep, and because of these necessities to make love that was not love at all but a confusion of limbs and purposes, a sexual limbo, the unquiet grave.

"Touch me," she pleaded, standing so close to him that her breasts grazed his chest.

"No, not now," he said indistinctly, "not yet." And as he spoke the words, and moved away, he knew he loved her.

A cab took him back to the same hotel. He had a different room now, a floor lower, but still overlooking the hotel's formal garden. Stone didn't bother to unpack, except to lay out his pajamas on the bed and put his toilet articles in the bathroom. He checked the Luger again, took a couple of extra clips, then went downstairs. It was only early evening and he had time. He collected his mail and had two drinks in the cocktail lounge while he went through it. A long business letter from Gordon again apparently untampered with told how sorry he was that the interview with Karst had not produced a manuscript. Stone had written him a brief note reporting that Karst had no book, sure that Decani's boys would be censoring his mail and hoping that would mislead them. Tonight's phone conversation with Decani indicated that, if they read his letter, they were not mislead.

A heavy square embossed envelope with a monogrammed VW and a Sutton Place address was a note from Valerie. It was a surprise, for Stone had not heard from her once in the years since their divorce. The letter's contents were even more surprising. It read:

My dear Warren:

I ran into your "partner" Sam Gordon the other night—and our cordial detestation of each other showed so clearly that even my husband caught it. He—Sam Gordon, that is—told me you were in Yugoslavia. It sounded like you were leading a much more interesting life than you used to!

A "discreet" inquiry on the telephone the other evening about your "past" and "sexual peculiarities" sounded like that anyway. I couldn't tell if someone was investigating for business reasons, or you were getting married again, and someone was checking up in advance! I hope I told them just enough to pique their interest and not enough to get you into trouble—or at least not any trouble you didn't want to get into!

I'm going to have a child in a few weeks and wanted you to know. Just why—I'm not quite sure. I am sure now—for the first time—that those rip-roaring quarrels we had were not only your fault—as I used to imagine they were! Perhaps I should have had your child—or seen a headshrinker sooner—and things would have been better. I don't know.

But I want to wish you well—and for you to wish me well too.

Yours,
Valerie

The note was so characteristic, full of dashes and exclamation points, yet chastened now. He was glad and sorry for her at once. They had even quarrelled about that, because he couldn't understand how all those expensive and "good" schools had failed to teach her to punctuate properly. Priggish of him, he knew, but undisciplined of her too. I shall have to write her a note, he thought, but was surprised how remote Valerie and her concerns seemed. Already his mind was churning with how he would get to see Alexandra Karst, and what he would say to her; and trying to banish from his mind Eleanor Hvar's painful confession about lovers and sleep.

A brief note from Townsend was among the letters too. Dated the same day it requested that he call the Embassy as soon as he returned. Stone decided he would call the next day.

When he had finished reading the mail, Stone went to the porter's desk and loudly, but not too loudly, announced that he wanted to leave a call for eight the next morning. He was very tired, he said, and didn't want to be disturbed, so would they please not put through any more phone calls. He took the elevator up to his floor, the third now, and went to his room. He changed to a dark shabby corduroy suit, a black raincoat, a pair of gumsoled shoes, and an old Basque beret which he pulled down well over his forehead, so part of his face was hidden and part of it in shadow. All I need now, he reflected uneasily, is burnt cork and it'll feel like 1944.

He took the stairs down to the second floor, carefully avoiding chambermaids and guests alike. No one saw him. He rang for both elevators. One came with people and Stone let it go by stepping around the corner of the elevator bank so the occupants couldn't see him. The second arrived empty, and he took it down to the cellar. As he got out, he pressed the button sending it up to the fourth floor, then walked into the cellar's semi-darkness and tripped over a trash barrel which echoed noisily as a bass drum. Someone from the hotel kitchen adjacent shouted, "Drago?" and Stone made a thick answering noise in his throat, found an exit, and was out in the street next to the hotel. As he walked slowly away, he looked over his shoulder. No one was following him.

He found the trolley he knew passed close to Karst's house and waited for it to begin pulling out of the terminal before he jumped onto the rear platform. No one got on after him. The trolley was jammed and he was unobtrusive in the crowd.

The conductor took his *dinars* without a second glance or a word. When it arrived at the stop halfway up the hill, Stone waited until everyone had stepped down and the trolley begun to move on again before he jumped off. Again, no one followed and those who had gotten off before him had already dispersed.

At the top of the hill he could see the lights of Karst's house. Slowly he walked through the winding streets, doubling back on himself several times. A few dogs barked or whined, some people hurrying home passed by, but no one paid him any attention. That way he went by the chambermaid's house twice, and the third time, with no one else on the street, he strolled casually into the hallway, and quickly turned the picture hook. Before the wall had receded three paces, he had slid into the passageway, pressed the switch and closed the wall behind him: the whole operation had taken less than a minute.

He raced up the passageway, past the room with the paillasses, noticing in passing that the two he and Karst had left in the middle of the room had been picked up and stacked with the others. When he got to the wall, he put his ear to it, but heard nothing. How he wished Karst had remembered to put some periscope arrangement there. He took the Luger out, turned the lights in the passage off and pressed the wall switch. The wall rolled back. He stepped out, pressing the switch to close at the same time, and watched the fourth wall of Karst's study come silently shut behind him. The dark outlines of Mirko Sutnjak's sculptures on the desk seemed a reproof and his eyes slid away from them.

Voices, one of them a child's, could be heard, probably from the kitchen. Stone walked warily to where he could see Alexandra Karst sitting at the kitchen table with her son standing before her. Mirko Karst's face was a mass of scratches and bruises, one eye black and blue, and swollen shut. His mother was bathing his face with a steaming cloth she kept soaking in a pot next to her on the table. Neither one saw or heard him. He had hoped both children would be asleep, but there was no time to lose. "Madame Karst," he called hoarsely in French.

"Who is it?" she cried, and stood in front of the boy, a kitchen knife in her hand. Then, as he stepped into the light, she recognized him, and laid the knife back on the table. Stone put his Luger away. But Mirko Karst's face did not change expression. Putting a finger to her lips, she went and turned on a small radio. Instantly, it poured forth rock n' roll. She led him out onto the back steps of the house, having first cautioned the boy to remain and given him the soaking cloth to hold over his puffed eye.

"I just returned from Llubljana tonight and found out that they had taken your husband."

"I told you they would, Mister Stone. I told Konstanty too. It was inevitable. There was nothing else they could do." She moved and talked like someone hypnotized.

"What happened to the boy?" Stone asked.

"Some of his school friends called his father a lunatic. Mirko fought them. They were five against one. They threw him down and one kicked his face."

Stone felt as if he would explode—into anger, into tears, into fragments.

"And the little girl?"

"She is more fortunate. She does not begin school for a few months yet."

"And your husband?" he asked, feeling foolish, as if calling a roll.

"Decani came for him four or five nights after you were

here. They, the ones at the top, wanted his word that he would publish nothing abroad without their approval. Konstanty refused."

"So they took him?"

"No. Decani pleaded with him, for the sake of all they had endured and fought for during the war. Konstanty said that he could not give such a promise precisely because of all that they had endured and fought for in the war, and because of all those who had died."

"The next night Decani came again and they took him. Konstanty was sarcastic, and asked if they would confine him in the prison where the King had sentenced him under the old regime. Decani said no, they would not put him into prison, but in a mental hospital, and give out that he had had a nervous collapse. Konstanty turned white, but he did not protest. He asked if the children and I could visit. Decani said only I could, no one else. But it would not be good for the children to come to such a place, or to see people in such a condition anyway, and Konstanty agreed."

Stone took a deep breath. "I spoke to Decani on the telephone a little while ago. That's why I'm here. He will let your husband go free if I tell him where the book is."

"No," she said softly.

"I am willing to do it," Stone persisted.

"No," she repeated. "My people tell a story of one of our great heroes, Karageorge. When he was a young man he fought in a rebellion against the Turks and the rebellion failed. There was only one chance, to escape to Austria, and he and his stepfather fled. But before they came to the borders, the old man lost his courage. He decided to turn back and ask the Turks for mercy. Karageorge knew the old man would get no mercy from the Turks, only torture and cruelty, and so he took his gun and shot his stepfather dead."

How could one answer such a story? Stone despaired. It pressed down with all the weight of history and myth and national character, tyrannical and magnificent. "But Karst would be alive," Stone countered feebly.

"No." She shook her head. "That way Konstantin Karst would only be walking dead."

"And what do you think a mental hospital will do to him?" Stone kept on.

"No, I said." She seemed hypnotized no longer. "Did you think, Mister Stone, that Konstanty didn't know what he was doing? What the risks were? It was a *conscious political act!* Do you hear? *A conscious political act!*" She had spoken the last sentences so forcefully that the boy came out onto the steps, perhaps thinking he had been called, or imagining that his mother needed help. She put her arm around her son's shoulder, murmuring something that seemed to satisfy him, and the boy looked up at her, his face a beautiful, breathing wound, and Stone felt tears start to his eyes.

"We do not cry here," Alexandra Karst grated, "Do you understand, Mister Stone, we do not cry."

Stone nodded, not trusting his voice to answer.

Stone made his way back to the hotel without incident. No one saw him leave the wall, and though the trolley going back to the center of town was not so crowded, he did not seem to be conspicuous. When he had left the trolley terminal, he took his raincoat off, tucked the beret into its pocket, and carried the coat over his arm. If anyone who had seen him saw him now, he would be harder to identify.

Decani was in the hotel lobby waiting for him. "Mister Stone," he cried, "thank heaven you're here. We've been looking everywhere for you."

"What for?" Stone asked.

"We were worried about you. Lili . . . Eleanor Hvar phoned and they wouldn't put her call through to your room. When she insisted, they did and you didn't answer. She became alarmed, thought something had happened to you and called me. Of course, I came right over. Your room looked peculiar too, your pajamas laid out and your luggage unpacked and you not there. And your having told the night porter you didn't want to be disturbed . . ."

". . . I didn't, but I couldn't sleep, so I went for a walk."

"You just walked out?"

"Right through the door," Stone said. Decani's eyes flicked to the trick side panels of his glasses and behind him Stone saw a rotund, small, bald-headed man seated on a couch reading an Italian newspaper. He was so inconspicuous, even effaced, that Stone had trouble remembering what he looked like the moment he took his eyes off him, but he had no doubt that this was the man who had been assigned to watch him for that evening.

"You're all right then?" Decani asked.

"I suppose so."

"What's the trouble, Mister Stone, uneasy conscience won't let you sleep?"

"Maybe, but I would have thought that was more your department."

"In my department, conscience is a luxury I cannot afford," Decani said.

"You should have some such luxuries then," Stone replied moodily.

"You haven't changed your mind, have you?" Decani asked. "About Karst, I mean."

"In a way, yes." Decani was startled. "I've decided to go home," Stone said, making his voice as surly as he could. "It'll take me a day or two to rest and get a plane reservation, but then I'm leaving. My presence here has only led to danger for myself and for others . . ."

". . . for Karst?"

"Not only for him. For Eleanor Hvar, even for you."

Decani mock-bowed. "You're very considerate."

"I dislike violence."

"Don't we all?"

"No, Doctor Decani, I don't think so." After Decani declined his offer, Stone lit one of his own cigarettes. "I've talked to your writers and critics, your editors and your professors, and I've got a valise full of books and manuscripts to take back—"

"—but not Karst's?" Decani said.

"No. Not Karst's."

"Well, I hope we meet again, Mister Stone." He put out his hand. Stone shook it.

"I'm sure we will, Doctor Decani. Somehow, I'm sure we will."

By the time he showered and got into bed, Stone was already half-asleep, feeling he could sleep a whole night and day through without a break, as he had felt in those sleepless days and nights in Belgium and Holland when Slater had driven them so mercilessly. "There'll be plenty of time to sleep later. We hold this road with plenty of perimeter on both sides and take more so those Limey tankers get up to Arnhem, or a lot of jump boots are going to be hanging from crosses." Slater, Slater! The name rang in his head. My dead good friend. Trained to be a microbiologist and wanting only to kill bacteria, fight only disease, dead in the Dutch mud. Slater. Whose life crack-shot Stone, and his expert's medal, could have saved and didn't. Slater's bony, hawk-nosed face blurred into Karst's

Lincolnesque one and then ran into Mirko Karst's bruised little-boy features. If only I had killed quickly, without thinking and all those complicated scruples. Kill! the wind shrieked in his ear like a bull-horn. Kill! Now hear this. His grandfather's grave voice strode slow-paced across his mind like boots on cobblestones in a great Biblical rhythm: "For we wrestle not against flesh and blood, but against principalities, against powers, against the rulers of the darkness of the world." "Did you hear that, Warren?" he thought he heard his mother say, and his grandfather calling. It was the telephone ringing.

"Warren?" Eleanor Hvar asked hesitatingly.

"Yes."

"Did I wake you?"

"No," he mumbled, "not at all."

The phone was silent except for the hum of the wires. Then, "I want you to come to Dubrovnik with me, Warren. Will you?"

She *was* asking him! He tried to be alert. "Didn't Decani tell you I was going home in a day or two?" he asked slowly, carefully.

"Oh, no," she exclaimed, "not yet. No, Petar didn't say anything about that. He just told me you were tired. Say you'll come, Warren, for me, for a vacation."

"Look, Lili, I couldn't take another ten days like the last ..."

" ... it won't be like that," she interrupted. "I promise you it will be different."

You had to give them credit, Stone thought fuzzily. He'd only just told Decani he was going and they had a plan to keep him here working—and a good one. He guessed they really didn't want him to leave, or to put it more accurately, they really wanted that manuscript. Even as he took the ironic tone with himself, he knew how hurt he was. There it was, all laid out like a welcome mat, a tryst in Dubrovnik with the beautiful Eleanor Hvar, the marvelous Lili Sutnjak. She sounded so sincere and straightforward, but he was too tired to believe her. He willed himself to believe her, tensing himself as if to leap a hurdle or scale a height, but he faltered and stumbled.

He had his own appointment in Dubrovnik, with those manuscripts, for Karst, for himself. Something wily inside him warned him to feign reluctance. This was his chance, and Decani and Eleanor had handed it to him on a platter. "I don't know," he said, "I've brought enough trouble and danger . . ."

". . . and happiness," she replied.

He was stunned.

"But this will be a vacation . . . and in Dubrovnik. Oh, Warren, Dubrovnik is so beautiful and I'd love to show it to you." There was a jubilance in her invitation that Stone admired as consummate art.

"Let me sleep on it," he said.

"All right," she said, after a very long pause. She sounded disappointed, rebuffed, very tired. "Sleep well, Warren."

"Good night, Eleanor," he said. He hung up the phone and turned his face into the pillow. He would have wept except that he remembered Alexandra Karst's, "We do not cry here," and refused himself the luxury. But it was a long time before he fell asleep.

THEY LEFT for Dubrovnik on a gloomy morning two days later, so early Stone had to be up well before dawn to be on time for the flight. At the terminal, where they were to take the bus to the airport, he waited for Eleanor Hvar, feeling out of sorts, and still very tired, though he had done little more than sleep for the two days, and the weather and early hour made him feel worse. The terminal, a small store with counter and baggage scale, irritated him further because of its blatant class-consciousness. All kinds of people were there, obviously differentiated by property, and the poorly dressed with their tied-up bundles and battered, roped luggage were shunted aside while the more prosperous looking were given attention and priority. The only people doing heavy work were dispirited-looking elderly women mopping the floors and cheerful, wiry Albanians, dark and mustached, who loaded the luggage, their invariable fezzes and plaited-thong leather mocassins giving them a touch of country.

He was cheered when Eleanor Hvar arrived in a black suit with a small leopard-skin collar, the suit tailored so severely, no doubt by design, that it made her body seem lush beneath. Her hair, once again done in the way she had worn it when first he met her, was held back by a matching headband of leopard and black velvet. They greeted each other formally, shyly shaking hands.

At the airport all flights had been cancelled until further notice, but they were assured that sometime during the day planes would fly. Eleanor Hvar apologized, saying that their planes had no radar equipment and, therefore, didn't fly in bad weather, but Stone was suitably and irritably monosyllabic in reply. The weather may hold like this for days, he thought, I just can't sit here in the airport. I've got to get to Dubrovnik. But he knew the sense of urgency was even more that he wanted to be away from Belgrade with her. They sat in the lounge and in the café, not saying much, avoiding each other's eyes, until Stone suddenly saw them like newlyweds on a honeymoon and burst into laughter. She looked concerned so he told her why he had laughed. No sooner were the words out, when the deeper melancholy of her face made him regret it.

His honeymoon with Valerie had been at a beach house friends had lent them in Westhampton. Though the war was over for several years he had not been able to stop fighting it. His nightmares were still so vivid, he couldn't sleep without pills or large doses of whisky. He no longer believed law had any reality; in the major issues of life, force ruled and the rule of law was reserved only for relatively trivial matters. Instead of "going into the law," as his grandfather had phrased and planned it, Stone drifted into publishing as a reader, then an editor. In books he found some meaning, some beauty, some refuge. Massinger's line, which Slater had taught him and so often repeated, was written over every portal, on every face. "Death hath a thousand doors to let out life. I shall find one." But unlike him, Slater had accepted that as part of the natural order of life, one of the rules, bacteria eating bacteria right up the "Great Chain of Being" to man killing man. "Even when members of a species cooperate," Slater said, telling him how his best biology professor had reconciled Darwin and Kropotkin, "it's to kill or avoid being killed." Slater had loved the Elizabethan playwrights because they were full of the lust of shedding blood; he had even, in his own curious fashion, loved the war. How many quotations from those bloodthirsty Elizabethans he had heard first from Slater's mouth! Stone remembered many of them, too many perhaps, but surely Massinger's most frequently of all. And he had looked, knocked on many doors.

One of them opened on a stupid cocktail party for a fifth-rate author whose very pomposity was pear-shaped and whose vanity matched. The writer was holding forth on how baseball was America's only true art, a folk wisdom, its notion of order and competition together—"umpired justice" was his barbarous phrase—and the guests stood around him in hushed awe. Stone and Valerie, unintroduced, looked at each other at that line and went into a gale of laughter. They were studiously ignored, but for the few barbed "Philistines" flung at them by the finer spirits there, and a short while later he and Valerie had left the party together.

One evening, some months later, they had gone to his place for an after-dinner brandy and to listen to a new Mozart quartet he had bought. A heavy snow had begun to fall which made getting from his apartment in the Village to hers on Park Avenue in the '70's difficult and she had stayed the night. They went to bed together for the first time without ceremony or comment, and her coldly competent sexuality repelled, then overwhelmed him: she had experience and imagination and both were sources of delight in bed, but there was, even then, something lacking. Yet, for the first time since the war, he slept afterwards, deeply and without nightmares. They saw each other more often after that, and with regular sleep and love-making, his inner wounds began to scar over and heal. Once, as he was dozing off in bed, Valerie, propped on one elbow, the line of her arm, armpit and breast graceful as ballet, looked down into his face and said, "You know, Warren, I think you just find me easier to take than a sleeping pill." They laughed uproariously at that, they always did laugh a lot together, even when things weren't funny, but it was true nonetheless.

Their honeymoon had been what the travel advertisements always promise but so rarely deliver: sun, sand, surf and sex. They swam, they played tennis, they sun-bathed, and they made love. Lying on the beach, the sun filtering through his half-closed eyelids, Valerie's smooth flesh hot against his, Stone thought he had at last found some peace. But before the honeymoon was over, the serpent had appeared. He hadn't known it then for the serpent, but when he picked up a book to read, Valerie invariably took it away from him, teased or excited him into sex, or diverted him into a walk on the beach or a swim or a set of tennis, and he let the reading go for a time. It was a long while before he realized the full extent of her hatred for books, that cold venomous fury which mocked them and him for reading them, and anyone for talking about them. Books were stupid words strung together by scribblers' fantasies and greed for money and notoriety. They were thin and pallid excuses for living. He had not realized from the first that, at that author's cocktail party, they were laughing at the same pompous idiot but not for the same reason.

He had already begun to think of starting his own small publishing house, but he didn't have enough money. When he talked to Valerie about it—she had considerable money of her own—she refused to give him a dime for anything to do with books. And she began her first determined efforts to get him to change his work. But he, too, was stubborn: the written word remained one of the few things he still cared about and when Sam Gordon came along with the idea of a literary agency, it seemed like a good second-best to the publishing house—and it required nothing of Valerie, not even her acquiescence.

The plane did eventually take off and Stone told it all to Eleanor Hvar as if talking about someone else, while they flew toward Dubrovnik above the grey-flannel clouds or beneath them, over spurs of the Dinaric Alps whose stony summits were bald and whose sides were covered with green moss and red furze. He told her because he knew he loved her, and because he wanted her to know he understood when she had said the other night, "It has been long and lonely, and I like to sleep."

"But why?" Eleanor Hvar whispered. She had sat listening tensely to it all, unmoving, her face averted.

"I don't know," Stone replied. "Valerie has, or had, an explanation. Pat and fashionable, but probably not altogether untrue. Her father was a writer, a very successful commercial writer, always talking of his books as 'Great Art,' and using them to mask his indulgences. He indulged himself on everyone around him, particularly on his wife and daughters, but it was all for 'Art,' for the 'imperishable Word.' And perhaps it was—for him. Her mother finally had her fill of it and divorced him when Valerie was about thirteen or fourteen, a bad age for a girl, and there was a newspaper scandal along with it that made things worse.

"When it came down to it, Valerie stopped trusting words,

because of her father, or the kind of people she knew, or just because life was like that for her. Words were too unreliable and imprecise a means of communication; her body, she thought, was better and she used it like a virtuoso. In a way, of course, it was; but there were only a very limited number of things that could be said that way. . . ." He let his voice trail off. How could he explain that to her?

"I know," she said. "It was like that between Mirko and me, from the beginning."

But before she could continue, the plane took an abrupt plunge and Stone felt the old lurching free-fall feeling of his stomach. "I'll tell you about that another time," Eleanor Hvar gasped, looking as if she was about to retch. In a few moments, after a steep, stomach-turning bank, they were below the cloud layer in a driving grey rain, flying between two mountains into a small single-runway airfield. They had arrived.

Stone's first glimpse of Dubrovnik was from a high hill in Ploce, just outside of the city. From the airport they had had a hair-raising ten-mile bus drive over a winding road that hugged the precipitous mountain edge and looked two- or three-thousand feet down to great black rocks and choppy green rain-driven sea. The plane's steep landing had made Eleanor Hvar's ears ache, and the occasional glances Stone stole at the rocks as they rode along in the bus filled him with vertigo, so they both sat rigid and silent in their seats. Stone's fear increased because the bus-driver who, though he drove with flair and an apparently sure knowledge of the hairpin turns, took his eyes from the road to talk to friends behind him, occasionally also took his hands from the wheel to emphasize a point he was making, and made Stone envision the bus tumbling off the edge onto the rocks below. The bus driver was blithely unaware of it all and soon began to sing with a bleached-blonde young woman passenger he obviously knew who looked like a prostitute, but had the angelic sweet soprano of a choir girl. The songs were sentimental ballads whose tunes Stone recognized, but the unfamiliar Serbo-Croat lyrics gave them a charm he knew they lacked and made him recall Valerie's comment that she loved music because it had no words, and especially Italian opera and French *chansons* because she couldn't understand a single one of the damn stupid words being sung.

Then, unexpectedly, they came around a turn and Dubrovnik was laid out below. Directly above it, groping clouds had broken open to permit a huge cone of pure yellow light to funnel down on the city. Its rainbow edges fell just outside of Dubrovnik's sun-beiged battlements and towers, and the great wall that protected its little square of earth from the mainland. The variegated greens of cypress, pine and palm swayed in the yellow light, as did the red-shingled roofs, a few strikingly white towers, and a melon-shaped church cupola. In the sheltered harbor, guarded by a breakwater and a fortress, a flotilla of small boats rode the peacock blue waters. Everything in Dubrovnik seemed in sunny technicolor, everything outside black as old films.

"This is where you get off," Eleanor Hvar said.

The bus had parked at the side of the road and across from it was his hotel. A threadbare curtain of rain still came down where they stood, but a thousand yards ahead sunshine began. Stone asked if she didn't want him to go with her, but she shook her head and confidently patted her handbag to remind him that she still carried the little black Walther automatic. He'd only have to come all the way back with his luggage, she told him, and getting transport was one of the few difficulties in Dubrovnik because no wheeled vehicles were allowed within the walls. Besides, she usually had an earache after a flight and if she could lie down for a short nap it would disappear; if she didn't, it would get worse. She pressed a slim card into his hand on which was engraved, "Eleanor Hvar, 7 ulica Od Margarite, Dubrovnik, Dalmatia." "You can see it from here," she said, pointing vaguely toward the outer wall of the city. "Just inside the wall facing the sea. You won't have any trouble finding it. It's on the top floor." She held his hand tightly, then released it with a whispered, "Give me an hour, but don't be too long."

While Stone registered, the desk clerk peered over his shoulder and gave him that second quick look and the, "Oh, are *you* Mister Stone?" that told him they were prepared for him. Well they should be, Stone tried to reassure himself, I have a reservation. The Luger under his jacket was cold comfort.

In his room, Stone threw himself on the bed to nap but he couldn't avoid thinking about the danger, or of making love to Eleanor Hvar when he went to her apartment. He knew he loved her, and thought she might even love him. Or was it, with him as with the others, simply her loneliness and need to sleep? Perhaps it was only that which had driven him to Valerie. In any case that left him an American now committed to getting Konstantin Karst's manuscripts to publication, and her a Yugoslav working for Decani and committed to stopping him. Even if she weren't, how could he get her out of the country, and would she go with him? Should she be asked to drop her life ties here to try to create new ones in America? And would they let her into the States and how would she be treated? Investigated, interrogated and perhaps even kept for a long time in custody until she was so embittered that whatever chance she had for a new life and whatever feeling was between them would be soured or killed? If she remained and he got out alive, they'd never let him back into the country either, for once Karst's books appeared, they'd know who was responsible and the name Warren Stone would go on their permanent *persona non grata* lists.

Restlessly, he got up, went for a cigarette and stood at the window looking out at Dubrovnik's stone walls, ramparts and citadels. His room faced the sea and the city and, between the promontory the hotel sat on and Dubrovnik, a blue bay nosed its way into the land and made a short strip of beach. On the bay small boats bobbed and a stubby ketch, its stern shaded by a white canvas canopy, made for the open sea. The rain had lifted and the sun poured down on the palm trees around the hotel making their wet fronds glisten as if sprinkled with gold sequins. They looked, he thought, like an evening-dress fan his grandfather once showed him that had belonged to his grandmother as a young girl. Below, the sound of the sea pounding the rocks soothed him. It was like a tropical paradise, far from Karst and Decani and Townsend and Kucic.

When he had watched for a long time and grown calm, he looked at his watch, and decided he still could shave and wash before he left for Eleanor Hvar's. In the bathroom, propped on the glass shelf over the washbasin that held two cellophane-wrapped waterglasses was a neat square white envelope. Impatiently Stone tore it open. Inside, in a curious rigid up-and-down cuneiform kind of handwriting was written in French:

Mister Stone:
You had your appointment with Karst just the same. Now I have mine with you. I promised to kill you the next time we met, but I did not succeed. We shall meet soon and here I will not fail. No man slaps my face.

It was unsigned but apparently Kucic had followed him all the way to Dubrovnik, to that very room, easily and without wasted time. He was in Dubrovnik, waiting.

OUTSIDE, a violet dusk had settled on the city, darkening Dubrovnik's tawny escarpments with winy shadows and staining the sea purple. Homer's wine-dark sea was not so far away, Stone thought, as he walked across the drawbridge into the city. He found his way into a square with a tall ugly campanile, then on to a broad cobblestoned street of matched buildings which was the *Placa*. It was crowded with people taking their evening stroll, out staring or being stared at, the Balkan version of the Spanish *paseo*, or had it historically moved from the eastern end of the Mediterranean to the western end? If Kucic was already there, he might be following and the *Placa* looked like a good place to lose him, so Stone paused to examine shopwindows, stopped at a café for a *slivovicz*, and watched the crowds go by until the street lamps came weakly to yellow life.

When it seemed certain no one had followed, he let himself be carried by the eddying crowd down the *Placa* until he was able to slip into a darkened side street so narrow that he could, with outstretched arms, almost touch both sides of the roadway. Overhead, straightfaced buildings bulked so close together that only a sliver of darkening sky was visible. Every window was filled with plants or clothes hung out to dry, and the smell of mildew mixed with the aroma of flowers hung heavy in the narrow street. A flock of pigeons coasted gracefully into the gutter before him and, as he approached, fluttered heavily and clumsily into the air like old men staggering away from a table after having eaten too heavily.

A shattering crash sounded only steps behind him and Stone spun into a doorway, Luger out, prepared to make a stand; but no one was behind him. A stone block, probably a heavy piece of cornice, had fallen from one of the buildings exactly where he had stood only seconds before. Shutters were opening, casting oblongs of light on to the street, then windows opened and heads peered out. There was a little talk, high, questioning, then the windows were closed, the shutters put to, and the darkling silence flowed back. Gun in hand, Stone went back to the piece of cornice and tried to lift it. It was so heavy he could barely move it, at least two hundred and fifty pounds. He looked up but night had clotted between the buildings and he could see no one. Had the stone's fall been accidental? He heard noises far above on one of the roofs and moved back into the shadow of the houses, his gun trained upward, his eyes squinting into the darkness, but he saw and heard nothing more.

Did the coping stone explain Kucic's note, why Kucic had given him warning of his presence in Dubrovnik? In the instant before that stone cornice was smashing his life out, was he to have understood that Kucic always paid his debts? Compliments of the totem pole. For the first time he began to think of Kucic as a madman whose mania had been channelled into a cause that could profitably exploit his love of murder. Stone had the feeling that against such madness he had no chance, that he was going to be killed, to die even before he could once make love to Eleanor Hvar. "Death hath a thousand doors to let out life. . . ." Or was he going mad? Was he beginning to imagine things? Why should Kucic try to kill him before he got the manuscripts, or learned where they were? Or was it someone else?

Stone slipped down and sat on the house step, his back against the door, listening to his own hoarse breathing. When his head began to swim, he let it sink between his knees and sat there resting until a pair of bare feet interposed themselves between his eyes and the cobbles. He looked up and saw a little dirty-faced boy of eight or nine standing wide-eyed before him, staring at the Luger dangling from his hand. Stone hurriedly put the gun away and stood up. The boy squeezed past him into the doorway and then glancing back fearfully, fled into the house.

Stone took even more precautions about continuing to Eleanor Hvar's but he had little confidence that he could shake Kucic and his confederates if they'd been able to follow him thus far. He supposed they used the roofs, for there was almost no place to hide in the narrow streets. But how had they got from street to street? And was it Kucic? or Decani and his people? Or was he beginning to imagine things?

Eleanor Hvar's house was like the others, three stories high and squeezed between the adjacent buildings, but on her street the salt smell of the sea was stronger and the night breeze blew fresh. He went up to the top floor where, thumbtacked to the door, was a duplicate of the card she had given him. There was no answer to his knock so he knocked again. The door gave and, alarmed, the Luger in hand once more, Stone stepped softly into the apartment, cautiously closing the door behind him. To the right it was dark, but on the left a faint light glimmered and Stone moved warily through a narrow corridor into a large front room flecked with the faint light of a sliver of waning moon. A book-lined studio with a large working desk, the room was much like the one Eleanor Hvar had in her Belgrade house, and on the desk was another Mirko Sutnjak sculpture. A nude in white stone, it seemed in the uncertain moonlight to shudder and breathe like flesh. It was of a woman, head hung modestly and face turned shyly away. Her arms, like powerful wings outstretched, shielded and bared her simultaneously, marking the tormented curve of her back and waist, and the full insistent breasts, nipples large and erect. A clump of thick stone hair hung in a massive wave over her forehead and her angry fingers burrowing beneath it seemed to be tearing her scalp. Legs akimbo, she sat on both buttocks, one haunch folded under her. Her other leg, propped up and bent at a powerful knee, stamped its foot solidly down on the desk. Folds of stony material were draped loosely over her thighs so that they fell between her legs and hid her sex. Above, her belly had been scooped out, leaving only a heartless hollow, not the totally empty space Sutnjak had cut through his bronzes, but something more anguished and pathetic, a tortured emptiness backed by straining muscles, aching rib cage and the body wall behind. That it was Eleanor Hvar, or her younger self, Lili Sutnjak, Stone knew immediately and with absolute certainty.

In the shadows a crouching black panther and leopard moved together that Stone, with abrupt relief, recognized as Eleanor Hvar's black suit and leopard collar draped over a chair and stirring in the night breeze. Beyond, on the large studio bed, turned on her side and swathed in a blue tartan robe, Eleanor Hvar slept. Her hair flowed around the pallor of her face like a dark fall, cascading past her shoulders and over her arms and back and breast. He had never seen her with her hair down and for the first time the phrase, as he thought it, struck him not as a cliché but as meaningful. He wanted to reach out and stroke the flowing plaits, submerge his fingers in them, but instead he went back through the rooms to make sure no one had come in before him, then bolted the door and breathed easier.

When he returned to the front room, she stirred uneasily. He put the Luger on a table, sank into a chair and watched her slow, rhythmic breathing. In mid-breath, she opened her eyes full and looked into his, with instant recognition, as if in sleep she had known he was there. Though more beautiful with her hair free, she was also more unfamiliar. She put out her hand and he went to her, but as their fingers touched her fear burned through them like a palpable disease. The trembling of her body in his arms at once snuffed out the passion their abstinence had aroused and his fear had heightened. An anguished tenderness sharper than pain shocked him, a desire only to protect her from suffering, from her past and her future, to shield her nakedness even as he was uncovering it. And he knew what he felt was another kind of love. But when she touched him, a separate lust nourished a voracity for her flesh which when it was done was still unfed, and her unstopped cry in turn was not a release but a torment.

On the moon-drenched bed they lay together, her face against his heart, his tangled in her hair. Beyond the windows the surf boomed and inside Eleanor Hvar began haltingly to talk. Mala Palic, the girl who introduced her to Mirko Sutnjak in Belgrade had been his mistress, and when the Gestapo sent Mala to Banjica concentration camp, Sutnjak was not eager to take Eleanor with him to his new hideout. She was not a Party member, she was too young and too beautiful, and therefore too conspicuous. But he pitied her and felt responsible because he had used her as a Party courier. With the Germans looking for her and her not having a place to hide, he had little choice, so against his better judgment he took her along with him. They hid out in the secret stockroom of a commercial laundry where the former owner, now dead, stored pilfered linens which he later resold. Only two Party members who worked in the laundry knew of the room's existence, one of them, the night watchman, had hidden them there.

Eleanor Hvar was only sixteen then, Mirko Sutnjak twice her age. At first, they were very proper: they put a blanket on a rope between them so they could undress in privacy and sleep separately on the floor on their bedbug-ridden mattresses. The laundry was unheated at night and soon the cold drove them to sleep together on one mattress and cover themselves with the other and their partition blanket to keep warm. When Eleanor told Sutnjak she was a virgin, he would not make love to her, but one night, drunk, he did. "It was wonderful, but not like that more than two or three times," she said. "Either Mirko treated me like a prostitute when he was drinking, or like his daughter when he was sober. Neither made me happy. Though I was only a girl, I wanted to be treated like a woman, and however inexperienced I was, I knew the difference.

"And then I became pregnant and Mirko stopped making love to me altogether."

At first she thought he was angry with her, that he didn't want to be burdened either with her or with a child, then perhaps that he thought she had tried to trap him into marriage by becoming pregnant, but neither was the case. Though she did not want to marry, he insisted on a formal wedding ceremony. "He had some idea about the child and I being his future, his purity, the only part of him uncontaminated by life and the Party and his fear," she explained. "He was a Croat and a Catholic, and though he had broken with the Church long before, I think he thought of me as some kind of holy

204

virgin he had desecrated and had to make whole by marriage and giving the child his name."

Stone sat up in bed, and reached for his jacket pocket. He lit cigarettes for them and then lay back as they smoked and she continued to talk. "I wanted Mirko to make love to me, I asked him. But he couldn't seem to bear the thought. He was drinking very heavily and when he did try, he wasn't able. But other nights, in Belgrade and here in Dubrovnik too, he came home smelling of other women, prostitutes, with whom he had been."

She grew quiet, watching the smoke rings she blew rise toward the ceiling, expanding and thinning until they disappeared. "I was so young, too young to understand, much too young to help. And it was wartime and there was little I could do. He was so terribly afraid. The fear was worst of all for him. Mirko knew he was going to die, and he wanted to live. Every time he went out on a mission or even went to a *kaverna,* he was blue with fear. Each time he came back alive and unwounded, he would make his sculptures, wood, bronze, stone, with their insides carved out. No matter where we were, he found time and strength and tools and materials, and he told me that only because of us, the baby and me and his sculpture, was he able to go out again each time he had to. What he didn't admit was that he needed the drinking to help him too. And he couldn't paint any more; like love-making, he tried and he couldn't."

"Karst said that in the mountains he was braver than all the others," Stone asserted.

"Oh, yes, Mirko was brave. He was even reckless, but it was because he was so afraid, he had to be. He couldn't show anyone how afraid he was. Except me, and I couldn't stand to see him cry."

And so, Stone thought, he drank and tore the guts out of

himself and his sculptures. Of course Mirko Sutnjak was afraid. Who wasn't, except the madmen and the imbeciles? But to be brave meant to go on doing what had to be done anyway, even though you were afraid. Yet he knew that some did not seem to be afraid at all, Karst and Kucic, for example, and he remembered Slater humorously insisting that he wasn't afraid because he was a Calvinist and knew that he was one of the elect and predestined to survive; and if he wasn't, then it had all been taken care of in advance anyway, so there wasn't anything he could do. Though that had been one of Slater's typically sly and self-mocking jokes, a part of him had believed just that: the one with your number on it got you and couldn't be avoided.

"In the beginning, when he believed in the cause," Eleanor Hvar said hesitantly, "it must have been easier for Mirko, but by the time I met him he was no longer a Communist except in name. Sometimes I really think he hated them. He was always on the wrong side, being accused of bourgeois tendencies and deviations. But he loved the country and was convinced that only the Communists were fighting and could save it from the Nazis. They would win and after the war all Eastern Europe would be theirs."

"You mean he wanted to be on the winning side?" Stone asked, thinking how right Sutnjak had been.

"No nothing so crude, Warren. Mirko was many things, but not a crude man. He wanted to remain in the Party because he thought there were good people there, idealist cadres, who could and would eventually make the Party and its beliefs different. I think he got that idea from Max and Max's father, Doctor Nikola. And the best of those cadres he believed was Konstantin Karst. Karst would eventually lead them. Mirko was a Croat and Karst a Montenegrin, but he trusted him all the more."

206

They finished their cigarettes before she spoke again. "Mirko used to say that I was his sister and Konstanty and Max his brothers. He loved only us three. He was an only child like myself, and perhaps we were more like sister and brother because of that. He would sometimes point at my belly and say that when *it* was born, he would have a fourth person to love ... and his fill."

Silently, Stone lay there elated by her head in the crook of his arm, her hair spread on his shoulders, her flesh against his. The faint night wind blew across them, the surf sounded in the distance, and he felt peaceful and absurdly happy. In a little while her breathing and the rise and fall of her breasts told him she was asleep and that gratified him deeply. The happiness spread out inside him like sunshine warming his blood. Yet there seemed little enough reason. He still had to find Karst's manuscripts and get them out of the country. He had only a short while before almost been killed, and Kucic was in Dubrovnik pursuing him. Probably Decani and Townsend were not far behind. Although at last he had made love to Eleanor Hvar, the ghost of Mirko Sutnjak stalked between them and the white stone sculpture of what had once been Lili Sutnjak was there on the desk as a reminder. At best, their love-making, however moved for her he had been, had not been very satisfactory, for either of them. And, most important, what was to become of them? Even when his arm grew cramped and his uncovered flesh was chilled by the night air, the happiness continued to suffuse him with its warm glow. And then, as he turned to cover her with her tartan robe, his flesh stirred and he touched her again, slowly waking her from sleep, himself moved by a new, fiercer urgency that she matched.

While they were eating dinner in the small old-fashioned kitchen, the telephone rang. It was Decani, and the moment Stone heard the metallic voice crackling from the earphone, his elation vanished. He and Eleanor Hvar were no longer an oasis; they were a beachhead, or an outpost surrounded. Her answers to Decani were brief, almost curt, and when she hung up, her jaw was set. Stone asked nothing and waited until she had put the Turkish coffee and *slivovicz* on the table and lighted her cigarette. "That was Petar Decani," she said without prompting. "He's here in the city. He called to warn me that his people had tracked Mister Jazak to Dubrovnik."

"Yes, I know. Jazak left me his calling card," Stone said calmly, handing her Kucic's letter. She read it quickly and returned it without comment.

She stared into her coffee cup as if trying to read the thick black grounds, and said, "He asked about you, Warren, and I told him you were here."

"In Dubrovnik? I'm sure he already knew that."

"No, *here*." She tapped the table with her fingernail.

"You mean he wanted to visit you tonight?"

She nodded.

"It's like that, is it?"

"No. It *was* like that."

"What did you say?"

"I said he couldn't. You were here."

"And?"

"He said to send you away."

"Well," Stone said, getting up. "I was just going anyway."

"Oh, sit down," she said, with an impatient wave of her hand, "and don't be such a fool." She poured more coffee and *slivovicz,* then continued, "I don't expect you to understand what happened between Petar and me, Warren. I don't understand it all myself. But this I do know: Petar saved me from the Gestapo and he nursed me back to life. And over the years, when I had few friends, he was my friend, my good friend."

"So you were grateful?" Stone said, the jealousy bile in his throat.

"Warren, forgive me their language, but don't be such a damn bourgeois. Of course, I was grateful. I'm grateful now, still. Petar Dacani *risked his life for me,* not once but many times. And it wasn't the way it is in your Hollywood moving pictures. During the war, when we had no food, he gave me his rations. He gave me his blanket in the snows. He . . ."

". . . all right," Stone interrupted, putting up his hands. "I believe you."

"I was grateful and there was no other way to show my gratitude. Mirko was dead, and then who knew which of us would die tomorrow. It didn't mean much to me. And Petar really cared for me and wanted to marry me. When I refused, he never married, he always hoped I would change my mind."

Stone tried to match her likeness of this tender and loving Decani and the man he knew, the staring-eyed, blue-lipped man standing ecstatically over the *banderilla* he had just driven into the loden coat's neck, or coldly stomping the chambermaid's foot and slapping her face with his pigskin gloves. But the pictures of tenderness and violence were like separate images in a camera view finder that he couldn't get to fuse.

"And Petar suffered too," she said softly, her eyes narrowing, ". . . when there were the others."

An uncontrollable shudder shook him and she leaned across the table, over the coffee cups and *slivovicz* glasses, and kissed him. Sitting back, she said, "Our worlds are so very different, Warren. We have been too poor, too oppressed, too often tortured and put to the sword to have your Anglo-Saxon notions of chivalry."

"Decani had them?"

"He loved me," she said simply.

"But not enough to tell you that Karst ordered your rescue from the Gestapo, that Karst too kept his eye on you, helping you into the university, with your scholarships to England, with your first translation jobs. And when Maxim was looking for you after the war, Decani told him you were dead."

She was shocked. "Is that all true?"

"Every word of it," Stone retorted, but he was already ashamed of his outburst. He had used Karst's real concern and generosity as an instrument of his own pain and jealousy, as a riposte against Decani and he was disgusted with himself.

"Why didn't Petar tell me?" she asked, hurt and perplexed.

"Probably because he wanted you to feel indebted only to him, perhaps . . ." Stone hesitated, "because he loved you."

"Konstanty really did those things?" she asked in a hushed voice. "For me?"

Stone nodded.

"Why didn't he say something, or come to see me?"

"He's not that kind of man, I suppose. He's obstinate and proud, a bull-headed Montenegrin, I think Decani called him. He didn't want you to feel indebted to him. Because of the talk about Mirko's death, he wanted you to come to him by yourself, freely, because Mirko was his best friend and you were Mirko's wife. And then, too, I guess he felt that he was Vice-President and you ought to show him the respect of his office by coming to him."

"There were so many who wanted to go to university after the war," she mused aloud, "so many who wanted to study abroad. I wondered why I was chosen. I wasn't a Party member, I was of bourgeois origin, I was . . . I thought I was lucky. And it was Konstanty Karst. But why should he do anything for me after he killed Mirko?"

"Konstantin Karst didn't kill your husband."

"Then who did?"

"Karst doesn't know. Maybe this totem-pole man, Jazak, or Kucic."

"But why?"

"He doesn't know that either. He thinks Kucic is a Russian agent, and he knows Kucic hated Mirko. And Kucic was with them in the mountains. He could have done it."

"You believe that? You believe him?" Her face turned blindly toward him, eyes brimming with tears.

"I believe him. Karst is no liar. Did you know that he named his son after Mirko? A murderer would have to be pretty cold-blooded to name his own son after someone he'd shot down, especially when that someone was his best friend."

"His son, his son. Mirko. Mirko Karst," she repeated, as if tasting blood on her tongue where she had bitten it. Desolately, she began to cry.

Stone took her in his arms, knowing he couldn't comfort her, that her losses were inconsolable, but he offered the best he had. "I love you, Lili," he said. "Don't cry. I love you."

She began to laugh and cry together, parodying his words, her voice so hoarse with tears it sounded like a raven croaking. "I love you, Lili. Don't cry. What's easier to cry about than I love you? What's more painful or promises more unhappiness? I love you too, Warren. Don't cry. I love you too. I love you too. I love you enough so that after our trip I told Petar I wouldn't work for him to get that manuscript of Karst's, though it's the first favor he ever asked of me in return for all he's done for me. And I did work for him to get Karst's book more for myself, for Mirko, because I hated Karst, rather than for Petar. Now you tell me it wasn't Konstanty who killed Mirko at all, so I dirtied myself working for the UDBA for nothing, worse than nothing, for something against Karst that was un-just, and against you, whom I already loved then. I didn't even help Petar by getting that damn manuscript.

"And when I told Petar I asked you here to Dubrovnik for a vacation, that you'd soon be going away and I wanted to be with you, I thought he would be sick and I couldn't stand that either. I love you too, Warren. Don't cry.

"I love you enough so I'd probably even stop sleeping with other men if I had you." She pressed herself against him and he held her head tightly against his chest.

"Come home with me," he said thickly.

"Come home to America with me," she mocked him again. "The home of the brave and the free. Do you think we just go and tell them we're in love and they'll let me out? Or that your new Senator McCarthys and Congressmen Walters, whatever their names are now, will let me in? I love you, Warren. Don't cry. But don't expect passports and visas and the rest to love us or cry for us. They won't."

It was on the tip of his tongue to tell her about Karst's boat, but he bit it back. He had talked too much before; he wouldn't again. And he was by no means certain that Karst's man, or manuscripts, or the boat would show. "We'll manage something, somehow," he promised lamely.

"I love you, Warren," she replied bitterly. "Don't cry."

Although Stone wanted to stay the night, to comfort her, to make love to her again, he left because she wanted to be alone, and because he wanted to give Decani no evidence so blatant as staying the night. Before pushing him out of the door, she kissed him so grievingly, so desperately, it was more as if she were kissing him good-by than kissing him good night.

THE STREETS were empty, the shadows hung on the buildings like animal carcasses and in the distance Stone heard the hooting of owls. As he hurried, his heels were stark on the cobblestones and he heard an echo plainly behind him, but could discern no one following. At the *Placa,* he had to make a choice and he hesitated only a moment, then walked down the center of the broad street, giving himself plenty of room to keep from being surprised from either side, yet knowing he made a perfect target. But the footsteps were gone. Relieved, he made his way out of the city walls, slowing his pace and walking easily. Just beyond the walls, as he went past the huddle of squalid shacks where bundled bodies lay sleeping on the ground and a few old mules were tethered, someone clapped a hand over his mouth, pinioned his arms and lifted him bodily off the ground. So swiftly and expertly was it done that he couldn't move. As he was drawn into the shadows away from the road a drum-roll bass voice cautioned in quiet German, "Don't be afraid." A resonance in Stone's skull vibrated and Antun Vuk's, "Be not afraid. . . . I bring you the thing from Master Karst," sounded. Furiously, Stone tried to tear himself loose until the bass voice said calmly, "Mirko Sutnjak is my brother."

It was Karst's man! The man held him for a few moments more until he stopped struggling, then let him free. "Mirko Sutnjak is my brother," he repeated for good measure. In the shadows before him Stone saw a man easily over seven feet tall and wide as a door. "You are Mirko Sutnjak's brother?" Stone reiterated, impressed by the sheer size of the man. The great head nodded and a hand proferred a small card, one of the two he had given Karst. So this was what the second card had been for. Karst had anticipated that he might be skeptical of only a single sentence to identify his courier.

"I'm Warren Stone," he said, putting out his hand.

"I know," the cavernous voice whispered. "I am Branko Georgevic." A hand twice the size of his own enveloped Stone's fingers in a crushing handshake and Stone winced. "I am glad you have arrived. I read in the newspaper that they took Konstanty to a mental hospital."

"Yes. They want him to give them . . . what you are to lead me to. They even offered to free him if I would give them the . . . material," Stone said.

"That is not freedom," the huge man snorted derisively. "That is like that mule there, tied to a stake. Konstanty would not accept that."

"No," Stone corroborated, "he wouldn't."

"Do they think you have the material?"

Stone shook his head. "They think I will lead them to it."

Georgevic tugged a black, thick, drooping mustache, then replaced the grey cap he was wearing, tugging it further over his forehead. "You have not been easy to approach," he said. "Many are following you. Among them our own people. And there is not much time."

"I didn't think you would come to me so quickly," Stone said.

"I did not intend to. But tonight the Doctor Petar Decani and his UDBA scum arrived from Belgrade. And he is talking to the soldiers, the militia, the sailors in the port. They sit up there," he pointed to the mountain looming behind the city, where lights like yellow eyes seemed to look down on everything below, "on Mount Srd and watch everything. Ever since Napoleon and his General Marmont, there is someone up there on the hill watching us. Aggh! But they too will not expect us to move so quickly, therefore it is better that we should."

"When?"

"Tomorrow night."

"So soon?" Stone was dismayed.

"There is no time for delay. The more swiftly we move, the greater safety and chance for success. And tomorrow there will be no moon, as you can see." He looked up to the heavens and the waning slice of moon. "Are there other tasks you must do in Dubrovnik first?"

"There is someone with whom I came here," Stone said, hearing the irrelevancy.

"A woman?"

"Yes." He had the feeling that Georgevic already knew all about him and Eleanor Hvar, had perhaps been the man dogging his footsteps since he left her house.

"Above the entrance to the room where Ragusa's Grand Council used to meet is carved: *Obliti privatorum publica curate.*"

Forget your private concerns and proceed with public matters. An appropriate motto, Stone thought, and the gentle obliqueness of Georgevic's reproof seemed almost too delicate from a man of such physique. "Tomorrow night, then," Stone agreed.

"Good. I will not come to the hotel for you. Better that few or none should see us together. As soon as it is dark, take the road up towards the mountains, away from the town. I shall meet you along the road."

"All right."

"You will *not* come back to the hotel. But you must look as if you intended to return after a short while. Leave everything behind. Your clothes, your luggage, everything you cannot easily hide on your person. There must be no suspicion that you are going anywhere except for an evening walk."

"And if I am followed?"

"Avoid that, if you can, but not too openly. If you are followed, do not waste too much time with evasion. I will look after those who follow you."

"Anything else?"

"No. Tomorrow you are a tourist. Tomorrow is your day to enjoy the beauty of Dubrovnik, this little walled enclave that was once the great empire of Ragusa. And to enjoy your lady. Good night, Mister Stone." He tipped his cap.

"Good night, Mister Georgevic."

"Ah, a moment. You may need this," Georgevic added, putting the Luger into his hand. "I had to take it to assure myself you would not be rash before I could persuade you that I *was* Mirko Sutnjak's brother," he explained, and then he was gone. Stone had not even felt him take the Luger.

Though he had been a long time falling asleep, Stone awoke early. Outside the day was clean and sunny and in the brilliant light, Dubrovnik, like an animal that overnight sheds a tawny skin, had turned white. From his bedroom window, everything in the city, buildings, walls, towers, all seemed whitewashed. Beyond, Mount Srd towered bleakly, a squat threatening fortress-like building, that must have been the yellow eyes of the night before, and a gigantic white crucifix on its crest combining malevolence and benediction in one brooding weight over the city. Above them, a red and white skeleton radio tower stood poised to send both their tidings.

It was too early to call Eleanor Hvar and Stone wanted to think through what he would do before he did call: if he was leaving that night, there wasn't much time.

After breakfast he walked into town and through the market place. Long rows of wooden tables were piled high with peppers, apples, carrots and other fruits and vegetables, and against the side of the adjacent church cabbages mounted a third of the way up the church wall like a mound of light-green skulls. A peasant with an old-fashioned scale and metal weights was selling them to people whose faces had the look of ancient, roughhewn wood carvings. But none of the market's color and movement dissipated either his melancholy or his sense of being stalked, nor did its vitality disperse the sense of death threatening. When he walked past a cluster of boys playing marbles in the street who, staring at his foreign clothes, began to chant loudly in English, "Here comes Mister Detective," he almost drew his Luger. Only after he had left them behind, gingerly making his way through a bevy of yowling cats foraging and fighting for scraps, did he see how funny the incident was and wondered what stray Hollywood movie had brought such an odd tag-line to out-of-the-way Dubrovnik, and what strange quirk of human nature had enshrined it in those boys' memories. It was not the English that surprised him, for after all Dubrovnik was a tourist center, but that curious menacing line.

If he left that night without telling Eleanor anything, it was straightforward, if not simple. But if he asked her to come with him, it was no longer either. Even if he didn't tell her that they would leave that night but got only her general agreement to going, he couldn't be sure she would go that evening when the time came so suddenly on her. And would Branko Georgevic take both of them?

At the end of the *Placa* he came to a magnificent multi-faced stone fountain, crowned by a biretta-like oval of red brick. Though the fountain's sculptured faces were now eroded and distorted by loss of features, a nose broken off here, an eye worn away there, they still spewed water musically into a trough that skirted the entire fountain. The combination of the time-worn faces and flowing water had the same effect on him as the fortress and crucifix on Mount Srd, as the peasant and his scales and mound of skull-like cabbages, as the glittering marbles and eyes of the boys and the nonsensical threat of their, "Here comes Mister Detective." The stairs leading up to the city's walls were only a little way beyond and he walked toward them as much to leave behind that poignant fountain and its reminders of historical erosion as to leave behind his own thoughts. At a small wooden table next to the bottom step a lean old man sat reading, his head covered with a floppy white sun hat, a green celluloid section in its brim shielding his eyes. Without looking up from his book he stopped Stone and wordlessly tapped the sign on the table top: 200 dinars it read. Stone laid the money on the table. An old hand with prominent blue veins and liver spots swept the money up and motioned him past. Stone felt he had placed a bet and lost, and the croupier had not even noticed him.

He made his way up the steep stone stairs, feeling a little dizzied by the height as he looked out over the unguarded edge, but as he mounted higher the pattern of the city spread out beneath lightened his mood. Red, orange and brown tile roofs were splashed among the white walls and festooned with drying laundry. Flowers and vines garlanded balconies, terraces and windows. It was a little like being God up there, Stone reflected, seeing the city laid out at his feet as if its secret life were open to him. Women were sweeping, cleaning, hanging bedding out of the windows to air. Between lime and blue shutters, he saw others darning, knitting, cooking on a small two-burner stove, an old white-haired carpenter hand-sanding a chair, and a lazy, graceful naked arm reaching up from the darkness within and closing a shutter. In the narrow streets, children kicked a soccer ball and people stopped to gossip. Women carried milk, fruit, vegetables and long brown and white loaves of bread on their heads and in string bags. Hidden piazzas and gardens were suddenly and bloomingly revealed. In one, a young girl carried a demijohn to a spigot in a wall; in another, nearby, a Franciscan monk, the tonsure on his head a small white sun, was watering the lemon and orange trees in the monastery's open court.

Beyond the city walls a green tide of trees swept up the hillsides, dark cypress, lush umbrella pines, fig trees and carobs, chestnut and oak, cutting the clear intense light with their restful shadows. Palm trees and spiky wild cactus were everywhere, a semitropical contrast to the dour medieval ramparts, and the combination brought back stories his mother had read to him as a boy about the Crusaders trying to storm the walled city of Acre in the Holy Land. A mule, heavy-laden with panniers, was being urged uphill by its impatient driver by having its flanks beaten with a stick. A honking motorcycle, driven by a girl in a red sweater, zoomed by and left them in a cloud of dust. At the water's edge, boats were moored and some beached, and on the jetty and breakwater beige fish nets hung drying in the sun. Men sat on the concrete pier fishing and talking, and in the harbor a boat jammed to the gunwales with passengers chugged slowly out towards one of the islands, a man in torn white shorts, naked from the waist up, holding the big rear rudder firm. A woman in black gathered driftwood along the shore and just up the bank from her, another, whose bright print apron and blue kerchief Stone recognized even at that distance, having seen her only a short time before in the market place, carried gold-framed paintings slung over her shoulders by a rope. Stone remembered them as very ugly mezzotints of *The Last Supper*.

It was not an idyllic scene, but the way life seemed to be for many men, without hatred, violence, or murder. But not for me, he thought, not for us. Then angrily he brought himself up short for the self-pity. If I take her with me and we are caught, she is doomed. But isn't she doomed anyway if I leave her here? "It has been long and lonely, and I like to sleep." Was that enough? And then I am obligated to her in a way I wasn't to Valerie, couldn't be to anyone from my own culture. Committed. The tie that binds, for which divorce would be no solution. And what if these few weeks have been wrong, an illusion, and I've made a mistake? Or if she has? And there was always the possibility that she might betray him to Decani's men, for whatever reason—hatred of Karst, continued gratitude to Decani, love of country and people always—if he told her about Karst's manuscripts, Georgevic and the boat. *Forget your private concerns and get on with public affairs.* Ragusa's adage was good; if only it were that simple.

Stone continued his long climb to the top of the wall and then walked to the corner tower. A small café was there, or had been, half in a room set back into the tower, half on a projecting platform outside. A zinc-topped wooden bar stood inside in the corner of the room and next to it a new white refrigerator, its door ajar, its shelves empty. Chairs and tables were piled one on top of the other, and near them a big potted philodendron flourished. Just outside, the floodlights that illuminated the battlements at night reflected the sunshine and one of them, broken, was surrounded by shards of glittering glass.

At that level the city below seemed almost remote. The faint sounds of human voices, barking dogs and crowing cocks and the muffled clangor of church bells drifted upward, distant and unreal. Beyond, the sea lay in blue, green and black stripes, and Stone heard the faraway sound of breakers pounding the beach. Less than a hundred miles away in that direction lay Italy . . . and safety.

What startled him, Stone didn't know, but when he spun around a powerfully built young man in ill-fitting brown tweeds was pointing a camera in his direction. Good argument for Decani's trick glasses, Stone thought, slipping out of the man's way to let him photograph the panorama. The man dropped the camera from his eye and Stone saw a heavy-jawed face of Asiatic cast with dark almost Mongolian features. The man spoke and Stone replied in English, then French and German, but they could find no common language. Finally, the brown tweeds produced a grimy pad and a tiny stub of pencil and patiently, combining drawing and pantomime, indicated that he wanted his picture taken against the background of the tower. He showed Stone how to focus and trigger the camera, carefully repeating his instructions three times to make sure that Stone understood, and then posed, dark, unsmiling, sinister. Stone grinned and said, "Say cheese." The man showed his teeth, Stone snapped the shutter and handed the camera back.

Another pantomime, this time more intense and urgent: he must now return the compliment and take a picture of

Stone. The same uneasiness afflicted him and Stone shook his head, refusing again and again, until, to get rid of the man, he gave in to his insistence and agreed. He stood tensely, as the man brought the camera up to his eye. The man's finger went to another button on top of the camera, and Stone dived to the floor. The shot sounded flat, like a slapped face, and he heard the bullet tear into the bar behind him. Before he could get to his feet, the tweed suit had hit him in the head with the camera and knocked him off balance. Behind the camera came the man. The man aimed a kick at his head and Stone twisted his ankle sharply and brought him down to the ground. Then he had his Luger out. "All right, get up," he ordered. The tweed suit got the point: he stood up. "Hands on your head," Stone said, gesturing with the Luger. Reluctantly, the man complied.

Who was trying to murder him now? Last night he might have been mistaken about that cornice; in this city slowly crumbling under the weight of its history, that part of a building gave way and a coping stone fell to the ground might only have been accident. His feeling of being stalked might be merely imagination. But this camera man was no figment, nor was there any question of the man's intentions: the man had been waiting there for him with a plan worked out to kill him. Kucic had nothing to gain from killing him at this juncture, because he had not yet found where the manuscripts were hidden. Moreover, by now, it was personal vendetta; if anyone was going to kill him, Kucic would reserve that satisfaction of doing so for himself. Townsend, too, was not ready until he had Karst's work in hand, however angered he might be. Only Decani might not care. His purposes were satisfied if Karst's work didn't leave the country; getting the books was secondary and didn't matter so much. And now Decani had another motive: he knew that Eleanor Hvar had spent the night with him and Decani loved her, was jealous. But enough to kill? Enough to risk the possibility that Karst had another emissary and that he might be a decoy?

"Decani?" Stone asked. The man's face was noncommittal. "Kucic? Jazak?" Not a muscle moved. "Townsend?" The man laughed in his face and Stone fought down the urge to pistol-whip the information out of the man, but even as the idea flickered through his mind, he knew that kind of face wasn't going to give anything until it had been badly battered and he couldn't do that kind of interrogating. "All right, then, you'll tell the police, *polizei, militzia,*" Stone threatened, but the tweed suit only shrugged. Holding the gun level with the man's belly, Stone walked closer to him, hoping to get his wallet or some papers, to see if he could find out whose cat's paw this man was, though he was sure that if the set-up had been so carefully prepared the man would not be carrying identification papers. Abruptly, the tweed suit brought his forearm swinging down and caught him a stunning blow on the wrist, knocking the Luger from his hand. Then he butted him to the ground and they grappled, rolling over and over until the tweed suit was on top, a glass shard from the broken floodlight in his hand and trying to cut Stone's throat. Stone fought to hold the man's arm back but slowly the glass lowered. Mustering all his strength, Stone bridged, rearing desperately, and threw the tweed suit over, reversing their positions and now forcing the glass shard in the man's hand toward his own windpipe. The tweed suit's bared teeth and growling were like an animal's, and so was his own soughing breath and beating blood. Unexpectedly the man went limp and as Stone jerked back to keep from cutting his throat, the man spit in his face. Instinctively, Stone dropped the piece of glass and wiped his eyes with his sleeve, but by then the tweed suit was up and running fleetly along the wall.

Stone picked up his Luger, sighted it on the man's back right under the heart, and steadied his elbow. At that distance he could surely kill the man, but he couldn't make himself squeeze the trigger. The tweed suit turned to see if he was being pursued, tripped, lost his footing, and with a bizarre, arm-flailing pirouette, fell over the parapet. His shrill, retreating howl followed him like a streamer. Stone walked cautiously to the spot and looked over the parapet. Down below the tweed suit lay spread-eagled and still. Slowly, Stone went back and picked up the camera. He slammed it smartly on the ground so that the back popped open and whatever film was inside, if any, was exposed. He dropped it over the parapet and watched it plummet down and land in the shrubbery near the body. Like a sleepwalker he put the Luger back beneath his jacket and hurriedly picked his way along the wall toward the harbor. There had to be another exit there, and he didn't want to go back past the man selling tickets. This time the old man might look up from his book and remember a face.

How he got down from the wall, Stone couldn't remember, but he found himself near the square before a building with open doors and he went inside to sit down. It was a church whose window drapes had been drawn so that it was dim and quiet as evening inside, and in the artificial dusk a nun on her hands and knees was cleaning and straightening the carpet at the altar steps. Stone sat in a pew for a long time, his face in his hands, deliberately keeping his mind blank. Then he got up and walked slowly down the nave and up the aisles looking at the paintings and religious images, and in every crucifixion seeing that spread-eagled tweed suit, aware that Karst's manuscripts had taken another life. While he walked, the nun did not look up from her tasks, and he turned out through a side door. He entered a small, square garden full of rosebushes and grapefruit trees, with an ancient well in its center. The air was heavy with the scents of citrus and roses together, slanting beams of sunshine bubbling with motes were like cool white sparkling wine, and the silence was tangible enough to touch. Above him, on a balcony supported by graceful Romanesque arches and pillars, several white-robed and hooded Dominican monks walked separately and in silence behind a balustrade, their hands telling beads, their pale faces half-hidden and unearthly. A typewriter pecked in the distance, birds sang, and the silence grew richer, more healing. Stone leaned against one of the cool, smooth pillars and breathed in the silence and the peace.

Then, like a series of twisted spotlit ikons, the deaths lit up and blacked out in his brain—Antun Vuk, his head lolling; the loden coat, the *banderilla* in his neck; the tweed suit, lying dead at the foot of the wall; Decani's crumpled black-leather raincoated henchmen—and the agonies—Karst in a mental hospital; the chambermaid dragging her foot in a cast; little Mirko Karst's bruised face; Eleanor Hvar's "It has been long and lonely, and I like to sleep."—and the problems still facing him—Karst's manuscripts, his rendezvous with Branko Georgevic and Eleanor Hvar. "Death still hath a thousand doors to let out life. I shall find one," Stone assured himself. In that lovely, pacific garden he felt gross and earthy, altogether an intruder, and with a last lingering look, he turned and went out.

Eleanor Hvar was waiting when he arrived. They had lunch in the study, on the large desk, at the feet of Sutnjak's stone sculpture, and while they ate she apologized for crying every time she was with him. It wasn't usual, she protested, she wasn't a crying type and hadn't cried once in all the years since Mirko's death. How much better it would have been, he thought, if she had been able to cry during those years, and he remembered her bitter mockery of his, "Don't cry, Lili. I love you." He soothed her by saying that she was tired, had been working too hard.

"No," she said shyly, "it's not fatigue. Only that you've peeled a layer off my feelings."

"And you several off mine," he replied.

"You know," she said, suddenly gay, "it's true."

"What is?"

"Man is made for happiness as a bird is made for flight."

He looked at her, puzzled.

"A Russian poet, Korolenko, I once translated," she explained. Then, together, they began to laugh.

Throughout that long sunny afternoon, as she led him around the city, one part of his mind struggled to make a decision about the evening impending and the future, and another listened to her describe Dubrovnik's past. Almost all the rivers of European history seemed at one time or another to have flowed through there. The city's beginnings were lost in prehistory but its earliest Illyrian settlers had been killed, plundered and conquered by Greeks, Romans, Ostrogoths, Huns, Avars, Franks and Slavs, and merged with all of them over the centuries. At first, two separate communities had been built on the site, separated by a narrow channel, one to seaward on the rocks by refugees from Greek Epidaurus and Roman Salona, the other on the landward side in the oak forests by the Slavs who had come ravaging down from beyond the Carpathians in one of the barbarian invasions and stayed. One town was called Ragusa (after the rocks), the other Dubrovnik (after the oaks), and eventually time and mutual interest had fused the towns and blended their peoples.

Never more than six thousand inhabitants in the city proper, or forty thousand in the entire state, on a small strip of unproductive land, Ragusa had nevertheless become a world maritime and commercial power and established a Republic that had maintained its sovereignty and integrity for five hundred years against all comers—Byzantines, Venetians, Hungarians, Turks—with a diplomatic skill that was both uncanny and Machiavellian. In the clash between the Christian West and the infidel Turk, Ragusa succeeded in astutely playing one against the other, or cravenly paying one or the other tribute, an inspired neutrality which little compromised its own native Roman Catholicism, but little demonstrated its Christianity. By playing both ends against the middle, this little "Athens of the Slavs" had created an impressive culture and advanced social institutions, and kept outsiders from breaching its fortresses and walls or shedding its people's blood. Insiders were kept from breaching similar walls of caste and class imposed by their rigidly autocratic and aristocratic rulers as well. Hardworking shrewdness made Ragusa rich and so widely known were the Republic's ships, and so powerful its overseas and overland commerce, that the English word *argosy* was a corrupt version of the name Ragusa.

"As you can see," Eleanor Hvar commented wryly, "our present-day government learned a good deal from the success of the Dubrovniki."

Two things finally finished Ragusa, one natural catastrophe, a devastating earthquake, and a second political

227

catastrophe, Napoleon, whose armies under General Marmont had finally put the quietus on the Republic in 1808, and left the fortress on Mount Srd as a perpetual reminder.

But if Dubrovnik was only a shadow of Ragusa's former glory, only a tourist resort and a minor port on the Adriatic coast, it had an antique grace that touched Stone's heart. And as Eleanor Hvar led him through its churches, cathedrals and monasteries, its collections of Titian, Raphael, Vasari and Tiepolo, its fountains, statues, campanile, its palaces, with all their marvelous juxtaposition of Gothic, Renaissance and Baroque, and rolled the fine names of its builders off her tongue—Michelozzi of Florence, George of Dalmatia sometimes known as Orsini, Onofrio de la Cava—Stone could feel Ragusa's pulsebeat. Finally, in the Franciscan convent, when she showed him a fifteenth-century painting of St. Vlaho, or St. Blaise, the city's patron saint, holding a model of the Ragusa that was then, Stone saw how little five hundred years had changed it outwardly. Some sense of its tragedy was born in him and with it the irony, that fatal combination of changing circumstance and character which had turned a once vigorous and vital community into a backwater, like a lovely starfish, dried, blanched and fossilized left high on a beach by the ebbing tide of time.

But behind it all he still saw the tweed suit's sprawled body at the foot of the medieval walls and only just managed to avoid a tour of the landward walls with Eleanor Hvar. Instead, they strolled along the seaside wall, from the harbor fort of St. Ivan to the great Lovrjenac fortress, built to protect the city from the threat of rival Venice. There, she told him how the Ragusa nobility's motto had been *Pax optima rerum,* its coins inscribed with *Libertas,* and on the fortress itself on the battlements the maxim: *Non bene pro toto venditur libertas auro.*

There, too, with the salt wind blowing in their faces, Stone told her of Karst's manuscripts and asked her to come with him. Except for mentioning Branko Georgevic's name, he was now committed on all counts, and in her hands; if she wished to betray him, in either sense, it took only a phone call to Decani. "I love you, Lili," he thought. "Don't cry." But he didn't speak the words.

"Tonight? she asked finally.

"Tonight," he said, "in a few hours."

He had wanted to wait longer, to make love to her once more without this between them, to prolong that almost carefree pleasure of the afternoon, to avoid the pain of her refusal. But he knew he had delayed too long already: she had to have that little time left to think, to make her own decision.

Walking back to her apartment, and there serving tea and brandy, she was silent, her face telling him nothing of what she was thinking, of what she would do. She touched him then, at first as if for reassurance and then stirring his flesh, but held him off with an alluring retreat that permitted pleasure but no consummation until they stood together naked, facing each other, the late afternoon sun gilding their bodies. The curtains blew into the room like presences and there, next to her likeness, Mirko Sutnjak's stone statue, no longer so young or firm-fleshed as once she'd been, she looked somber, and Stone yearned for her with a terrible longing that was for the first time able to encompass their pasts however uncertain he was of their future. They made love with a kind of fumbling rage at their bodies for not melting, at their flesh for not obeying the outcry of their spirits to weld their separate worlds, with a ferocity that acknowledged a beginning and an ending and found both insupportable. And afterwards she did not have to tell him she would go: he knew.

They had dinner at his hotel and were finished just as the sun began to edge the horizon. Stone excused himself and went up to his room. Carefully, he emptied the loden coat's brief case and transferred the guns, the ammunition and grenades to his various coat and jacket pockets. He took his own pencil flash and made sure that he had all his money. For a moment, wistfully, he looked at all the things he was leaving behind and idly wondered who would take them. With the coat over his arm, nothing bulged too conspicuously, and he went down to the lobby where Eleanor Hvar was waiting for him. She took his arm, gaily, and as they left the hotel whispered, "I am quite sure we are under surveillance."

"I'd be surprised if we weren't," he answered.

In the thickening dusk they walked up the road toward the mountains. A quick glance over his shoulder confirmed that they were being followed. On opposite sides of the road and some distance apart, two men dawdled along; in the distance behind them a grey Mercedes was parked at the edge of the roadway. It was growing chilly and Stone put his coat on, and helped Eleanor Hvar into hers. As he did so, he was amused to see that the men trailing them didn't know quite what to do, and one stopped and began to pick blades of grass. An old black prewar Mercedes-Benz shot past them, braked screechingly to a halt, then backed up to Stone. Branko Georgevic was inside. "Look like you are giving me directions," he ordered, his eyes glued to the rear window mirror. Eleanor Hvar began to gesticulate, making turning motions with her hand, while Georgevic spoke. "About a thousand meters ahead, the road bends very sharply. As soon as you go around, those behind will not be able to see you for awhile. Run ahead as far and as quickly as you can." He waved his hand, put the car into gear, and roared off. The men behind, Stone noticed, were almost running to catch up to them, and the grey Mercedes had started into the road behind them rapidly closing the distance between them, but now they slackened their pace and the car pulled to the side once more and parked.

The road began to climb and grew narrower, its sea side shearing off so sharply that they had to cross to the mountain side to walk safely. But the men following were now on that side too and their grey Mercedes inching along a good way behind. Abruptly, the road rounded a huge rock boulder, turning back on itself by close to ninety degrees, and the men trailing them were blocked from view. Hand in hand, Stone and Eleanor Hvar began to run. Ahead, a heavy truck, its headlights dim, careened past, skidded, turned sidewise and blocked the road at the narrow sharp bend so neatly that the only way past was either to climb through, over, or under it. The old black Mercedes-Benz was waiting just beyond, motor running, and Georgevic had the car moving before they had slammed the doors. He drove very fast, not talking, while Stone peered back to see if they were being followed. Seven or eight miles later, Georgevic pulled off onto a dirt side road, then later into a bumpy field, and finally into a small clearing in a thick grove of stalwart pines. They all got out and Georgevic skillfully removed the car's license plates and then laid pine branches around the car until, in a few moments, it was so well-camouflaged that only if someone were looking for the car specifically would it likely be noticed. Then he turned and said in German, "I did not know there would be two of you, Mister Stone."

"Nor did I," Stone replied. "Mister Georgevic, this is Eleanor Hvar. Eleanor, this is Branko Georgevic."

"He said nothing about a woman," Georgevic declared, ignoring the introduction.

"No, he didn't know."

"And you brought her along?"

"As you can see."

"You are either a very brave man, Mister Stone, or very rash," Georgevic said, slapping the license plates on his palm with a resounding boom.

The comment required no answer, so Stone said nothing. They stood there glaring at each other until Eleanor Hvar said something in Serbo-Croat. There were a few brief sentences exchanged, then Georgevic embraced her and kissed both her cheeks. To Stone, he said, "Very well, then, we must go quickly." He took a collapsible spade from the front seat of the car that Stone recognized as a wartime American entrenching shovel the kind with which he, himself, had dug God knew how many foxholes. Georgevic, the spade on his shoulder, set off up the mountain, his long legs quickly carrying him a good distance out in front of them.

They hurried after him and Stone asked in English, "What Serbo-Croat charm did you use on him?"

"I told him I was Lili Sutnjak," she said. "Georgevic knew Mirko. They were together with Konstanty in the mountains and I remembered hearing his name, and the stories of the Montenegrin giant. Georgevic is the brother of the man who married Karst's sister, the uncle of the boy why was murdered in your hotel room in Belgrade."

"Antun Vuk," Stone said sadly.

She nodded.

"Everything in this country is a family matter, everyone knows everyone else."

"Ours is a small country, Warren, and the leaders and intellectuals a very small group. They all know each other, or about each other. Often from the war. And right over those mountains, in Bosnia, Herzegovina and Montenegro, the family is as close as five fingers in a fist, and blood feud the way of life for many."

The path wound irregularly along the contours of the hill as if originally made by animals grazing along the slope. Behind them, below, was the road, and beyond it the sea. They passed vineyards and olive groves, the trees silver-leafed, and at last came to a thick stand of oak trees where Georgevic waited for them. He took Eleanor Hvar's hand and plunged into the underbrush. Stone took her other hand and followed, through shrubs, nettles and briars, a thick, clinging undergrowth, until in a few minutes they came to a small meadow where humps of grey, lichen-covered stone bulked out of the ground. When they were quite close, Georgevic's bass boomed, "Bogomil tombstones." On them were crude carvings, like the drawings of disturbed children, schematic, poorly proportioned and awkwardly unnatural, without detail or perspective, but with the stark simplicity and power of elemental things passionately felt and primitively shaped. One showed a man bracing a spear into the chest of a charging bear; another giant suns and hands, shepherd's crooks, spears and bows and arrows. But the most moving showed a frieze-like string of dancers, like the cut-out dolls of kindergarten, their hands joined at shoulder height, somehow made tragically beautiful by their impersonal, identical figures, without faces or features, and their flat inability to convey the human form. Over them flew a great bird with fringed wings, the hawk of death, and in Stone's mind, repetitively, the childhood refrain sang, "Ring around a rosie, a pocket full of posie, all fall down."

In the still remaining light, he had to run his fingers over the surfaces to corroborate what he thought he saw in the stone, but he had no time to linger because Georgevic was leading them toward a small rise, where a rounded head and rounded arms became a man-shaped stone cross tombstone stitched with broken Cyrillic letters. Georgevic stopped before it; next to it, another low, plain, more recent gravestone with carved Latin letters read: Mirko Sutnjak, and his dates.

Eleanor Hvar began to tremble and Stone put his arm around her shoulders. "Is it . . . ?" Stone began, and Georgevic nodded. "Why didn't you tell her?" Stone asked angrily.

"I thought she knew," Georgevic apologized, "or I would not have brought her here. I thought that was why you had taken her with you, to see his grave."

"No," Eleanor Hvar gasped. "I never knew where Mirko was buried. I thought they left him in the mountains, unmarked."

"They did," Georgevic said softly, to her directly. "After the war, Konstanty and I went into the mountains together and brought him back here."

"But why here?" she asked.

"So he could look down on his beloved Dalmatia and the sea."

"And why in a Bogomil burial ground? He was a Catholic."

Georgevic shrugged. "I don't know. Konstanty didn't explain, but I am sure he had reasons. He placed him next to one who lived many years ago," he pointed to the human-shaped cross, "because he thought his epitaph should be Mirko's." He touched his fingertips to the worn Cyrillic letters, put his face close to them, and read:

Here lies Luka Vladosalic. I was a bold hero. I beseech you, brothers, disturb not my bones. You will be as I am, but I cannot be as you are.

234

Softly, mournfully, Eleanor Hvar began to chant, her face pale as the small, white gravestone she faced, and the giant Georgevic took his grey cap off and bowed a head of thick black ringlets like Antun Vuk's.

"What is it?" Stone asked gently, when she had done.

"A poem one of our Partisans wrote. Edvard Kocbek. I translated it once for an English anthology. It's called *A Prayer*:

> I am
> and I was
> and everyone
> will be able
> to forget me.
>
> And nevertheless
> I have to say:
> I am
> and I was
> and I shall be,
> and therefore I am more
> than oblivion,
> immeasurably more
> than denying,
> immeasurably more
> than nothing.
>
> All that arises
> is eternal,
> birth is stronger
> than death,
> more endurable
> than despair and loneliness,
> more solemn

than pain and sorrow,
more solemn than damnation.
I shall never
cease to be.
Never.
Amen.

When Eleanor Hvar turned away, Georgevic picked up the spade and began to dig at the foot of Sutnjak's grave. He dug rapidly and was three feet down before Stone heard the sound of metal strike metal. Quickly, Georgevic brought up a rusty, corroded box, broke the lock on it with a swift stroke of the spade, and threw it open. Inside were four neat packages wrapped in pliofilm: Karst's manuscripts. Georgevic handed them to Stone, dropped the license plates he had taken from the car into the box, then carefully replaced the box and filled in the hole. When he had covered the fresh earth with leaves, twigs and vines, everything looked as it had before.

To say something, anything, Stone said he thought the Bogomils had disappeared after the Turks had occupied Bosnia in 1463, that most of them had become Moslems, and that it was difficult if not impossible to identify families today as being of Bogomil origins. Almost curtly, Georgevic replied that the attachment to Bogomilism had come down in families privately, even surreptitiously, over the centuries, handed down from father to children, but such families remained reluctant to identify themselves publicly as of Bogomil derivation.

They followed Georgevic still further up the slope along a sheep trail through meadows and thinner stands of cypress and pine until they came to a shepherd's hut under a canopy of old oaks. Made of raw stones and mortar, except for its slate roof, the hut might have stood there for millenia. Inside, Georgevic lit a candle and motioned them to a crude wooden table and the equally crude wooden chairs around it. From a shelf he brought a jug of *rakija* and gave it to Eleanor Hvar. She drank, choked, and passed it to Stone. He took a long pull of the burning liquor and handed it back to Georgevic, who tilted the jug back and let the liquor run down his throat as if it were water. Eleanor Hvar seemed stunned. She put her arms on the table, then her head on them, and closed her eyes. Stone set Karst's manuscripts on the table next to her dark head, and Georgevic, with a pitying look at her, nodded toward the door. "Better to leave her for a time," he advised softly.

Outside, they sat on the cold ground, the irregular jutting of the cabin wall sharp in Stone's back. "We must wait for nightfall," Georgevic said. "Darkness is our ally." Stone took out his cigarettes and offered one to Georgevic, then lit one. He did not feel pursued or harried, only sad and remote from his own predicament. "Darkness is our ally," he thought. "Yes, and what an equivocal ally." Georgevic brought him back with a sentence. "There is another who follows you besides Decani," Georgevic said.

Stone told about the tweed suit he had met on the walls of Dubrovnik and what had happened, but Georgevic did not think that was the man: he thought the tweed suit was one of Decani's men. The thin totem-pole figure of Kucic loomed in his mind and Stone described him to Georgevic. When he was finished, slowly, contemplatively, Georgevic spat.

"You knew him?" Stone asked, astonished.

"I knew him," Georgevic answered flatly. "He's from Sarajevo, just over the mountains." His head indicated the direction behind them. "I met him there." In the silence there were the rustling stealthy movements of small animals, and off on the horizon night gathered like a black fist. "My father was ambitious for me," Georgevic began, "he did not want me to be a shepherd and a fisherman as he was. Sarajevo had a *gymnazium*, like nothing we had in the mountains, so my father sent me to stay with his brother in Sarajevo so I could go to the *gymnazium* there.

"In school I come to know Zora Kucic—only her family name was really Stanasic. Kucic was a Party name *he* took. Zora was his older sister, the first-born, beautiful, with long black hair and eyes dark as the ocean bottom. She wanted to go to the university, to become a children's doctor, for she was very intelligent."

He stared at the darkness, moistening his lips with his tongue, trying to dislodge a tiny fragment of cigarette paper stuck dryly to his lower lip. Impatiently he rubbed the cigarette paper wisp away with his hand and began to talk again, at first in a hoarse whisper, then normally. "Zora introduced me to her brother, Kucic. He was only a year younger than she was and a class behind at the same *gymnazium* we went to but already man's hand was against him and his against every man's. Even his sister's. He loved Sarajevo, almost the only thing he seemed to love, and he was a part of it—the Turkish part. Sometimes it seemed to me, and to Zora, that four hundred years of Turkish brutality and violence had been reborn in him, in one man's bad blood."

"Was the family of Turkish blood?"

"How does one know in a city where Bosnian and Turk have been locked in battle and in embrace for centuries?" Georgevic shrugged. "Years later, when I saw that scar Konstanty had carved on his forehead, I thought it was a proper mark of Cain, shaped like a faded white Sarajevo minaret. 'Allah is great and Mohammed is his prophet. Come and pray,'" Georgevic intoned. "Kucic had that wild Moslem fanaticism transformed, as if five times a day he heard his own muezzin chanting, 'Lenin is great and Stalin is his prophet, and I, Kucic, his executioner. Come let us kill in the name of the prophet.' "

"That murderous fanaticism," Stone mused, half to Georgevic, half to himself.

"Oh, yes, his family was Bogomil and their mark was on him too. But the Moslem was in him, an Oriental fever you could see in the way he loved to kill and in the way he treated women. . . . Especially in the way he treated women," Georgevic added, after a significant pause. His eyes closed as if he were napping, but he went on talking in a low voice. "Kucic didn't want Zora to go to the university. He didn't want her to go out with men. Though he was a Communist by then and in the Party, and supposed to be a 'free thinker,' he wanted to keep Zora veiled and hidden from the eyes of the world, as in a harem."

"But he didn't succeed?"

"No. Of course not. Perhaps it would have been better if he had. But I stopped him. Zora went to the university and I went with her. I helped her, in spite of what Kucic wanted, and his raving did not frighten me. The more fool I. I wanted to marry Zora, but she refused me. And because I, too, was a Communist and knew a great war was coming, I did not insist. But those were not her reasons."

Something crashed in the brush, then scurried through the undergrowth, its sounds echoing in the distance. Georgevic had instantly tensed, already half on his feet, like a runner about to sprint, but when the silence returned, gracefully, slowly, he sank back on his haunches, his shoulders erect against the stone hut. "Zora said she was cursed," he continued, "that I would be better off with another woman, any other woman. I could not understand why. She would not make love with me. I knew I was not ugly. I knew she had feeling for me. So, because I was young and foolish, and did not believe there were secrets the human heart could or should keep buried, I made her drunk. She was not used to drink and it was not too difficult. Perhaps it was even what she wanted."

He flipped the flaming butt in a long arc away from him and watched it burn in the dusk. "I made her drunk and I made love to her," Georgevic said, almost talking to himself now. "I was not surprised not to be the first, but her abandon, her wantonness, took me unaware. Lying there, the taste of her still sweet in my mouth, my heart swollen with love for her, she told me I was the second, but the *very first outside of her family.*

"I thought she spoke with the drink and was confused, but she made me understand, clearly, made me listen to how her brother had been before me, had forced her at first a long time ago, until after many times she hungered for him and hated him together. And so it was still, she said, and showed me the purple flowers he had only recently marked on her flesh that, in my passion, I had not noticed."

The tiny coal of the cigarette still smoldered on the ground and Georgevic rose, strode over and mashed it out beneath his heel. When he came back, he sat down as if suddenly hamstrung. "I was a simple boy from the mountains then, and I was horrified and frightened. I believed she was truly accursed, that she had committed the deadliest sin. First, I wanted to kill her, then him, then kill both of them, but I was paralyzed and I did nothing.

"I couldn't study, I couldn't stay in Sarajevo without seeing her, and I couldn't bear to face her. So I went back to my father's house." Georgevic laughed, a sound harsh and racking as a cough. "He, poor man, could not understand what had happened to me, to his favorite son. I was no longer the same boy. And I couldn't explain. But God rest his soul, he said nothing. He gave me tasks that occupied my hands, if not my thoughts, and wearied my body so that at the day's end I fell from my feet into sleep.

"But still I couldn't keep Zora from my mind, nor Kucic. I knew that unless I did something I would go mad, so the next spring I returned to the university."

The quiet was tied tense as a knot, and even as Stone asked, as a part of him wanted to hear the inevitable, another part of him shied away, wanting not to hear, or to hear a happier end. "What did she do when she saw you?" he asked Georgevic.

"When I saw her," Georgevic said slowly, "it was as if I had waited without sleep through the longest night of winter for day to come. But it was too late. Our moment had passed. I asked her again to marry me, in spite of what had happened with her brother, and I meant it. But too much had been said, too much revealed. It was poisoned. We were polite, but strangers. Or worse, perhaps, not quite strangers. It was done though I didn't know it then and tried to persuade her. But Zora knew, she knew."

"And Kucic?"

"He had already gone to Moscow."

"So she was alone?"

Georgevic stared through him, unseeing. "I don't know. There was talk of many men, of her taking them as men take women, greedily, expertly, unfeeling.

"When we finished the university, she went to the faculty of medicine, and I came back home. She became a childrens' doctor and returned to Sarajevo. I remained in the mountains

241

and on the sea, as the Party ordered me to, until the war came."

"What happened to her?" Stone made himself ask between clenched teeth, unable to speak her name. "Did she marry?"

"No, she never married," Georgevic answered, "she did not even fall victim to the Germans. In her life it was written that she could only be despoiled by her own. During that first summer of the war, Pavelic's cutthroat Croats, the *Ustachi,* came through Bosnia and Herzegovina like flame through wheat. They were going to make Croatia and Roman Catholicism more glorious, so they murdered Serbs by the thousand, men, women and children, to persuade them to convert to Rome. Nothing was beyond their efforts—rape, arson, torture, mutilation, slaughter—for it was, after all, *ad majorem Dei gloriam.* Some *Ustachi* collected the eyes and breasts and sexual organs of Serbs they had killed as if those were religious relics to display in the market places of their cities as marks of their bravery and fervor, and a demonstration of loyalty to their leaders and fascist allies."

Stone shuddered, the chill air tingling his teeth, burning his flesh. Always the burden of history; and always the burden of history, murder.

"Zora was still in Sarajevo, in charge of the children's ward of the hospital. The *Ustachi* found her there. She tried to save the children and in spite of her stubborn Bogomil pride agreed that they would all convert to Rome if they were left in peace. But even that was not enough. The *Ustachi* heroes had shed blood; now they wanted only more blood. They packed them all, women and children, into a railway convoy, like Jews, after they'd had a little fun raping, and bayoneting, and shooting the few male attendants. Then they took them to the mountains and drove them all over a cliff."

There on the bare hillside Stone saw that slaughter like a

nightmare made live, saw Zora Kucic violated and killed, and closed his eyes to erase it from his consciousness. When he opened them, Georgevic's huge bulk next to him was folded over, as if he had, himself, been bayoneted in the midriff, and he was groaning, his eyes wild and staring. "They drove more than two hundred women and children off the edge of a seven-hundred-foot cliff like cattle," he rasped. "They did not even have enough mercy to shoot them first."

The silence was anguished and prolonged. Stone heard his own heart beating in his ears, his teeth ached, his muscles twitched painfully; he wanted to do something, anything, about that monstrous event in Sarajevo, about Zora Kucic and his own Eleanor Hvar, but he sat there helpless, the ground cold and hard under his tensed buttocks, the irregular stones of the hut wall a goad in his back. If there was a hell, that was it and he'd been there before. Neither Slater nor the two Germans he'd killed in hand-to-hand fighting had been the worst hell of the war; at least, with them, there had been some illusion of a personal encounter with an objective, some purpose, however horrible. The worst had been the anonymous, statistical killing, fields of men harvested like grain by machine-gun fire, or shattered into bloody fragments by high explosives. Almost none of it made sense out there except the human blood and bones fertilizing soil that would some day produce finer wines and richer grains.

And none of that was as awful as those women and children herded over a cliff outside Sarajevo, or the thousands, millions of others who had perished that way, or before firing squads, or in cattle cars, or in death-camp crematoria. The statistical millions few remembered . . . even as statistics.

Georgevic took an old gold pocket watch from under his jacket that reminded Stone of his grandfather's watch, Roman numerals and all, which still sat in his safety-deposit vault back in New York. For an instant, Georgevic's face looked back to the hut's door, then turned more urgently to his watch. "I will need two, perhaps two and a half hours, to bring the boat back. It will depend on whether they have alerted their sea patrols or not."

Stone proffered the cigarette pack again and they lit up a second time. Georgevic pointed down the hillside with the glowing cigarette end to where the earth plunged into the sea. In the dying light a small cove and narrow beach were visible. Georgevic indicated a footpath that led down from the back of the hut, in the opposite direction from which they'd come. "That path will take you straight to the beach. Twenty minutes or half hour to the bay from here. There is only one place to be careful, where you cross the road."

Stone looked at his wrist watch. "Two hours then?"

"Yes. Better earlier for you so I do not have to wait."

"Of course."

"You are armed?" Georgevic asked.

"Yes," Stone replied. "And you?"

Georgevic shook his head. Stone took the Webley-Vikers out of his coat pocket, all the ammunition he had for it, and one of the grenades, and silently handed them over. As Georgevic stowed them in his pockets, he asked, "Who was driving that truck?"

A white grin split Georgevic's swarthy face and his black mustache seemed to preen itself. "A friend. An old friend. He was taking some olive oil and cheese into Dubrovnik. It is usual for him to do so about this time. He knows and he will tell nothing."

Stone smiled back. "It was well done."

Georgevic accepted the compliment with a wave of his

hand. Then, as he was about to leave, he hesitated, and looked at the hut. "She will come?" Georgevic asked.

"I don't know."

"You must be firm," Georgevic said. They shook hands and then he glided away and in seconds was lost from sight among the trees.

WHEN STONE came back inside the hut, Eleanor Hvar's face was in her hands and he pried her clutching fingers loose and kissed them, but she did not acknowledge his presence. "Read me some of what Karst wrote," he asked, trying to distract her from her melancholy, "I want to see if any of this has been worth the candle."

The manuscripts had been well-packed, in three layers: heavy brown paper, oilcloth, and pliofilm. Stone unwrapped each manuscript and placed it in front of her. Unseeing she stared at the four neat piles of paper, then picked one up. "This is called *Earthbound*," she said in a flat, expressionless voice, as if reciting by rote. "It is dedicated, 'To my wife, Alexandra, who was always skeptical.'" She leafed through the pages for a time, then remarked. "A novel about our collectivization in the Voivodina. It tells about two families, friends for a long time, and intermarried, who are divided about it. A very powerful beginning." The second was a book of poems, titled *My Brother's Keeper,* its dedication, "For Mirko, brother, comrade and keeper, who lived and died a hero." The third was called *The Unwithering State,* a polemic dedicated to "Dr. Nikola Grout, who long ago taught us what socialism really is." The last was Karst's autobiography, *The*

Black Mountain, with the epigraph: "For Mirko's widow and unborn son, casualties of the war; for my wife and living son, casualties of the revolution."

She went on reading, apparently unmoved by the dedications, translating a chapter from the novel, a section from the autobiography on family feuds in the Montenegrin mountains during World War I, the slaughter, savagery and splendor which Karst remembered as a child, or had been told about. Then, a few poems, one of them a haunting lyric which began, "Speak to me, Mirko, my brother's keeper,/ And tell me how shall I shape my life," an impassioned personal plea to a dead friend for guidance through the thickets of life. Last, she translated a part of *The Unwithering State,* a fiery critique of the Communism Karst had known and helped to impose on his country.

"No party, class, group or individual," Karst had written, "has drunk from that Pierian spring which provides solutions for all earthly ills, panaceas for all human difficulties. The state capitalism which calls itself communism, that unwithering state which continues to grow like the green bay tree in power and privilege, instead of keeping its prophesy and promise to wither away, is already, has already been forced to concede more and more freedom, privacy and initiative, but always short of the citadel of the monopoly of Party power and wisdom. And without that citadel being stormed or relinquished, all the rest is a Potemkin village, a façade by a dark river of blood, which may have misled leaders and intellectuals, but not often the people.

"And those countries called capitalist which gave up the name and many tenets of classical capitalism long ago will now have to accept even more changes which technology and human reason have brought to dubious flower in our century.

Here, too, a citadel remains to be stormed, or relinquished, the concentration of economic wealth and political power. Property, privilege and power must surrender to man's need for economic security, for meaningful work, for the possibilities of human freedom and fulfillment. Increasingly, property and power must be, have been, and are being separated, but still more sweeping concessions must be made concerning the material wealth a man may acquire and retain in his lifetime or pass on to his heirs. And without that citadel being stormed or relinquished, all the rest is a Potemkin village, a façade by a green river of illusion and coercion which has not only sometimes misled leaders and intellectuals, but often the masses as well.

"In spite of the prophets of doom and despair, progress is a fact of history and an opportunity. The mass of men is better off today than ever before and their chances for tomorrow are still better if reason, freedom and science are encouraged and brought to bear. Industrialism, whatever its ugliness and its shortcomings, will feed and clothe and house better than ever before. Machinery will have eliminated the physical wants that have dogged man's footsteps through history. It is not the machine which must be destroyed, as the Luddites had it, but the man who controls it must increasingly be brought to control himself and its use to make a better society.

"Nor is it merely economics which is at stake. Human freedom is at stake, and therefore human personality and human life. We who have loved the people, must learn to love men; we who have enshrined the masses, in order to cater to their baseness or exploit it, must now enshrine the individual to develop and fructify him. Choice must *not* be between capitalism's atomized and aliented wage-slave, or communism's hive-like and aliented drone. A plague on both those houses! A free man, self-made and self-making, a man who

248

is part of and partakes in human society must be made to flower, a man in whom socialist humanism and amiability inceasingly grow instinct as animal competitiveness and ruthlessness grow increasingly extinct. But neither competition nor cooperation may be finally extinguished, neither the animal in man nor the man in the animal, for both are natural to human beings and they live and make progress with and by the two.

"And it must be accomplished in freedom, for in the longer run, no social system can be imposed on a people against the grain of its character and its history . . ."

". . . in the long run we're all dead," a voice interrupted. It was Townsend, standing in the doorway, a small submachine gun, the kind called a "grease gun" during the war, cradled in his arms. Behind him was the grimmer, broader bulk of Grout, silent, a black Colt 45 in his fist, and over his right shoulder a worn leather knapsack that looked like a diplomatic dispatch pouch.

Deliberately Stone reached into his pocket for a cigarette and heard the safety on Townsend's grease gun click off. He brought the cigarettes out and lighted them, one for himself, the other for Eleanor Hvar, surprised to see his hands steady, the flame unwavering. Very slowly, he lay the pack on the table. "You know, of course," he said, "that when I get back to the States, I'll raise Cain about this."

"You already have. We gave you a chance to cooperate, but you wouldn't," Townsend replied.

"I'll accuse you of stealing my private property, and I'll go to the courts."

"No one will believe you. What evidence will you have? We have the word of two reliable, long-term government officials against yours, a literary agent." The last with scorn. "And we could keep it tied up in the courts for a long time, anyway. I'm sorry, Stone, that this has to be the way. You've stumbled into an undeclared war and in it sometimes civilians get roughed up. We have to use every means they use to fight them, or we're lost, so it's not according to Hoyle or the Marquis of Queensbury. We must have Karst's book. I mean," he amended, gesturing at the manuscripts with the grease gun, "those books."

"You're going to have to kill me to take those manuscripts," Stone said, very quietly. "They were entrusted to me in confidence, and they are my responsibility."

"If I have to kill you, Stone, I will. Make no mistake about that. I might even enjoy it," Townsend said grimly.

"Don't be a fool, Warren," Grout advised quietly. "This isn't the time for grandstand plays. And weren't you the one who poked fun at words like duty?"

"Besides," Townsend added, "why kill yourself for that kind of high-flown rhetoric anyway?" He nodded at the manuscript Eleanor Hvar had been reading from, and still held in her hands.

"Is that your opinion too, Maxim?" Stone asked.

"No. Not exactly. Karst is an optimist, he always was. And there's a great deal to be said for the pessimists in our time, the prophets of doom and despair. Our century, with its Auschwitzes and Vorkutas, and with that Big Bomb, says very little for human progress or gives very little on which to base much hope. But what Karst writes is true and inevitable, if there is to be any more history and any more mankind, though many"—with a sidelong glance at Townsend—"will think what he says is Bolshevik."

"Besides, Max, your friend Karst is always better with words than with making political institutions, isn't he?" Townsend said.

"That's true," Grout replied reluctantly, "but the word is sometimes more important than the political institution, isn't it?"

"Man doesn't live by political institutions alone?" Townsend grinned crookedly. "Maybe not. Maybe not. But he doesn't live by words without political institutions either. . . . The manuscripts, Max."

Stone stood up and Townsend aimed the grease gun at his midriff. "Move away from the table, please, Mister Stone," Townsend requested politely, and ominously. Stone didn't move.

Like a croupier raking in the chips, Grout pulled three of the manuscripts to his side of the table, careful not to block Townsend's line of fire. Still holding the 45 in one hand, he nimbly rewrapped them and dropped them into his leather sack. Then, when Eleanor Hvar had still neither moved nor spoken, he took the last manuscript gently out of her hands. "That one, Max," she said so softly Stone strained to hear, "is dedicated to your father. 'To Dr. Nikola Grout, who long ago taught us what socialism really is.' "

Grout hesitated. "It is, Lili?" he asked. "Is it, Warren?" His normally florid face seemed as white as his cropped hair. Stone nodded, absentmindedly, still trying to think of a way of striking back, for once they took those manuscripts, his chances of recovering them were almost nil. Like a fish out of water suddenly resubmerging, Grout dipped his head and resumed his swift wrapping of the last manuscript. All that could be heard in the hut was the crackling of brown paper and oilcloth, then the squeal of pliofilm until a heavily accented voice said in English, "Thank you, I will have that bag now."

It was the totem pole. Saturnine, in black coat and homburg, he looked like a diplomat dressed for a formal dinner except that in his hand he had a machine pistol. Townsend whirled and Grout, depositing the last manuscript in his leather bag, made a slow about-face from the table. "I've been expecting you," Stone said.

"And I have been looking for you," Kucic replied suavely, "as my note informed you. Put your Luger on the ground, Mister Stone." To Townsend, he said, "You will place yours next to it." And to Grout, "The bag and the pistol next to it." Grout stepped forward and dropped the gun and bag together. Seeing Townsend tense, Stone, to distract Kucic, made a large hopeless gesture of throwing his gun next to the leather bag and said loudly, "I didn't know you could speak English too." It didn't work. Before Townsend could bring the grease gun to bear and press the trigger, Kucic shot him in the head. It was such close range that the shot blew part of Townsend's skull away and the memory of the German he had killed in Holland swam dizzily in front of Stone's eyes. The next instant he and Grout tried to rush Kucic, but the totem pole backed off, kept the machine pistol trained on Eleanor Hvar, and said, "I can probably kill all three of you with one burst, but I shall surely kill her." They halted, Townsend's body between them and Kucic, still twitching at their feet, but already dead. With his shoe Kucic shuffled the grease gun to the door, then Grout's 45 and Stone's Luger, and last the leather sack of manuscripts, but he did not take his eyes or the machine pistol off them.

Inwardly Stone cursed himself for not having been prepared, and for having thrown down his gun. Townsend had been right after all; if all three of them had tried together, one of them was bound to have killed Kucic. But now, without weapons, they were helpless. And what was to prevent Kucic from killing them. He'd promised to do so, and why shouldn't he? "How did you find us?" Stone asked, hoping delay would give him an idea, an opportunity.

"I followed Mister Townsend and Mister Grout. I had confidence that they would find you," Kucic replied courteously.

"Then you didn't follow us?" Stone said.

Kucic shook his head. "I would have found you anyway. The man who cut the gravestone with Sutnjak's name told one of our people."

"Our people?" Grout inquired.

"Yes, our people," was Kucic's bland retort.

Stone looked quizzically at Grout. "Konstanty told me about Mirko's grave a long time ago," Grout explained. "I went there twice after the war, and knowing Konstanty's macabre romanticism and political cunning, it wasn't hard to imagine he'd bury his books at Mirko's feet. It would be his idea of poetic political justice. From there, it was easy to track you here." But even as he told his story, Stone felt he was leaving something out.

"Well, gentlemen," Kucic said politely, "you will please lie on the floor." Slowly, they kneeled and then stretched out, like Moslems doing obeisance to Mecca or Orthodox prostrating themselves in front of the iconostasis. This is a nightmare, Stone thought, his face only a few feet from Townsend's bloody shattered head. "Now, Madame Sutnjak, your turn." Kucic took a coil of rope from his pocket and tossed it across the table. "Tie them up, and tightly, please." Still holding the machine pistol at their chests, Kucic demonstrated. He wanted their hands and legs behind them, ankles and wrists tied together, so they would be completely trussed. A brace of pigeons, not a pride of lions.

But why was Kucic tying them up, why bother to rope corpses, Stone wondered. Why didn't he simply shoot them and take off? Kucic had been talking, slowly but compulsively, as if he couldn't stop tasting the savor of his own words, and Grout's short grunted sentences egged him on. Always the words, prelude to, accompaniment with, explanation after the act, even or *especially* the act of murder. They had to have the last word.

". . . Moscow thought Karst was leadership material. He was orthodox, defended the Party line. He was implacable with those who faltered, or deviated, or split. And, like most Montenegrins, he loved Russia, was pan-Slav."

"A zealot. Was that enough for leadership?"

Wordlessly, mechanically, Eleanor Hvar was tying up Grout. When she had finished and begun on him, Stone whispered, "Eleanor, my pocket, other gun, grenade," but she seemed not to hear or understand. Stone felt sick to his stomach, as if he were going to throw up from the cloying smell of Townsend's blood. But he was not afraid: instead, he wanted only to kill. He wanted to murder Kucic with his own hands. "I've arrived," he thought grimly, "at where commitment ultimately leads." And another part of his mind replied, "Yes, but where else?"

"No," Kucic was saying, "Karst was brave, intelligent and well-educated. He wrote and spoke well. Most important, people listened to him. He was being groomed for the Number Two man, to lead the country into the Soviet camp after the war."

"Without his knowing, of course."

"Of course. But he had to be watched, because he was sometimes too outspoken, too militant . . ."

". . . too much the zealot," Grout interjected.

254

". . . and sometimes influenced by bad friends," Kucic relentlessly completed his sentence.

"And not enough the zealot too," Grout said. "Besides, the zealot turned and became the worst of enemies, the heretic, didn't he? The avenging archangel who knew every one of your weaknesses as he knew his own."

"*Because they were his own,*" Kucic agreed. "By then, politically, he no longer mattered. Like most fallen archangels, he had no party, no faction, no followers. In short, no power."

"But he did matter, because even abandoned, in a no-man's land between all our battle lines—yours and ours and his own people's—Konstantin Karst mattered. No one else could tell what he had to tell. And your people knew his temper well. You knew he would tell it, and to the world," Grout said, almost triumphantly.

"Yes," Kucic said quietly, "and that's why I am here. For those." He nudged the bag of manuscripts with his shoe. "I would have preferred to kill Karst, for this," he touched his fingers again to the scar on his forehead, "as I shall kill your friend, Mister Stone, for having slapped my face, but the Center would not permit it. And perhaps it is better, for one so proud of his reason, to remain in a mental hospital. He will suffer far more. The Center did not want to make Karst a martyr, a *cause célèbre,* a source of friction between our two states and parties. They wanted only to see that those manuscripts were not printed, and I have them now."

"The bad friend was Mirko Sutnjak?" Grout demanded.

Kucic nodded, his fingers still exploring the white scar across the bridge of his nose. "Hurry!" he barked impatiently at Eleanor Hvar. "Decani has patrols everywhere, looking for you. We do not have the whole night." Then he turned to

Grout and calmly continued, "Sutnjak was a born deviationist, a bourgeois, a romantic, a Dalmatian with the soft Italian love of the flesh. A sensualist. A bad influence on Karst as in another way you and your father had been. But you Grouts were far away, in America, and Sutnjak was here, at Karst's elbow. He fought against the Molotov-Ribbentrop Pact, against the policy of treating the socialists as social fascists, and he talked such nonsense as socialist humanism and artistic freedom."

"So you killed him?"

Kucic made a small formal bow. "It was necessary. At first, the orders were to turn him over to the Germans. So, in Belgrade, I arranged to have his mistress reported to the Gestapo. We had our connections with them, and it was very easy. But Sutnjak escaped. Again we gave him to the Gestapo through the Italians, in Dubrovnik, but as usual the Italians were too late. Sutnjak escaped again, to the mountains, to join Karst. Finally, there, the orders came to liquidate him, and to make it seem that Karst had done it. Why, I do not know. Maybe the Center wanted to have a hold on Karst, or on me. But those were the orders, and I carried them out."

Stone had been watching Eleanor Hvar's face as he told the story, but her expression did not change. She seemed not to have heard, but went on tying him up methodically.

"But why then? Sutnjak agreed with Moscow's line at the time, a nationalist resistance," Grout persisted.

"Those were the orders. The Party makes men and breaks them in its own way and in its own time. Sutnjak was a bourgeois, anti-Russian, a Yugoslav nationalist. Unreliable. He had to be eliminated."

"And *you* were the instrument of the Party," Stone said sardonically, squirming against the ropes Eleanor Hvar was tightening around his wrists and ankles.

256

"I *am* the instrument of the Party, its unrelenting Bogomil hand," Kucic replied seriously.

"Why Bogomil?"

"The Party understands the men it needs. To be the instrument I am, a kind of Angel of Death, one must be a very special type of man. Bogomils are very special types of men."

"Yes, patriots who wanted their independence, who wanted Bosnia free and their religion separate from Western Roman Catholicism and Eastern Orthodoxy," Grout reminded him, not unkindly. "But you've betrayed both: your country and your religion."

"That kind of Bogomilism is dead and buried. Under those tombstones back there with Sutnjak. Mine is different, even if it did come from that older kind. My father was a pharmacist in Sarajevo, a mean, small, melancholy man. Jesus, Maria, I can still smell the stink of his drugs in my nose! He was Bogomil, like my mother, but he'd been educated. He laughed at her, at Bogomilism, at religion. He despised her, and my sisters, and all they believed. He called himself a rationalist, who believed what he could see and touch and smell, and he read French books to show he was different from and better than the neighbors. He was a great believer in progress. After the Turks were gone, he loved the Habsburgs because they brought their progress with them to Sarajevo.

"My father!" he laughed vengefully. "During the war, the first World War, he volunteered for the Austrian army and they sent his division to fight against his beloved France, not against the Italy he'd hoped to conquer. When he came back to Sarajevo, he believed in nothing, neither in Cartesian reason nor in Austrian power. He believed in the Bogomil forces of darkness."

"And you became a good Marxist?" Grout asked incredulously.

"By myself. Between my mother and father I became a good Bogomil," Kucic said cryptically.

"Good enough even for the NKVD, eh?" Grout commented ironically.

"The NKVD is the vanguard of the Party as the Party is the people's vanguard," Kucic retorted, his voice rising sharply. "It is the Party's steel soul and iron fist, to be used . . ."

". . . to kill," Stone grated.

". . . to push back the forces of reaction, to make a new, better world," Kucic insisted excitedly. "I was an instrument. You know the words in *The Internationale?* 'Tis the final conflict, let each stand in his place.' I stood in my place. I learned to kill as one learns a science, with a gun, a garrote, a knife. I learned to speak languages, to cross borders, forge passports, live underground. I became a professional revolutionary. Killing is necessary. With some people there is no other way. No persuasion, no re-education, only liquidation. If we are to change anything, they must go, be eliminated. I fought in Spain and here with our own Partisans, because I believed that. And I believe it now. We are the future of history. 'The earth shall rise on new foundations, we have been naught, we shall be all.' "

"And you couldn't forgive Mirko Sutnjak because he knew that was not the way life should be lived," Stone said. "You're a weapon, not a person, a human pistol the Party points at people it wants killed."

"Sutnjak," Kucic replied contemptuously. "He wanted to drink, to paint pictures and carve little pieces of wood, and make love to women. Is that a man? I did not drink or carouse with women because there was a job to be done."

"Is what you are a man?" Stone asked, genuinely horrified.

Eleanor Hvar finished knotting the cords around his wrists and stood up. Kucic motioned to her and she walked around the table toward him, hands in her coat pockets, her face still starched and ironed. With his free hand, Kucic touched her breasts and said, "Is this what makes a man?" Awkwardly, he pulled her head to him by the hair, and with his leg held her against him, body to body, then glued his mouth over hers. Stone tore at the ropes until the booming blast of the gun, once, twice, slowly separated their bodies. The machine pistol dropped from Kucic's fingers and he clutched his side. Blood poured over his hands and a wisp of black smoke floated up from Eleanor Hvar's coat pocket.

Kucic began to shriek, single words, exclamations, as if they were being torn out of his mouth like teeth. He staggered toward her, his bloody hands groping, and she took out the Walther automatic and with a steady hand shot him twice more, in the chest. He stared at her as if she had committed some completely gross and improbable impertinence, then his knees buckled and he fell at her feet. For a full minute, he lay there curled up like a child, crooning two words over and over again until he died. In the long silence that followed, Eleanor Hvar stood staring down at his body, dazed, the gun still aimed, until finally she murmured, "Bogomil! Bogomil!" and fainted.

While they fumbled untying each other, Stone asked what Kucic had screamed.

"Woman! Slut! Bitch! Whore!" Grout's voice shook. "Until the end, when he was dying, he kept repeating, *Mama, Zora, Mama, Zora.*"

"And the Bogomil?" Stone said.

"In old Slavonic," Grout answered wearily, "Bogomil means 'God have mercy.' "

"Why did he wait to kill us? It would have been so easy for him to give us a burst and run."

"He had to tell us. He wanted us to know who he was, what he had done."

"The last word?"

"The last word." Grout's head dipped. "You see, Warren, you made one mistake. Kucic was not a weapon. He was only a man."

As soon as they were untied, Stone picked up his own Luger and Grout's 45, reached for the diplomatic pouch, and announced, "Max, I'm taking those manuscripts."

Grout, still squatting on the floor, rubbing his wrists and ankles, looked up and said, "Sometimes you surprise me, Warren, you really do." He looked stunned and suddenly older, and there was a fatigue in him so profound and apparent that his bulk seemed to have shrunk and withered.

Together, they revived Eleanor Hvar, sat her in a chair, and poured some of the *rakija* into her. When she could talk, the first thing she sputtered was, "Is he dead?" They nodded in unison. "I thought he was. I killed him, didn't I?"

"If he owed anyone a death, he owed it to you," Stone tried to comfort her.

"There was no other way, Lili," Grout added.

No other way, Stone thought. Grout was probably right, but then, of course, so was Kucic. The unrelenting Bogomil hand. But he had relented, at least long enough to tell them, to tell them off, to speak his piece. Probably there was no other way to deal with the Kucices of the world, or was there?

"What makes a man like that?" Eleanor whispered.

And Grout's response was an epitaph for Kucic, words so like those his grandfather had spoken that Stone could hear the old man's dry, precise voice in his ears, ". . . the evil man is born with his wickedness as the snake is born with its poison fangs and its sac of venom, and the one can as little change his nature as the other." Grout's words had the same old-fashioned timbre as his grandfather's. *Evil* and *wickedness*: they were not words one heard much any more.

She sat in the chair, vacant-eyed, watching as Stone gathered up the bag of manuscripts, the grease gun and machine pistol, and her little Walther automatic, while Grout searched Kucic's body. Kucic carried no papers other than three passports in three different names, none of them Kucic, one Yugoslav, the others Bulgarian and Romanian, and large quantities of cash in all three currencies. Besides the machine pistol, he had a revolver in a shoulder holster, and a knife in a sheath. Grout separated each of the cigarettes Kucic had, sliced open the heels of his shoes and the lining of his clothes, and even the cuffs of his trousers, with Kucic's own knife, but he found nothing. "A real pro," Grout said, admiring and grudging at the same time. "They train theirs well."

Stone looked at his wristwatch. There wasn't much time left; he should be starting for the beach: Georgevic would soon be there. Grout caught him looking at the watch. "Georgevic taking you over to Bari tonight?" he inquired.

"You never quit," Stone replied angrily, "do you? Even when Kucic was going to kill us, you kept right on at it, finding out what you could, adding your one little piece of information to another, so you could make a mosaic and see the big picture."

Grout looked shamefaced. "I guess I'm made that way, or have been made that way. That's how I really found you, though, Warren, those bits and pieces added together and a little knowledge of what Karst's character was like."

Stone was forced to grin. "Just like a little jigsaw puzzle, huh? All right, then, I guess we have to take him along with us, Eleanor, don't we, so he can't explain it all to Decani?"

Eleanor Hvar's expression changed. Life and sadness seemed to flow back like blood into her face and her features became mobile. "I am not going, Warren," she said slowly and very distinctly.

Though he had never entirely believed she would go, never hoped that anything so good could happen to him, her refusal came like a blow that sent something inside him reeling from its impact. "This afternoon . . ." he faltered.

". . . this afternoon was a long time ago."

"But why, why?"

"How can I explain to you why?"

"Try, I'm not so stupid."

She got up, and put her arms around his neck. "Warren, I love you," she said. "It does not seem like it now, but that's not the whole story. They are part of the story too." She shuddered at the two corpses on the floor. "And Mirko's grave out there."

"Come with me, Lili, please come with me."

"I can't. *All my dead are here, buried here!*" She shrugged helplessly. "My father and mother, my son, Mirko . . . oh, how can you understand that?" she cried.

Even as he protested, "But that's the best reason you could have to leave, to go somewhere else where you can make a new life, create a new life," Stone understood it all right. He understood because at home he had his own dead, some buried, some not, his mother and grandfather, his father, Slater, though that had been in Holland, and Valerie too, now giving birth to another man's child in a different marriage, another and different Valerie because the woman he'd known had died, or been reborn, on an analyst's couch. Yes, he understood. You buried your dead and sometimes they returned the compliment. But who ever had scratched those words on the Bogomil tombstone that Georgevic had read had touched the nub of it: "You will be as I am, but I cannot be as you are." And soon, soon.

"You Americans," Eleanor Hvar said, trying hard to joke, "you believe in happy endings."

"No, Eleanor, only in new beginnings," Stone replied.

No one spoke for a while. Grout, still kneeling over Kucic's corpse, was staring out into the night trying hard to look as if he had heard nothing but Stone knew every word had sunk into his brain.

"You're sure?" Stone asked her once, a last time, straight and not pleading.

"For now, I am sure," she answered.

"Remember what you told me up on the walls today, that even in the 18th century Ragusa's ships sailed to America? Well, they still do."

Tears welled up in her eyes but did not fall. She nodded. "I'll remember."

"All right then," he said, after a pause, "there are things to be done."

Grout stood up. "Yes," he said, "a great many."

Stone handed him his 45. "Here, Maxim, you might need this yet."

"Thank you, Warren, I shall remember that."

"We can't leave the bodies here to involve . . . our friend. I imagine you'll want to take Townsend's body back to Belgrade and send it home for burial."

"If I can."

"Have you got a car?"

"Not too far from here."

"Good. Can you let Eleanor off somewhere safe, so she can get back to Dubrovnik? The quicker the better. As long as she is staying in this country, she shouldn't be caught with you."

"Unless Decani has all the roads blocked, I think I can manage that," Grout said.

"I can get back alone very easily," Eleanor Hvar said. "Remember, I was a Partisan for almost four years, and I know this countryside well."

"What will you tell Decani when you get back?" Stone asked.

"I'll tell him you took me for a walk in the woods, but that I wouldn't and you lost me." Irony glinted in her grimace.

"And you, Maxim?"

"Unless they catch me with Townsend's body, nothing. I've never been here. Otherwise, Townsend was hurt in a hunting accident. I'll stick to that. In fact, it will probably be the official story for everyone."

Using Kucic's knife they cut two saplings and with his rope tied them together to make a rough stretcher. They laid Kucic's coat on it, and then Kucic and Townsend's bodies. Stone saw some blood on the floor and threw sand on it and rubbed out as much of the stains as he could. Then everything looked in order, or at least as it had. "I guess that's it," he said.

The three of them stood there awkwardly until Grout picked up the jug of *rakija* and said, "We should have glasses to make a farewell toast and then smash them against the wall in good local style." He raised the jug, smiled at them, and said, "To a safe journey—for all of us," and tilted the jug back. Eleanor Hvar gazed at their faces as if to reassure herself of their presence and to remind her of them in their absence, and said, "To life." She drank shortly and when she passed him the jug her lips were still wet as if she'd just been kissed. For an instant Stone recalled that green-gold ingot of *rakija* in Karst's hand in the garden that day and his toast to freedom. It seemed almost appropriate to make that same toast again, here, now, but Stone knew his would be to a different freedom, from corpses, from memories, from the burden of past failures. Or was that a different freedom? Was that what Karst too was driving at? "To reunion," he said finally, then he drank and when he was finished, he snuffed the candle out with the bottom of the jug and left the jug standing next to it on the table.

They took the path that led sharply downhill from the back of the hut, Eleanor Hvar carrying the grease gun and machine pistol while Stone kept the bag of Karst's manuscripts slung over his shoulder yet managed, with Grout, to carry the two bodies on the improvised stretcher to where Grout's car was concealed in a clump of trees that grew in a small half-hidden gulley only a little way from the road. The car was the same big black American one with *carte diplomatique* license plates. Grout opened the trunk and lifted Townsend's body soberly into it, and covered it with a car rug. As he did so, he declared abruptly, as if expecting contradiction, "He was not a bad man," but Stone made no rejoinder. Like his answer to Eleanor Hvar's question about Kucic, that too seemed an epitaph, this for Michael Townsend, and when Grout closed the trunk, an interment. Only Eleanor Hvar did comment, "He is *your* generation of Gletkins."

"The Rubashovs are all dead," Stone said. "Your Gletkins have seen to that."

"No," Grout amended, "not all." And Stone had the feeling that he was not only talking about Konstantin Karst but about himself.

Together they hauled the stretcher with Kucic's body swiftly across the road to another stand of trees and put it down there. "Do you think you can manage it down to the water from here by yourself?" Grout asked.

"I'll manage. It's not too far now."

"Better to cut him loose and carry him over your shoulders."

"I'll see how it goes."

Grout measured him appreciatively. "You'll do," he said. "That war record was no exaggeration. You're a lot more than just a literary agent." He meant it for a compliment but Stone only felt it as a weight.

At the car Stone offered Grout some of the arsenal he'd accumulated, but Grout refused. "I did take the cash, though. The passports I give to you." He handed them over. "The cash we can put to good use."

"And what were you and Townsend hunting with?"

"Rifles, Warren, U.S. Marine Corps rifles. We have some at the Embassy. But I was so upset by the accident, I left them behind and someone probably stole them." He put out his hand. "Don't worry, Warren, diplomats are trained to lie, its one of the graces of their profession. Besides, I don't think they'll stop me. The diplomatic plates help."

Stone shook his hand. "Good-by, Maxim."

"Oh, not good-by, Warren. I think we'll be seeing something of each other yet," he said, and sounded glad of it. "Coming, Lili?" he asked, opening the car door for her.

"No, Max. You go south, back up through Titograd, Pec and Kragujevac to Belgrade. I'll just walk in the other direction, toward Dubrovnik. It is simpler and safer that way."

Grout hesitated, then nodded. He leaned over and kissed her cheeks. "Mirko would be proud of you, Lili," he said huskily. He drove the car quickly and powerfully up onto the road and only when he was several hundred yards away from them did he turn on his riding lights.

SHE CAME into his arms, quivering. "I killed him, Warren," she murmured, "I killed him."

"If you hadn't, he would have killed us all."

"Does that make it good?"

"No, better. The best we could do." His fingers dug into her shoulders and he buried his face in her hair. "Come with me," he said.

"I can't. I must stay here, at least for awhile. Until all this . . . until . . . I don't have to uproot myself or cut off my roots to be transplanted."

"You'll grow new roots."

"I'm not twenty any longer."

"So much more reason to decide, to go now."

"I need time."

"Time is what we have least of."

"Time is all we have."

"That, too, Lili, that too," he said, but the irony was weak.

She tugged the strap of the leather pouch. "Well," she said consolingly, "you got one thing you wanted, Warren. They are good books and they will make a sensation. And lots of money."

"Was it worth it all?" he asked. "I don't seem to care very much right now."

"You had no other choice, though, did you?"

"It looks that way," he admitted reluctantly, but he knew he had had a choice and had made it. And even if that was an illusion of choice, he'd taken it as if it were choice itself, freely given and freely accepted, so the responsibility was his and remained. "When this blows over," he said slowly, weighing the words, "can you get another fellowship? Come to London to study or work for a while? We've been thinking of opening a London office . . ."

". . . Warren, Warren, you're as bad as Max. *There's nothing you can do now—except wait.*"

"There's always something you can do," he said, hearing the lack of conviction in his words. "Besides, I *have* waited. For a long time."

"And I too."

"And in the meantime it will be back to Decani—and the others," he added bitterly.

"Perhaps," she said slowly. "If it is too long, probably."

"For the time being, I wish you were less honest," he exclaimed.

"Why, so that later I might be more?"

The remark struck home and he was silent.

Automobile headlights burst suddenly over a rise, came surging along the road toward them, and together they fell to the ground. The car swept up, lights flashing, and then past, and they lay together in the darkness, their breathing openmouthed and quick. She reached for his hands and when she found them took them through her clothes into her breasts as if bringing him home. And when he was holding her, feeling her heartbeat against his palm, she burrowed beneath his shirt and discovered his flesh. Hands on his sides, each of her fingers in the hollow of a rib, she held him as if she would join herself to his very blood and breath. "I have learned from you, Warren," she whispered, her fingers tightening until he felt her nails, "I have learned so much from you."

The words moved him more than any "I love you" might have, and he said, "And I from you, Lili." He kissed her mouth, then her breasts, as if in them, in her, he were plumbing depths of himself, falling through abysses beyond anything he had yet been willing to risk, and as he fell he heard his own voice ringing in his head. "I'm lost," it said, "hopelessly lost." He lay there enveloped in a cloud of her warm flesh, listening to the wind disarray the leaves and flutter the steady hum of night sounds.

"It's late," she reminded him, and her breasts, like live things withdrew from his hands as she freed herself from his embrace.

They got up together and he asked, "Can I write?"

"It is better not to," she answered, and he knew she was right.

Without words she turned and began to walk along the road back to Dubrovnik. When she had gone only a little distance, his voice ripped "Eleanor" from his throat. She turned and stood still, but did not retrace her steps. "Tell Decani," Stone called after her, "that some day he's going to look behind him with those trick glasses and turn into a pillar of salt." She nodded gravely, as if understanding something more and different from what he had intended, then waved, a halting, constrained motion that was acknowledgment and good-by. Stone strained his eyes to tears to keep her in sight to the last possible moment, and then she was lost in the shadows. Viciously, he kicked the bag of Karst's manuscripts, packed them over his shoulder, collected the grease gun and machine pistol. He crossed the road to the other side just as another car's headlights came down toward Dubrovnik. He hid behind a tree but it did not look like one of Decani's or a police patrol, and as it sped by he hoped it would stop and give Eleanor Hvar a lift back to Dubrovnik.

For a while, letting his legs carry him down the uneven slope toward where he thought the beach was, Stone dragged Kucic behind him on the improvised stretcher, but it was awkward and too noisy. Finally, he stopped, put all the guns into the diplomatic pouch with Karst's manuscripts, thinking ironically of the phrase, "words are weapons," and kept the Luger in his belt in case. He took Grout's advice, cut the body free of the stretcher, and lifted it, fireman's carry, over his shoulders. Despite Kucic's height he was surprisingly light to carry, lighter than the guns and the manuscripts in the pouch seemed to be. Well, Stone thought, after all that had happened, it was appropriate for him to be leaving the country that way, loaded down with a dead man and a small arsenal. And also, he reminded himself, with Karst's manuscripts. But without Eleanor Hvar.

Dispirited, tired, not yet having caught his second wind, Stone moved down the slope, slowly, gropingly, feeling the burden of Kucic on his back and the pouch's leather strap cutting into his shoulder. Man the maker and man the pack-animal: even the atom and automation hadn't changed that yet. And in the Balkans less than in many other places. The night had grown chill but sweat poured down his face and chest, coldly trickling down his back and sides. In the darkness, he felt his way, stumbling, tripping, underbrush tearing at his clothes and flesh. Twice, he lost his footing and fell painfully to his knees, and all along he remembered how he had carried

Slater back to the battalion aid station that same way, covered with Slater's blood and refusing to believe that Slater was dead, and now he wondered if what ran down his face and hands was his own sweat or Kucic's blood.

The night grew darker and Kucic's corpse and the pouch heavier with each step. Sweat ran into his eyes and he tasted its salt on his lips. Though the land still inclined sharply and he smelled salt water—or was that too only his own salt sweat? —Stone wasn't sure he was headed for that narrow strip of beach where he was supposed to meet Georgevic. Try as he would to keep from thinking of her, he kept seeing Eleanor Hvar walking the road back to Dubrovnik. Yet he admitted shamefacedly to himself that part of him was relieved that she had turned back. At least a clear-cut decision had been made, perhaps the most sensible one for this time and place. Even more, and he was still more ashamed of that, he was glad that the decision had been hers, had relieved him of the final responsibility. Her not coming with him made escape easier and did not involve her if he was caught. But that was scant apology. If he was caught! He couldn't afford to be caught, with the manuscripts and Kucic's corpse, more for her sake than for his own, though he had made up his mind that if Decani did capture him he would say that he, himself, had shot Kucic in self-defense. Me and Sidney Carton, he thought." 'Tis a far, far better thing I do. . . ." But none of that made up for what he knew was cowardice in not accepting, insisting on, the burden of Eleanor Hvar's return.

As he came into a clearing of bald rock outcroppings, Stone saw in the distance the sliver of beach and the black bay water. They were not too far off and the sudden heady feeling that he might escape lifted his heart. He stopped, dropped the pouch and gently slid Kucic's body off his shoulders to the stony ground. Unencumbered, he stretched and unexpectedly found his mouth dry and all the rest of him wet and trembling. He was still afraid. After all there was no sign of a boat in the bay yet though in the darkness and distance he couldn't be sure. What if Georgevic wasn't there and didn't arrive? He had no alternative escape worked out, no fall-back position, as Maxim had called it. God, he thought, will I ever be free of fear? He sat down, back against a tree trunk on the edge of the clearing, and lit a cigarette, taking elaborate precautions to hide the flaming match and glowing butt. But that, too, reminded him of the war and the smoke didn't calm him.

He bent to pick up the body again and Kucic's face stared up at him. The lupine hardness, the semi-drooling leer, even the white scar that marked Karst's vengeance seemed to have been smelted into a seraphic calm touched with ecstasy. One of death's thousand doors had opened for Kucic and changed his face, made it simultaneously younger and older, but altogether different because it was without fear, without hatred, without life. "You will be as I am, but I cannot be as you are," he thought, recalling the Bogomil tombstones. That was it, Stone supposed, the answer to when a man was without fear, at peace. Swiftly, he shouldered his two burdens, corrected his angle of march and plunged into the trees once again.

When finally he came out on the pebbly beach, Stone was still thinking what the totem pole's life must have been like, a wolflike existence in which Kucic ran alongside the flanks of the herds of men to dash in, on NKVD orders, to bring some man down with a throat torn open. Stone tried to remember Kucic's other face, the one he'd met in Decani's office, on Kalemegdan, up at the shepherd's hut, its relentless evil, its casual cruelty as it had cut Michael Townsend down or forced itself on Eleanor Hvar, but the seraphic face kept obtruding, inviting him simply to turn his head to see it peacefully lolling just behind his shoulder. He forced himself to look ahead and there he saw Georgevic's fishing sloop, once white, but still graceful, anchored offshore. Georgevic, pulling strongly on the oars of a dinghy, was heading in toward the beach. Stone's biceps began to quiver violently, in spasms so painful that he had to put Kucic's body and the pouch down and sit next to them, kneading the painful knots out of his muscles.

When the dinghy came close inshore, Georgevic shipped his oars and waited. Stone stripped down to his underwear and tied his clothes into a roll with his belt. There were no breakers and he made three slow wading trips out to the dinghy, where the water was just under his chin, the first with Karst's manuscripts and the guns held over his head, the second with his bundle of clothes, and the last with Kucic's body slung over his shoulders, dragging him under and forcing him to gulp mouthfuls of slimy sea water. Georgevic silently helped him get the corpse into the dinghy and then Stone swung himself over the side. "She did not come," Georgevic said, eying the body which lay face down on the floorboards. Stone knew he had not asked a question, only confirmed a conclusion, but he couldn't tell if Georgevic was pleased or disappointed.

"No," Stone answered, "she couldn't."

Georgevic nodded. "I feared it would be so." He took to the oars and began to pull for the sloop.

Once the dinghy was alongside, Georgevic leaped aboard the sloop and deftly tied on. Stone began to hand up the diplomatic pouch, his clothing and then Georgevic reached down to help him and lifted the body up, holding it under the armpits, drawing it up until he was face to face with it. A great animal roar and a flood of Serbo-Croat words that could only have been oaths came hurtling out of his mouth then, interspersed with only one word Stone could recognize: *Kucic*. His face distorted with rage, his mustache electric with hatred standing out like a cat's, Georgevic hoisted the body high over his head and slammed it down on the deck. He stood over it, glaring down on Kucic's seraphic face, still roaring curses and then kicked the body so hard that it rolled over twice, then lay there on the deck, its ecstatic face staring up into the night sky.

Wordlessly, Georgevic went to the side and together they brought the dinghy astern and secured it to the davits. While Georgevic at the helm nosed the sloop out of the bay, and almost silently and without lights took it out to sea, Stone, stripping off his wet underwear and rubbing himself dry with an old, faded yellow towel Georgevic taciturnly handed him, put his clothes back on. Then he stretched full-length on the boards and, without another glance at the diplomatic pouch, Kucic's body or Georgevic hulking at the wheel, closed his eyes. The shaking inside him vibrated with the slow rhythm of the ship's engine and he tried to let it soothe the tension out of him, lull him to sleep as if he were being rocked. But like one of those crowd scenes in the old silent films, his grandfather, his mother, Slater, Karst, Antun Vuk, Decani, Townsend, Grout, Kucic and Eleanor Hvar jostled one another in his mind, their movements like marionettes, their faces distorted and talking furiously though he could not make out what they were saying, nor understand their curiously urgent and threatening motions. Then, abruptly, they were Mirko Sutnjak's sculptures, blank-eyed and blank-bellied, presenting themselves to him in all their agony and terror. When Stone opened his eyes to drive the spectres away, the night was so black his eyes seemed still closed and his nightmare outside, in front of him, for it was as if day and the world had been burned to charcoal and ashes, and only a few, pale stars left as embers, tiny reminders that day had once been and might, remotely, be rekindled.

"Man is made for happiness as a bird is made for flight," she'd said. Happiness, Stone thought bitterly, happiness. What a pernicious idea, what an alluring travesty of human life, the "And then they lived happily ever after" of the fairy tales or the moving pictures. Happiness was that rapture on Kucic's face looking blindly into the night. Before Stone's eyes there flashed, as if they were constellations, the sights of Decani standing over the loden coat, the *banderilla* quivering in the fat man's neck, of Kucic cutting Michael Townsend down like chaff, of Decani's twisting purple lips and Kucic's slanting livid white scar. They were the matadors, the eternal footmen who held open the thousand doors of death to let out life, the custodians of evil. Even they moved in their courses, mysteriously as stars, tragically as other men. Stone felt himself steeped in the well of tragedy, knew it in his bones like an ancient ague, for this was the Balkan inheritance: only next door that painfully piercing inevitability of the human inheritance, if not born, had been formalized and made beautiful, then handed down to others to see and wonder and tremble at the condition of men.

But life sounded other notes while imprisoned in that tragic destiny. Notes of delight, lyrical melody, sometimes even a symphonic happiness almost too broad and intense to be borne by the human instrument. That he knew as surely as he knew the other. Not often, not many such happinesses. Most happiness was as small, intermittent and infrequent—perhaps even accidental and unlooked-for—as those pale distant stars. And if that idea, that blind and plunging commitment to searching for happiness in life was pernicious, it was also grand, one of mankind's consummate creations, no mean or unholy grail.

Living was bound up with that promised pulse of pleasure and spiral of joy. He had known it himself, quietly and rapturously, talking to his grandfather, listening to Slater read his beloved Elizabethans, making love to Valerie at Westhampton or walking the walls of Dubrovnik with Eleanor Hvar, hearing Konstantin Karst in his garden holding a golden isotope of *rakija* in his hand like freedom and the future themselves. Though the new world, his world, lifted up that ideal of happiness (if not its reality) like the lamp before its golden door, it had as ancient and honorable a lineage as the tragic sense, an impulse as old as man, everywhere alike and different, everywhere the lure to persist, the incentive to endure, the illusion that they might prevail, that all men needed to warm and soften their days in the wintry face of discontent and tragedy. If happiness was indeed man's creation, his artifact, its blinding pervasive quality might only be a carrot dangled before the donkey; but if it was, it was a carrot the donkey could sometimes nibble.

The steady beat of the engine and Georgevic impassive at the wheel seemed not to have changed when he opened his eyes, but the night was colder and no lights except the small, green-shaded wheelhouse light were to be seen. Thick, slow-moving clumps of cloud and fog rolled over them, some seeming to come out of the water itself, others bearing down at mast height, more a heavy layer above that. The pitch and roll of the boat were more pronounced and Stone felt his stomach and knees, and he was thirsty and ravenously hungry. Georgevic seemed to read his mind and motioned to the base of the wheel where Stone found dark bread, sausage and a jug of *rakija* in a sack. When he had eaten and drunk, Stone lit cigarettes for them and gave one to Georgevic.

Suddenly Georgevic's body stiffened. "Did you hear anything?" he asked.

Stone shook his head.

"There is something," Georgevic said with certainty. He stubbed out his cigarette and Stone followed suit. Georgevic turned the wheel sharply and steered for a nearby clump of fog limping low over the water. He cut the engine, flicked out the wheelhouse light and let the ship glide silently and eerily into the brown mist. Tensed, as if for a spring, he remained at the wheel, listening. Stone strained his ears but heard only the slap of waves against the ship's sides, the creaking of the mast. A sound like a bee's, a hum that for an instant Stone thought was a ringing in his ears, came to him, high and faraway. Georgevic pointed up at the sky at the same time as the sound began to pulse, and Stone recognized airplane motors.

"Airplanes," Georgevic whispered. "Two. I did not think they would be so swift."

Stone wondered if they had taken Grout or Eleanor and learned about Georgevic and the boat, and the bay from which they had left. "They know where to look, don't they?" he said.

"They should," Georgevic replied. "They know the route as well as I do. Many have used it. And Decani surely knows. Besides, where else could you go from Dubrovnik except Albania?"

As the drone of the airplane motors grew louder, Georgevic at first seemed deliberately trying to ignore them. But the quaver of the engines was closer now and louder, and he seemed almost to vibrate with them. There was no conversation because the ship had nosed into the open and Georgevic was concentrating on steering it back into cloud and fog. Without the ship's engine, relying only on wind and current, it was difficult. Finally, he maneuvered them into a thick cloud once more as just above them the airplanes' highpitched roar beat down like thunder. The planes seemed to be hovering over

277

them, dipping lower each time, as if the pilots knew that they must be down below, hidden. But Stone couldn't see the planes and he assumed they hadn't been able to see the boat either or they would have attacked. He reached for the diplomatic pouch and, not allowing metal to clink on metal, took out Kucic's machine pistol and Townsend's grease gun. The machine pistol he passed to Georgevic, the grease gun he kept for himself. If they were spotted, they wouldn't have much chance fighting back with those, but it was all they had.

The airplane motors pounded over them in a climax of sound as if at any moment the planes would break through the mists to find and rake them with machine guns and cannons. Abruptly, one of the airplanes broke off and roared northward, leaving its companion still droning above them. The single plane racked in slow, tight circles above them, its engines straining. Georgevic spoke grimly. "We cannot wait too long. But he does not have too much fuel either. If he stays up here for more than half an hour more, we must go ahead and take the risk, or we cannot get you to the Italian coast before daybreak. And I cannot come far back enough by noon to make it look like I was truly fishing."

"Why is he circling? Do you think he spotted us?" Stone asked nervously. "And the other one, did he go for help?"

"Perhaps. Though more likely he'd radio if he saw us and stay. Probably he's trying to cover the more northern route, of someone heading along the coast through the islands and then going over to Pescara. This whole area is cloudy and foggy and the one above is assuming that this is about where anyone leaving Dubrovnik and going toward Bari would be and would hide. He's hoping to catch a glimpse—if he can."

Stone had a violent urge for a cigarette, and tried to distract himself from that and the ring of sound over them by remembering Eleanor's figure fading into the gloom. Suddenly the roar of the airplane motor stopped. In the silence the sea noises and their breathing were loud. "He's cut his motor to see if he can hear anything below," Stone whispered, wanting to shout, and having to clamp his voice down.

Georgevic nodded. "A ship's engine."

Both of them turned their faces up, tensely waiting. Looking at Georgevic's fine brave mustachioed features, Stone could only remember the picture he'd drawn of Zora. What had happened to Georgevic and his love was not very different from what had happened to him with Valerie and Eleanor, only it was worse for Georgevic, so very much worse. No wonder Georgevic's first words at the beach had been about Eleanor Hvar, with all their inevitable certainty. "She did not come." A statement, not a question. "I feared it would be so." Georgevic had lived that before, and in conditions immeasurably more horrible than his own. With surprise Stone felt his teeth grinding and his throat filled with a choking lump. Time stopped: the hands and hours of his wrist watch disappeared in a blur; and then, momentaneously, as if he, himself, had come out of trance and begun to breathe, the airplane motor hiccupped into full-throated roar, so close it seemed only yards away. The plane circled above, the waves beat against the hull, yet Stone heard only his own heart beating in his ears until the airplane motor began to recede: the plane was climbing, heading east, back for Dubrovnik.

After a time Georgevic straightened up and began to move purposefully. The ship's engine coughed into life and the sloop leaped forward through the cloud and fog, his hand firm on the helm. It was time, Stone knew, to be rid of Kucic's corpse, and it was his responsibility, not something he could leave for Georgevic to do. If they were intercepted, it was going to be

279

tough enough, if not impossible, to stay alive without having a corpse aboard. "I'm going to throw him overboard," he told Georgevic just a little bit too loudly.

"There's canvas and rope aft, and some weights," Georgevic told him in answer.

Stone got them and then went forward to where Kucic lay. From the diplomatic pouch he took the small arsenal he had collected and held each weapon up for Georgevic to see, but the big man declined every one of them. Stone spread the canvas out on deck, and though touching the corpse or looking at the rapturous face made him feel sick, he swiftly rolled the body on the canvas, then laid the weights and all the weapons on with it: Kucic's own machine pistol, Townsend's grease gun, and Kucic's revolver. From his coat pocket Stone took the grenades and for a moment half-pulled the Luger from his belt, then changed his mind, and tucked it back. It might be time for disarmament, but it wasn't yet time for total disarmament. He pushed the three passports into Kucic's jacket breast pocket; only Eleanor's Walther automatic remained. Stone held it in his hands, his only souvenir of her, lingering over it for a moment. Then, with all his strength, he threw it like a baseball in a high, hard loop as far away from the ship as he could, and turned back to the body. He tried to figure out a way to make the grenades explode after Kucic's corpse was in the water and well clear of the ship, but he was relieved when he couldn't work out a delayed detonation. Something in him was revolted by blowing even a corpse to bits, however much more prudent that might be: the fish would be at it soon enough.

Quickly, Stone rolled the body up in the canvas, stealing one last look at that ultimate ecstasy on Kucic's features before it was hidden. The corpse lay there looking like one of his mother's Oriental rugs wrapped for summer storage so long

280

ago. Georgevic had watched him closely and now he tied the wheel down and came forward to help. He stood looking down at the dirty canvas lump and said softly, "We were in the mountains together when they brought him the news about Zora. For three days he lay in a cave with his face to the wall. Konstanty tried to get him to eat, to talk, to drink, even to get up, but without success. One morning he was gone and didn't come back for a month. Later, we heard he had gone to Sarajevo and killed a dozen or more *Ustachi*, mutilating them like a Turk or a Bulgarian, but we never learned if it was true and he never spoke of it himself."

Together they lifted the body onto the rail and Stone felt something should be, had to be, said, but what he didn't know. "Bogomil," Georgevic intoned hoarsely. "Bogomil."

"Bogomil," Stone repeated after him. "God have mercy."

And then they threw Kucic's corpse over the side and watched it sink heavily from sight.

The horizon had become a jagged white scar between fraying darknesses of sea and sky when they came on the Italian fishing smack. Georgevic signaled them, they hove to, and their captain came aboard. Georgevic bargained with him in fluent Italian; for some of Stone's dollars and the promise of more, the Italian captain would take Stone not to Bari but to the small fishing port of Vieste. From there, he assured them, Stone could get a bus for Foggia and a plane from there to Roma. They agreed, passed the *rakija* jug around to seal the bargain, and then Stone slung the diplomatic bag with Karst's manuscripts over his shoulder, turned away to double-check that he still had the Luger and ammunition for it, and then followed the Italian captain to the side. The captain preceded him into the dinghy where a fisherman sat waiting at the oars, an unlit cigarette stub hanging from his lips. Stone turned and looked into Georgevic's face. "There's no way to thank you," he said. "You know that."

"There is no need."

"Good-by Georgevic."

"Good-by Stone." They shook hands. "Do not worry," Georgevic said gently. "She will be all right, and I, too, will be all right."

But would they, Stone wondered, and how about Konstantin Karst and his family? And all the others?

Only when the Italian dinghy had pulled clear of the sloop did Stone see, for the first time, the faded black letters behind the bowsprit that read *Zora,* blurred and scaled by time, but still legible.

Note About the Author

ABRAHAM ROTHBERG is that rarity, a native New York who has traveled widely in Europe, Latin America and the United States, sometimes under U.S. auspices. Educated at Brooklyn College, the University of Iowa and Columbia University, he has distinguished himself as a university teacher, editor, journalist, political analyst and writer.

Long a student of history, with a special interest in Communist movements and personalities, Mr. Rothberg was for more than seven years editor-in-chief and senior political analyst for the Free Europe Press. He recently returned from a year as roving European correspondent for *The National Observer* and special correspondent for *The* (Manchester) *Guardian* during which he spent time in various Communist countries.

Though *The Thousand Doors* is Mr. Rothberg's first published novel, he is also the author of a four-volume *Eyewitness History of World War II,* editor of *Flashes in the Night,* a collection of short stories by Hungary's rebel writers, and of *Anatomy of a Moral,* Milovan Djilas' political essays, as well as a journalist, essayist, and short-story writer of distinction.